TEMPEST RISING: INFINITY'S END BOOK 2

ERIC WARREN

Part of the Sovereign Coalition Universe

ERIC WARREN

TEMPEST RISING – INFINITY'S END BOOK 2

Cover Design by Dan Van Oss: www.covermint.com

Content Editor Tiffany Shand: www.eclipseediting.com

ISBN 978-1-0966-6795-7

TEMPEST RISING

To my sister Katie

ERIC WARREN

The Sovereign Coalition Series

Short Stories

CASPIAN'S GAMBIT: An Infinity's End Story

SOON'S FOLLY: An Infinity's End Story

Novels

INFINITY'S END SAGA

CASPIAN'S FORTUNE (BOOK 1)

TEMPEST RISING (BOOK 2)

DARKEST REACH (BOOK 3)

JOURNEY'S EDGE (BOOK 4)

The Quantum Gate Series

Short Stories

PROGENY (BOOK 0)

Novels

SINGULAR (BOOK 1)

DUALITY (BOOK 2)

TRIALITY (BOOK 3)

DISPARITY (BOOK 4)

CAUSALITY (BOOK 5)

Sign up on my website and receive the first short story in the

INFINITY'S END SAGA absolutely free!

Go to www.ericwarrenauthor.com to download

CASPIAN'S GAMBIT!

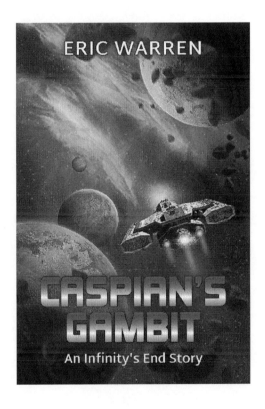

ERIC WARREN

1

Caspian Robeaux wasn't used to this.

Typically, when he sat at a bar and drank himself into a stupor the place was a seedy hole-in-the-wall. The type of place where illegal transactions were the norm and everyone who came in either looked like they wanted to fuck you or kill you. A place where he could disappear into the back wall and no one would give him another glance.

But this wasn't that place.

The bar was too clean, too sanitary for his likes. An automated bartender stood behind the polished wood surface separating them, waiting to take Cas's next order. When he'd come down to the concourse to get away from it all he'd hoped he'd be able to find a place to hide out for a couple of hours until he could get his head straight. But staring into the yellow eyes of the bartender as it glared back, he couldn't help but wonder if the bartender himself was a deterrent. As if he'd been placed there to make the patrons uncomfortable and keep them from overstaying their welcome. Perhaps that was how the Coalition kept their officers from getting drunk all the time. Back when he'd still been one, he'd never ventured in a place like this. It wasn't until after his arrest, parole, and escape-slash-exile before he started frequenting imbibing establishments. And sure, maybe the Sargan Commonwealth

7

wasn't the safest place in the galaxy, and you had to carry a blaster on your person at all times, but they knew how to set up a bar. And mix a drink.

"This tastes a little weak," he remarked, hoping to give the machine something to do.

"I apologize, sir. Would you like me to fix you another? I can adjust—"

"Just, pour another shot in this one, will you?" Cas pushed the small glass away from him.

"Yes, sir."

Cas glanced around the rest of the bar. It was empty, which didn't surprise him. These were duty hours after all; he wouldn't expect a bunch of Coalition officers to be skipping work to day-drink. It wasn't their style. And that was fine with him. It was a good thing Admiral Sanghvi had called him into his office early in the day, because after his news, Cas needed something strong and he didn't want to have to push through a throng of people to get it.

"There you go, sir," the machine said, pushing the drink back toward him. Cas had been too distracted to watch and see if he had added anything substantial to the glass or not. He picked it up and gave it a swirl before knocking the contents back into his throat, nearly coughing on the burn. "Better?"

Cas cleared his throat as the warmth traveled down his esophagus where it disappeared into the acid of his stomach. "Yeah. One more just like that."

"I'm sorry, sir. You have reached your daily allotment. You may return for another in seventeen hours, fifteen minutes." The bartender picked up the empty glass and it disappeared below the other side of the bar.

He should have expected this. "Fine. Then I'll take a bottle for the road." Cas glanced up to the hundreds of bottles of liquid perched on shelves behind the bartender, each varying in color and label. Alcohol from all over the Coalition.

"I'm sorry, sir," the machine repeated. "But bottles are only available for ranking officers."

"What if I said I used to be a Lieutenant Commander, would that make any difference?" Cas asked, slightly slurring the words.

"Only current ranking officers may access alcohol stores." The machine's eyes blinked on and off once; an indication Cas's question had now been reported somewhere. Ever since he'd found and modified his robotic traveling companion, Box, he'd become accustomed to their mannerisms. Where most humans saw a machine's eyes go out momentarily, Cas knew it was the signal that something inappropriate had happened or was about to happen, and someone needed to be notified.

He grumbled, wishing Box were here at the moment. He could shove right past the bartender and grab as many bottles as he wanted; or at least push him out of the way long enough for Cas to grab a Firebrand or Scorb.

"Is there anything else I can do for you today, sir?" the bartender asked.

Cas stood, his legs wobbling under him as he pushed himself off the stool. "I guess not," he replied, preparing to reach over to pay. He withdrew his hand at the last moment, remembering where he was. The Coalition worked without money. *Service is its own reward.* The mantra had been drilled into his head from the academy. But experiencing life outside the Coalition had shown him a different reality. One where people *were* motivated by money, and greed, and the accumulation of goods. And sure, sometimes maybe someone got a little overzealous and put out a hit on someone for not paying their bill, or stole someone else's transport to sell for spare parts, but were things really worse in the Sargan Commonwealth than in the Coalition? If you stripped everything down wasn't a little bit of murder and theft worth being able to drink as much as you wanted?

Cas's communicator beeped. "Boss?" Box said on the other end.

"Speak of the devil," Cas said, tapping the small device on his arm.

"I've been pinging you for the last hour. The Winston left without us."

Cas sighed, stopping at the door to the bar to stare out into the concourse where civilians milled about, moving from shop to restaurant to shop again. While Starbase Eight did have a contingent of permanent civilians, most of these people would be family members of Coalition officers, or off-duty personnel taking in the beauty of the station. He was the only one who was neither. "Yeah. Something happened. I'll tell you about it when I get back." Cas ended the call, closed his eyes, and pressed his fingers to his temples. Box deserved to know the truth, and Cas shouldn't have left him waiting on a loading dock for a ship he knew they wouldn't be taking any more. But after the meeting with the admiral, their trip to Procyon on the *USCS Winston* had been the last thing on his mind. He and Box had been about to board when the call had come in for him to meet the admiral in his office. And when he got there—

"There he is," a low, gruff voice came from somewhere off to the right.

Cas's eyes snapped open; his vision swam for a bit as the room righted itself. Three large men approached him from the concourse, their eyes fixated on him.

Oh shit. Maybe coming down here without an escort hadn't been such a good idea. Most people considered him a criminal, and with good reason. Cas took a step back into the bar, trying to remember if he'd seen a back exit or not. He didn't think he had. His comm chirped again but he ignored it.

The man in the front spoke up again first. "You think after what you did you can come in here and waltz around like you're a regular person?" He had at least six inches on Cas and looked like he might bench press small shuttles for fun. He was in civilian clothes but Cas knew, even through the fog of inebriation, they were officers.

"Listen," Cas said, backing up further into the bar with his hands up. "I'm not looking for trouble."

"Maybe you should have thought about that before you deserted," the one on the right said. He was smaller, but still a hefty guy. Had the three strongest guys on the station got together and decided on an old-fashioned beatdown?

"How is he even allowed to be down here?" the third one asked. He wore a shirt so tight Cas could see his pectoral muscles tighten and loosen as they grew ever closer.

"I guess you haven't heard." Cas took a few steps back but kept his eyes on the man's pecs. Through his inebriation it seemed like the safest place to look. "My warrant was rescinded."

"Yeah, by who?" the first one said, only a few steps away from Cas now.

"Admiral Sanghvi," he replied, stopping as his back reached the bar.

"How can I help you today, gentlemen?" the bartender asked from behind him.

"What the hell are you staring at?" the third one asked, having finally noticed Cas's gaze.

"Your…" Cas put his hands out in front of him, making a circular motion with them. "Are very nice." The man's eyes narrowed. "I mean why else wear a tight shirt if you don't want to show them off?"

"George, I think he's making fun of you," the one in the front said.

"No, that's not what I meant at all!" Cas said, scrambling. He wished he hadn't had that second Firebrand. "All I was saying was you should be proud of yourself. It takes commitment to go to the gym every day. Or in your case, five or six times a day."

"I don't care if you were pardoned or not." The middle one stuck a finger in Cas's chest. "We don't tolerate deserters in the Coalition."

Now *this* was more like it. Cas had been in his fair share of fights with the Sargans, and because there were virtually no police, other than the Guard, fights tended to be final. It gave the fighters a healthy respect for each other. Not like these guys. These guys were nothing but bullies with extra time on their hands. And since he was backed up to the bar, there was only one way out.

"Then I guess it's a good thing I came back." Cas pulled back and plowed his head into the face of the man in the middle, his forehead connected with the man's nose in a sickening crunch.

"My fucking nose!" the man yelled as blood splattered everywhere. Cas reeled to the right, holding his own head as he stumbled and eventually fell on the ground, his forehead pounding with pain. Wasn't headbutting supposed to hurt only the attacked, not the attacker?

"George, Ivory!" the man yelled, his words wet with fury. Cas pushed himself into a half-standing position and reached for his boomcannon, only realizing too late it wasn't there. Weapons weren't allowed in Coalition facilities. And as this realization washed over him striking a match to his adrenaline, something large and solid plowed into him, knocking them both back into a series of tables that toppled as they fell. Something metal dug into his side and he cried out in pain while pounding on what he suspected was the man's head, but he couldn't be sure. George or Ivory, depending on which one hit him, was all muscle and everything felt like hitting a steel beam covered by a thin layer of cloth.

Pain exploded in his head again, this time from blunt-force trauma and white dots peppered his vision. It was a good thing he was drunk otherwise he'd be in a lot more pain than he was. Another explosion of pain knocked some of the inebriation away as his adrenaline kicked into overdrive, willing his body to get out of the very bad situation he'd found himself in. He kicked with his legs but nothing connected while a robotic voice in the background was saying something urgent. But it seemed his ears weren't quite working like they were supposed to as he couldn't make out the words. All he could discern were the white dots and the increasing levels of pain in his face as something plowed into it over and over again.

This would be the fight that would kill him. And it was all because of the Coalition and their stupid rules about no weapons. Had this been a Sargan bar, it would have been over in seconds.

As he felt himself drift further and further into unconsciousness, the pounding finally stopped. Just in time for him to take a nap.

2

"He's going to need a few hours rest, the alcohol still isn't completely out of his system."

Evelyn Diazal stared at the guard in horror. "Screw the alcohol, what about his face?"

"What about it?" the guard asked, unperturbed. She glanced at her station.

"It's a mess! He needs medical attention!"

The guard shrugged. "He was the instigator of a violent crime on the concourse and injured two Coalition officers in the process. After he sobers up, we'll be processing him and handing him over to Coalition military for long-term imprisonment."

Evie threw up her hands, her dark brown braid falling off her shoulder and back behind her. "This is ridiculous. You can't possibly think he would take on three men larger than himself in a fight."

"If he was drunk enough, he would. Scans indicate his BA level at point-three-one."

Evie scowled. "That's impossible. The bartender is set to cut anyone off after two drinks. And no two drinks combined are that strong."

"He must have forced his way past the bartender. We got an alert he was inquiring about taking a bottle from the shelf for himself after repeated refusals from the bartender. I can only assume he got his hands on it."

This was infuriating. "Do you have this bottle? Better yet, let me see the surveillance footage. I want to see him steal this bottle, drink it, then pick a fight."

The guard faltered. "I'm sorry, Commander, I can't—"

"That's an order. Now," Evie said, her eyes stern on the guard.

She let out a long, slow breath and tapped a few buttons on the console in front of her, bringing up the video footage. It showed Cas sitting at the bar, then standing as the bartender took his empty glass away. He seemed to talk to someone on his comm for a moment before turning to leave. A moment later he backed up into frame again, this time with the three other men bearing down on him, his hands up. One of them stuck a finger in Cas's chest, to which he responded by headbutting the man, then toppling over to the ground. The other two tackled Cas at the same time and began beating his face in until the concourse guards arrived and pulled the men off him. The feed ended.

Evie turned to the guard, heat radiating from every part of her skin. The guard averted her eyes, staring off at the ceiling. "Get him out of there. Right now," Evie growled.

"But he began the altercation," the guard protested. "He made the first move. Surely we can't—?"

"Either he's out of there in five seconds or I'm taking this directly to the admiral. The same admiral who gave this man a full pardon not more than five days ago."

"Oh, he's...I see. Yes." The guard fumbled, her hands working over the controls. The suspension field between Evie and the cell dropped, yet Cas remained splayed out on the shelf that served as a bed.

"And I want the names of those other officers. I'll be putting in a formal complaint for harassment on each of them," Evie added. "I don't suppose they're still here."

The guard shook her head. "I released them an hour ago."

"Unbelievable," Evie muttered under her breath. She walked over to Cas and sat on the bench beside him. He groaned as she pushed his legs to the side. His face was covered in bruises and one of his eyes had swollen to the point where he probably couldn't open it if he wanted to. She smacked him on the side.

"Nnnggh," he said, attempting to turn over, but not making much progress and flopping back on his back again.

"Are you crazy? Why did you even come down here without an escort?" Evie asked.

"Sssleep," he mumbled. Evie gave him a hard smack on both his cheeks. "Ow, ow!" His one eye fluttered open. "C'mander Evelyn Diazal! What a pleasure t' see you!"

Evie rolled her eyes and turned back to the guard. "What's his real BA level?"

"Point-one," the guard admitted.

Evie grabbed him by the lapels and propped him up against the side of the cell. "You're not that drunk, now come on. Why did you come down here without an escort?"

He sighed. "You really don't know?" he asked, his voice much less slurred.

"I assume it had something to do with the new mission," she said, inspecting his injuries. They weren't minor but he wasn't in any immediate danger either.

"Bingo," he replied. "Brand-new mission. Which means…"

"Which means you don't get to go off on your exploration trip, boo-hoo. We have bigger things to worry about, Cas." It was no secret he wanted nothing more than to leave the Coalition and go off on his own to explore, in fact, that had been the deal offered him when Evie had first come to pick him up from the Sargans. But after what they'd heard in the admiral's office, there was a very good chance neither of them would be seeing any off-time soon.

"You're a great empathizer, you know that?" Cas touched the side of his face with his fingers. "What hit me, a truck?"

"A couple of off-duty officers thought you belonged somewhere else."

"I agree with them."

"C'mon," Evie said, standing. "We need to get you over to medical."

Cas groaned but stood on his own, wobbling slightly. "Room's spinning." She grabbed his arm and held on until he opened his eye again and glanced around. "Thanks," he said. "I'm okay."

Evie shot the guard another frosty look as they walked out, the doors opening automatically for them onto the concourse. "Why did you come down here anyway?"

"Well, since all my reserves were destroyed along with my ship, I had nothing on-hand to consume. And the only place you can get alcohol on this entire kilometer-wide station is here. So here is where I came." He gestured to the concourse above them. The concourse itself was laid out in a circle with giant windows that looked out into space above them. Below, were a variety of shops, restaurants, and stores, each with its own unique offering.

"Medical is down here," Evie said, pointing ahead. She'd rather get him back to *Tempest* and have their medical officer, Xax, look at him, but his injuries didn't seem major and getting to the ship dock on the other end of the station was a long journey. She tapped her comm. "Box, can you meet us down in station medical?"

Cas whipped his head at her, his face making a grimace.

"What's he done now?" Box's voice asked through the comm.

"Started a fight he couldn't finish," Evie said. "He needs protection until he gets back to the ship."

"Be right there." She cut the transmission.

17

"I could have finished it," Cas said, his attention back in front of them. "If *someone* hadn't taken my only weapon."

"Not my rule, nothing I could do." If she had her way, she'd carry her sword with her at all times. "And you knew that when you came down here."

"Still," he protested. "If I'd had it my face wouldn't look like this. And might I remind you the mind doesn't exactly work right when you've had a few and you're staring into the dead eyes of three giants."

"They weren't giants."

"Giants! Three meters tall, each of them. It's a miracle I survived." Evie took a deep breath as they reached the medical bay. "Is this really necessary?" Cas asked.

"You haven't seen a mirror," she replied. "And doesn't it bother you you can't see out of one eye?"

He twisted the unswollen parts of his mouth into a grin. "That'll go down in no time."

A nurse approached them. "How can we…oh." His hand going to his mouth as he got a good look at Cas's face.

"What?" He ran his fingers over his swollen eye.

"Sir, if you wouldn't mind coming with me," the nurse said. "I think your cheekbone might be fractured."

"What?" Cas asked, his one good eye going wide. He followed the nurse to a chair that hovered off the ground.

"Be gentle with him," Evie called as they were halfway down the hall. "He's fragile." She couldn't help but suppress a smile as Cas turned to scowl at her. She turned to take a seat as the doors to the medbay opened to reveal Box, all two-and-a-half meters of him. She'd been around him for a few weeks now but still wasn't completely used to the blinking yellow eyes and faceplate that covered what should be his nose and mouth but in reality, was only a speaker beneath. Cas had told her it was because he was supposed to be a mining bot of some kind, and the plating was to keep dirt and grime out of his primary components. Though Box had never worked in a mine a day in his life. He held a small device in his hand.

"Bar fight?" Box asked, walking inside and sitting down in one of the chairs in the lobby.

"I guess you're used to it," she said, taking a seat beside him.

"He's got a solid record," Box said, turning the device on. It showed an old net drama program. "Twelve wins, six losses. Two draws."

"Add one to the loss column." Evie stared at the show on Box's device. Ever since she'd known him, he'd been obsessed with fiction dramas. "What's this one called?"

"*Her Heart's Desire*," Box said proudly. "Care to watch?"

"I'm good, thanks," she replied. "Did he tell you he was coming down here?"

Box's eyes blinked a few times. "He never tells me anything. One minute we're standing next to the loading dock for the *Winston*, bags in hand and ready to take off, the next he's off to some secret meeting with the head of the station." Box paused the image on the screen, turning to Evie. "And I have to call him two hours later *after* our transport has already left to find out he's gone off on the station somewhere. I was still standing on the platform with all the bags!"

"Okay, yes, that's shitty," she said. "We got some bad news in the meeting and I guess he didn't take it very well."

"What kind of bad news?" Box asked.

She glanced around. Two cameras were positioned over the doors and another nurse stood watch at the main entrance, ready to accept any new patients that walked in. "Later," she said, her voice hushed. Normally she wouldn't tell Box anything. But after all they'd been through, not to mention the fact Box had kept her secret when she'd snuck onto Cas's ship and overheard him, she felt like she owed him. Not that it would matter in the long run anyway, Cas would most likely want Box to come along on the mission.

"Gotcha," Box said, his tone equally hushed. He unpaused the image and turned back to his program.

Evie leaned forward with her elbows on her knees, wondering if by this time next year any of them would still be alive.

<u>3</u>

Cas opened his eyes to bright light, squinting into it as dark shapes above him milled about.

"Can you stand up for me?" a soft voice asked.

Blinking a few times, Cas sat up on the bed and swung his legs over the edge, glancing down at his shirt, still covered in dry blood. Another bright light appeared in his eyes, first in the left then in the right. It dropped away revealing the face of a bearded man with a small contraption attached to his head which covered one of his eyes with a green glass. He was in his mid-forties and had kind eyes. "Mr. Robeaux, is it? Next time you get in a bar fight, learn how to dodge."

Cas was about to comment but instead kept his mouth shut. It would do him no good to argue about it now. "Am I free to go?"

"Yes, but you'll have lingering effects from the drugs in your system. You need at least two more hours sleep. Then you should feel fine," the man said.

Cas reached up and ran his hand down the side of his face, feeling no trace of swelling or bruising. They may be a corrupt organization, but the Coalition sure knew its medicine. Back in the Sargan Commonwealth, he would have walked away with at least a couple scars or an ocular implant to the damaged eye. "Thanks," Cas said, shoving past the man back into the hall. He turned to right, catching sight of Evie and Box sitting together, waiting. "Ah, crap," he said, turning the other way.

"Cas!"

He stopped, turning back to face her. Evie stood and approached him, staring at his face. "Not bad. Dr. Powell is one of the best in the Coalition. In and out in under fifteen minutes."

"Great," Cas replied, "I can make it back to my quarters on my own. I don't need you and Box as bodyguards."

Powell appeared behind him, raising the green glass on a hinge so it now sat on the top of his head. "He needs an escort. He's still groggy from the medicine."

"Thanks," Evie said. "We'll get him back safe."

Powell nodded. "Good to see you again, Evelyn." Cas's ears perked up. As soon as Powell was out of earshot, he turned to her. "Friend of yours?"

"Old friend." She placed her hand on his back and guided him back to the lobby where Box remained, watching his screen.

"You've made it out of scraps with Erustiaans, Sargans, and Kal-Magal and it's the humans who trip you up?" Box said without looking up.

"Hey," he replied. "There were three. The three biggest humans I've ever met."

"They're infantry soldiers," Evie said. "Here on leave from the *Persephone*. It's docked up beside *Tempest*. I've also made sure to file a complaint with their commanding officer," she added.

"Thanks," he said, "but you didn't have to do that."

"Despite your status now, you were still a Coalition officer once. You don't deserve to be intimidated and beaten."

He took a deep breath. "I think most people on this station would disagree with you." He turned to Box. "I assume you took everything back to our old quarters."

"By *my-self*," Box said, still not looking up.

22

"Look, I'm sorry I just left you there. The—I was shaken up."

Box closed the screen and placed the device in a small compartment on his side. "The meeting. I know, Evie has agreed to tell me all about it once we're no longer monitored. I'm very excited to learn the secrets of—"

"Will you shut up," Evie hissed, indicating the nurse at the station nearby. She hadn't looked up, but she was close enough to be within earshot.

"I think I need to lie down anyway," Cas said, leading them out of the medbay and back into the concourse. "Which way?"

"The quickest hypervator is over here," Box said, turning left. "Now make sure you stay behind me in case someone takes a shot at you. I've adjusted my scanners for sniper fire."

Evie smirked and shook her head.

"Yeah thanks a lot, the both of you. Makes me feel a lot better knowing whenever I'm in mortal danger the two of you are the ones I can count on."

***

The door to the room slid open, revealing sparse, white furnishings and three containers stacked just inside the doors. It was a standard room with a view of the starfield beyond as well as the normal amenities; bed, kitchen, bathroom. Ever since his ship, the *Reasonable Excuse*, had been destroyed while they were chasing the Sargans, Cas and Box had been staying here. Evie hadn't expected them to stay as long as they had, despite the harrowing nature of what they'd all experienced trying to retrieve the *Achlys*.

"Make yourself at home," Cas said, kicking his shoes off so they both hit the far wall as he plopped down on the bed, placing his hand over his eyes. "By Kor, I've got a headache."

"Probably a side-effect of the drugs. I'm sure it will wear off soon," she said.

"I'd offer you something, but all we have is water," Box said. "The juicer is under about a kilogram of Cas's unwashed laundry."

"I'm fine, thanks anyway." Evie took a seat at the small desk which was up against the wall beside the door. This was…cozy.

"I'm all auricular sensors," Box said.

"Do you want to tell him or should I?" Evie asked Cas who still had his eyes covered with his arm.

"You do it," he said, his voice noticeably softer. He'd be asleep any moment.

Evie adjusted her low ponytail and pulled it over her left shoulder, just like she did any time she was getting nervous. The admiral had told them everything in complete confidence, but Box wasn't a human and could be trusted to keep a secret. If she asked him not to reveal it, she was sure he wouldn't.

"It turns out our mission to find the *Achlys* was just a small part in a much larger plan," she said.

Box's yellow eyes blinked on and off a few times. She thought that might mean he was intrigued. Box was the first "sentient" robot she'd ever met and so it was hard to gauge what he was feeling.

"Okay," she said. "Let me start from the beginning. Admiral Rutledge might have been in charge of the *Achlys'* mission; but it came from higher up. Even back when he was a captain."

"Corrupt…" Cas murmured.

"Anyway," she said, ignoring him. "The entire reason the *Achlys* was dispatched to Sil space to capture and reverse engineer one of their weapons was in case of wartimes with an unknown enemy. And it seems last year that enemy finally showed up."

"What?" Box asked.

"The long-range telescopes that sit on the far edge of Coalition space, out between Archellia and Starbase Five picked something up a few months ago. We don't know who they are or what they want, but we know they're headed this way and we know they're extremely powerful. One of the telescopes caught them imploding a planet. Cas thinks it was target practice but Coalition Central doesn't know what to think. All we know is they're headed this way."

"How long?" Box asked.

"Based on our projections of their speed, another year if we're lucky. Unless they speed up, though they've been consistent so far. By our estimates their ships are faster than anything we have. Except *Tempest*."

His yellow eyes blinked on and off rapidly. "This isn't common knowledge," he asked.

She shook her head. "No one knows. Not even the fleet. We were only granted access because of the nature of our mission."

"What mission?" Box asked. "What would they need a worn-out engineer and a stellar robot pilot for?"

"Hey!" Cas said. "Don't talk to me about worn out, you under-powered, arrogant—"

"The *reason*," Evie interjected, "they need Cas is because he's the only person who might have a chance of getting through to the Sil. They want to send us back into Sil space to ask for their help. With their weapons technology they might have some method of combating or at least giving us a chance…"

"Are we so sure these aliens are going to be hostile? What happens if they get here and they want nothing more than to exchange ideas? Or pie recipes?"

"When in the history of any civilization in your databanks has that ever been the case?" Evie asked, dejected at the thought of the encroaching threat.

"The Claxians," Box said. "When humanity encountered them, they were more than happy to share their technology. If I'm not mistaken it led to the creation of the Coalition as it is today."

"Touché." She had to give him that one. "Okay, other than that *one* instance, when else?"

"I'm drawing a blank," he replied.

"The basic fact is we can't sit around and hope everything will be okay when they arrive," Cas said from under his hand. "Which means we need to get the Sil on board, despite having little to no contact with them ever since the *skirmish* a hundred years ago. And what little contact we have had has been nothing short of antagonistic."

"That's why they want you," Box said. "Because you sent the signal that saved the scout ship. When Rutledge wanted to capture it, you saved them."

"Didn't matter in the end," Cas said, sitting back up. "Rutledge still got his hands on the ship and the weapon. Which is what I tried to tell Sanghvi. The Sil won't care I was the one to help them. All they'll remember is the *Achlys* coming into their territory and stealing one of their ships."

"Now we don't know—" Evie began.

"Yes, we do. It's a suicide mission and he knows it. Instead of flying off to explore Procyon like I was supposed to, now I have to go back into Sil space to die a useless death."

Evie stood, fuming. "No one ever said you *had* to do anything. The admiral asked if you wanted to volunteer. No one is forcing your hand, but I can tell you without your help this mission is already doomed. If you come, we at least have a chance."

"He's sending the *Tempest*?" Box asked, turning his head from Evie to Cas.

"We need to be as quick as possible. On a normal ship, Sil space is at the very least sixty to seventy days away. *Tempest* can get us there in half the time." So far, the *Tempest* had been the only ship outfitted with the new, experimental Claxian technology which nearly doubled the current limits of space travel. The only trade-off was it needed a Claxian on board to operate it, and they were notoriously reclusive, preferring to stay on their home planet rather than venture into the stars. *Tempest* got lucky with Commander Sesster, but Evie wasn't sure how many more Claxians the Coalition could coax off their homeworld to bolster the fleet.

"No wonder he went to the bar," Box remarked, staring at Cas sitting on the edge of the bed with his head between his knees. Cas only grumbled something incoherent in response. "You can't abandon them; they need your help."

"Yeah, yeah," he said, staring at the ground.

"I've had enough," Evie snapped. "If he ever decides to leave his pity party let me know. *Tempest* leaves in a few days. We still have to finish the repairs from the battle with the Sargans." She leaned in close to Box. "See if you can keep him away from any more *establishments*."

"These work just fine, you know." Cas pointed to his ears.

Evie shook her head and left through the sliding door, not bothering to look back. Let him wallow in it for a few days. He'd come around…hopefully.

4

"Good job, Romeo. You pissed her off again," Box said after the door slid closed. Cas grunted and laid back on the bed.

"How many times do I have to tell you? It wasn't, isn't and never will be like that with her. Not all humans pair-bond."

"Most do."

He sighed and sat back up on his elbows. "Do you have any hard evidence to back that up? Or are you just spouting your own personal propaganda?"

"It's important to have a belief system. I've noticed most humans have one which means so do I. Humans couple. It's what they do. It's what most species do. Though a few couple exponentially. Some triple. Some...*quadruple*." The last word came as a whisper.

"I'm glad you find it all so fascinating." He didn't care Evie was upset. He didn't even care about being beaten up or needing surgical treatment. All he cared about was his singular focus—the only thing he'd wanted—moving further and further into the distance until it would be out of his reach forever. First it had been Veena and the Sargans in his way. Then he'd managed to get caught up with the Coalition again and it was supposed to be one job. One *simple* consulting job. And that had turned into a multi-layered mission upon itself.

And now, just as he could almost grasp his freedom it had been yanked away again by some mysterious threat thousands of light years away. A threat they didn't even know was a true threat yet or not, they had just made assumptions. And sure, the evidence didn't look good, but that didn't necessarily mean it was bad either.

He sighed. Who was he kidding? Of course, it was a credible threat. One of the direst since the war with the Sil over a century ago. Maybe even worse. Sanghvi told them the rest of Coalition Central had been informed already, and other preparations were being made; but forging an alliance with the Sil was a crucial step if they were to have any chance of confronting whatever it was that was coming.

"I assumed because you hadn't coupled since your time in the Sargan Commonwealth that you had bonded with the commander," Box said, bringing Cas out of his thoughts.

"By Kor, we have more things to worry about than who I am coupling with," Cas replied. "Don't you understand the magnitude of what's going on? What this means for us? We won't be able to go off like we wanted. We have to stay."

"And that's bad because…?"

He sat up again. "Because we don't like the Coalition?" Did he have to spell it out?

"No, *you* don't like the Coalition. I'm just fine with them."

"Even though they don't see you as sentient. Most of them anyway."

Box's eyes blinked a few times. "Some do. The important ones. Like Commander Diazal. See the funny thing is you never asked me what I wanted. If I wanted to go off into space to explore with you. You assumed I would be there by your side. What happens if I *want* to stay? What happens if I happen to like the Coalition?"

"What?" Cas leaned forward causing the room to spin again. When it slowed, he continued: "Where is this coming from? If I remember correctly you were as happy to get away from them as I was. Or has everything since Kathora been a lie? We used to always talk about how if we got away from Veena and the Commonwealth we'd go off on our own, explore the galaxy."

Box turned to him, staring him right in the eyes. "That was before we had the option of coming back to the Coalition. *I* was never banished; I just felt it prudent to leave for a while. And neither are you anymore. You can stay willingly. I like it here; they have centuries of media available. Centuries upon centuries. And the best part is you don't have to pay for any of it."

Cas made a face. "So, you like it because you can watch your shows for free?" he asked, deadpan.

"And the people are nice. Nicer than you, anyway." He paused. "Selfish jerk."

"What has gotten into you?" Cas asked, standing and walking over to him.

"I am an abomination no matter where I go. A sentient robot that shouldn't exist. Most people treat me like garbage. Some don't, and for the most part people are better to me here than in Sargan space. Don't you understand? I don't have a place anywhere. And ever since we lost the *Excuse,* I don't have a purpose anymore. I just…am."

"You've never opened up like that before," Cas said.

Box turned away from him. "I'm bored with this conversation. Go to sleep, the doctor said you need rest for your wounds."

Cas frowned, not sure how to react. He'd always assumed Box would stay with him no matter where he went. The robot was right; he'd never asked him what *he* wanted. And despite the fact Cas had made the modifications that gave him greater sentience, it wasn't as if he could go around telling Box what to do. He wasn't his master, or even his boss anymore. Without a ship to command, Cas had been reduced to a civilian as well. He stared at the crate he knew contained all his paper maps and charts of the local star systems. A dream further out of reach.

He knew he should apologize to Box, but something about it seemed wrong. Or at least uncomfortable. And he'd been uncomfortable for long enough. "I'm going out," Cas said, turning for the door. "I'll be back later."

"You better not be headed back to that bar," Box warned. "The commander will run you through with her sword if you get smashed again."

"No," Cas said. "I need to do something else."

5

His head pounding, Cas approached the security desk; the officer manning it barely glancing up. "Authorization?" the guard asked.

"Robeaux, Pi-four-seven-delta," he replied, rattling off his old security code without a second thought.

The guard froze for a moment, then glanced up at him again under the wide brim of his hat. "Did you say Robeaux?" Cas didn't respond, only stared at the man whose gaze was intensifying by the second. Cas was too tired and too fed-up to deal with another confrontation. If the guard wanted to start something, he'd have one hell of a fight on his hands, boomcannon or not. "Put your thumb on the pad." His voice sounded humorless, as if he expected the pad to explode as soon as Cas touched it.

Cas did as he was told and it lit up with a soft green.

"Son of a—" the guard said. "That shouldn't be possible." He double-checked his feed, peering at the screen then back at Cas then back at the screen again. Another guard had appeared off to Cas's right, standing close to the door he'd just come through. "Seems as though you have been granted access by a Lieutenant Commander Diazal. It's a good thing it wasn't up to—"

"—up to you otherwise you'd kick my ass, yeah, yeah. Can we just get on with it? Are you going to let me in to see him or not?" Cas asked.

The guard pursed his lips and drew back, tapping his feed monitor. "You have up to an hour. Follow Officer Blankenship." He indicated to the other man who had taken up position by the door. Blankenship turned and crossed the room to another door, tapping it with his hand. They slid open revealing a long hallway beyond.

Cas took up stride behind the man. "And Robeaux," the guard at the front said. "Don't come here again. Or I'll find a reason to stick you back in there with the rest of the trash."

Cas rolled his eyes but kept his mouth shut and followed behind the silent Blankenship. They traversed a long corridor until they came to a familiar area, hexagonal in shape. Each wall was actually a force barrier, beyond which was a room— or in some cases, series of rooms. In the room furthest to the left was one person, sitting at a table eating from a bowl. His was the largest cell in the group, multiple rooms sharing the wall with the force barrier.

"Thanks," Cas muttered to Blankenship, walking over and standing in front of the force barrier, willing the occupant behind it to look up and see him. Behind him Blankenship turned and left, his footfalls echoing in the hallway. "I guess they give the important people the biggest room. You look no worse for wear."

"Can't say the same about you. You look like a man troubled, Caspian." He finally lifted his head and the piercing eyes of Cas's former captain struck him just as they had all those years ago when he'd first joined the crew. He still had his beard, though Cas could swear it had gone a shade grayer since he'd last seen the man. He had the instinct to step back, but stood his ground, not about to let this man intimidate him anymore. Despite the fact he was the reason for everything bad in Cas's life in the past seven years. "You wouldn't be here if you didn't want something," Rutledge said. "So out with it."

"Aren't you even the least bit sorry? For what you did to me? For what you did to my career?" Cas asked.

Rutledge appeared to chuckle. "Of course, I'm sorry. But it was for the greater good. I assume you know that by now otherwise you probably wouldn't be here. You'd have taken off for greener pastures, just like you always dreamed."

"I *dreamed* of being a starship captain," Cas spat. "And you stole that from me."

"You stole that from yourself!" Rutledge spat back, dropping his spoon in his bowl and standing. "All you had to do was cooperate, to trust me and see the greater picture. But no, you had to go off and let your ignorance guide you. Did it ever occur to you that I only had your best interests at heart? I never wanted anything but the best for my crew."

"Maybe if you'd told me what we needed the weapon for I could have!" Cas yelled back.

Rutledge shook his head. "You're deluding yourself, son. Even if I *had* told you, which I was under strict orders not to, would that have made any difference in your decision? Would you still not have disabled the weapons to save those people?"

Cas didn't respond.

Rutledge sat back down. "I knew. I knew when I got you on my crew if anything morally ambiguous ever came up, you'd be the first one to dissent. The first one to speak out. And back then I thought I could show you not everything in this world is so black and white. Not to mention you were one hell of an engineer and I didn't want to be out there without you."

"What were you developing the weapon for?" Cas asked. "The telescopes didn't pick up the aliens until this year. Back then there was no threat, no impending doom facing the Coalition. So why take the risk?"

Rutledge smiled. "Haven't you ever heard it's better to be prepared than to be caught with your pants around your ankles without a belt?"

Cas furrowed his brow. He didn't think he had heard that particular phrase before.

Rutledge blinked a few times, resetting himself. "If I sound not-quite-myself, it's the meds they have me on in here. Messes with my mind sometimes."

"Why are you on meds?" Cas asked.

"To keep me docile. To keep me from pounding on that force shield sixteen hours out of the day."

"It's not very much fun, is it?" Cas remarked, recalling the short time he'd spent in this very prison five years ago before he'd been transferred to the Dren Penal Colony. He pointed the cell directly across from Rutledge, currently unoccupied. "That one over there, remember?"

"I know," the former admiral said. "Don't think it doesn't gnaw at me. The Coalition lost a good officer and I lost a good friend. I trusted you more than anyone. And you betrayed me."

"You betrayed the Coalition," Cas replied. "Or at least what the Coalition is supposed to be. Not what it's become. I don't even recognize this organization anymore."

Rutledge scoffed. "Son, it's always been like that. You can't run a multi-species, intergalactic conglomeration without keeping a few dark secrets. Without making some compromises. It's been that way since the founding days." He paused. "But you didn't come here to talk about ancient history. So, get on with it."

"I want information on how you finally captured the Sil ship. The *second* time. After you'd already sent me to my fate."

Rutledge sat back in his chair, a smirk on his face. "Is that all? Shit, son, I thought you were going to make this difficult. You want to know what happened, read the logs, it's all there. Sanghvi will give you access."

"I want your version of events," Cas said, intent on not letting this go. Rutledge had betrayed everything he'd believed in for this weapon and if Cas was going to even try and speak with the Sil, he needed to know every detail, every nuance of what happened. Not just the scrubbed-down reports. And since the rest of the crew was dead…

"Fine," Rutledge said, leaning back in the chair. "You want to see me squirm, is that it? Just remember I'm in here because what I was doing was *right*. And if you hadn't exposed me to the council I'd still be out there, working to make the Coalition safer. But the public can't know, so *someone* has to be the scapegoat. But if they've done what I think they've done, then you better watch yourself. Because you're about to step into the shoes I just vacated."

"What do you mean?" Cas asked.

"Dealing with the Sil is like dealing with death. No matter what you're gonna lose people. You should know that better than anyone. And who do you think will be blamed for those deaths?"

"It won't be my first officer, I can tell you that," Cas replied.

Rutledge regarded him, nodding slightly, then let his chair drop back down to the floor with a *thunk*. "It took us six months to get the *Achlys* repaired after the beating we took in Sil space. And another six to outfit it with new equipment. By the time you were halfway through your sentence the ship was back out there, patrolling the edges of Sil space. But they were ready for us. They weren't about to let us cross their borders again, not without a fight. You remember Soon? She took over as captain after they promoted me to admiral for saving the ship from your *treacherous ways*."

Cas bit his lip, doing his best not to take the bait. And he did remember Soon. The first thing that came to mind was her tough demeanor and no-nonsense attitude. She'd been the *Achlys's* second officer when he'd been on board and he'd been sure she would be the one to support him and stand up to Rutledge when they returned to Starbase Eight. But she'd stayed silent at his hearing, despite Cas's pleas for assistance.

"She took the ship out for months at a time, returning only to refuel or resupply. She was looking for any advantage. Eventually she got sick of skimming the edges and plowed in where she knew their smaller ships were likely to patrol. She got a scout ship to pursue her to the Atrax system, familiar with it?"

Cas shook his head.

"Surprising. I thought you explorers knew every system." Rutledge stood and grabbed a water from the dispenser beside the table. "Atrax is a very unique system. At the center a star collapsed into a black hole, but three of the planets orbiting Atrax Alpha remained in orbit, even after the star's collapse, hundreds of thousands of years ago. The whole system, frozen in a perfect balance, each planet keeping the other two from falling into the gravity well."

"Don't tell me, she destroyed the entire system to capture them," Cas said.

Rutledge shook his head. "Nothing so involved. But she did manage to disable their ship with some quick thinking and clever pre-planning on her part. I don't think I ever gave her enough credit as second officer. Soon was clever. Regardless, she sent a bunch of marines over to that ship and blew the holds. It only took them minutes to clear the ship and with a minimum of casualties. Because of her quick-thinking and strategy, the Sil never had a chance to call the others. They don't know we took it and they probably still list the ship as lost today."

"How *many* casualties?" Cas asked.

"Now Cas, do you really want—"

"How many?" He could feel a vein throbbing at his temple.

"Just ten. And they didn't suffer."

Soon had done that? Killed ten innocent Sil?

"I don't believe it," Cas said.

"It's in the classified reports," Rutledge said. "Right down to the coordinates. Black hole's still there if you want to go visit, but her actions threw one of the planets out of alignment. The whole system is fucked up now. Eddies and gravitational currents all over the place."

"What if there had been life on one of those planets?"

"She specifically chose that system because it was *devoid* of life. She might have been a risk-taker, but she wasn't stupid. Or a traitor to our cause." Rutledge eyed him, then sat back down, sipping his water.

"So, then what, she just brings the ship back and you start working on it?" Cas asked.

He shook his head. "We couldn't risk someone seeing it. That's why we had that drydock constructed out in neutral space. She took it there, and I met the ship with a team dedicated to taking that ship apart and learning her secrets. And we did, it just turned out we didn't know as much as we thought we did." He leaned forward. "There is something strange about those ships. Enough to even make me pause. But we had a mission. We had to make a weapon. But trying to figure that ship out was like unwrapping an enigma stored inside a mystery."

Cas remembered seeing all the dust on the drydock and the Achlys when they'd investigated. There had been so much it had piled up in the corners, like they had become some ancient tombs, lost in the desert.

"She was on the *Achlys* when they tested the weapon. In fact, I talked to her before I sent Evie to retrieve you," Rutledge said. "I guess their deaths are on my head too."

"You're damn right they are," Cas said.

Rutledge snapped his gaze to Cas. "The fact is I was right. We needed that weapon because now we're staring down the barrel of something we don't even understand and I can guarantee, had it worked, I'd be on the other side of this field right now preparing to install them on all our ships." He dropped his head. "If these aliens turn out to be as dangerous as they look—"

"—we're all dead anyway," Cas said, taking a deep breath. He'd seen the footage. He'd seen what they could do. The Coalition had nothing anywhere near as powerful.

"*Now* you understand. Let's just hope it's not too late."

6

Cas left the high-security brig with a bigger headache than when he'd entered. His encounter with Rutledge had drained him, but he wasn't ready to return to his room yet. There was something he needed to do first.

He got on the hypervator, taking it over to the ship docks and exited on the boarding level. The docking ring was a band inside the giant structure providing access to the ships and vice versa. The windows showed the ships docked inside the giant station, each of them floating in weightlessness despite the fact they were enclosed. Starbase Eight was one of the larger bases and the primary ship resupply and maintenance hangar for this sector. This side of the station could fit twelve ships at a time, or three of the larger cruisers, though those didn't stop by as often. Cas glanced over to the dock where he and Box had stood only hours earlier, preparing to leave on the *Winston*. But now the dock was closed and the space beyond was empty, waiting for the next ship to arrive and take its place. Cas sighed and made his way over to where *Tempest* was docked.

It was a sight to behold. Clad all in a steel gray, the ship was compact, its undercurrent engines tucked into its sides like wings, in order to minimize damage at high speeds. The undercurrent emitter was positioned on top, unlike most other ships and the shuttle bays—both one and two—were directly below the main half saucer that made up the front of the ship. It reminded Cas of a bird-of-prey, ready to swoop down for the kill. And it was a brand-new class of ships, only the second in its line: Dragon Class. The *Dragon* itself had been a prototype and wasn't in service. Which meant *Tempest* was the only ship outfitted with the Claxian's new drive, making it the fastest ship in the fleet. If he had to be on a ship for another mission, *Tempest* was about the best he could ask for.

He made his way to the docking latch, connected to the station by a long tube which he followed all the way down to the ship itself. There a young ensign greeted him with a brief nod. "I need to speak with Commander Diazal and Captain Greene," Cas said.

"I believe they're on the bridge." The ensign's voice betrayed no hint of emotion and Cas couldn't remember if he'd seen him before. It was very possible he'd passed him in the hallways and hadn't noticed.

"Thanks," Cas said, making his way to the ship's hypervator. Civilians didn't have access to military ships, not unless they were immediate family or had some purpose being there. Cas had been granted special access, just like he had to the high-security brig. Going straight to Rutledge had been a risk, but Evie had put her faith in him and provided access. He had to remember to thank her.

The hypervator opened on the bridge, which was in much different shape than he'd seen it last. Half of the stations were missing, and it seemed to be undergoing some kind of cosmetic change. Commander Blohm, the bridge engineer, approached him. "Back again, huh? We had a running bet if you'd show up or not." She wiped her hands on a rag and placed it in her pocket.

"Sorry to disappoint," Cas said.

"Didn't disappoint me," she said. "Zaal and I bet you'd come back. The others, not so much." She flashed him a quick smile and headed for the hypervator. Cas turned to watch her go, her long, blond hair which was usually down had been pulled up in an intricate design on her head. The commander had a difficult job; on any other ship she'd be the chief engineer. But since they needed a Claxian to run the new engine and Blohm was a human, she'd been made a liaison to Engineering via the bridge. It had worked out on their last few skirmishes, though Cas could always sense the tension she brought with her when she wasn't in Engineering.

Cas glanced over to where Ensign Blackburn used to sit: the navigation station. She'd been impaled by a piece of falling bulkhead in their battle with the Sargans and died on that very spot. And Cas couldn't help but blame himself. Had he taken down Veena when he'd had the chance, it never would have happened.

His eyes lingered there until he caught movement. Lieutenant Izak Ronde came into his view, wearing a scowl. He was tall, dark-skinned with vivid green eyes and a youthful face. Being the ship's helmsman Ronde had worked very closely with Blackburn and Cas couldn't help suspect he blamed Cas for her death as well. "Something I can help you with?" Ronde asked, his voice tinged with sarcasm.

"No," Cas replied, turning toward the commander's room which sat off to the side of the bridge. "Just here for the captain."

Ronde didn't reply.

Cas made his way across the deconstructed bridge as crews of workers glanced at him then continued their work resetting and moving the individual stations. Before each station had all been placed in a circular fashion around a central core which displayed 3D information to the entire bridge at once. But that core had been damaged in their battle with the Sargans and it looked as if they might be reconfiguring the bridge for a more traditional two-dimensional setup. Cas would have loved to stop and ask questions about the specifics, but he didn't have time. And his headache wouldn't have allowed him to enjoy much of it anyway. He approached the door to the captain's room and pressed a small button beside it.

The doors slid open, revealing Greene and Evie, both standing beside Greene's desk. He held something small in his hand. "Congratulations," Greene said. Evie nodded, taking the item from him, but it was too far away for Cas to tell what it was.

"Mr. Robeaux," Greene said. "Good to see you again." Typically, when people said that they were either being sarcastic or had mistaken him for someone else. But with Greene the sentiment was genuine. Cas could see it in the man's eyes. It helped Evie had done nothing but supported him since he'd been assigned to *Tempest*. "How are you feeling about our new assignment?"

Only he and Evie had been present with Cas in the meeting with the admiral. Cas could only assume that meant no one else knew about the specifics of the mission yet. "Ev— Commander Diazal didn't tell you?" he asked.

"She said you weren't feeling well and visited the medical ward on the concourse."

Cas couldn't help but feel indebted to her again. Even after his outbursts, she still hadn't given up on him. "It was a lot to take in," Cas finally said.

"I imagine for someone who should be on their way to Pyrocyon it came as a shock." Greene rounded the desk and took a seat in his chair. "Have a seat." He offered the two chairs behind them.

"Have you...made any decisions?" Evie asked, hesitant.

"I spoke with Rutledge," Cas said, prompting a look from Evie. "I wanted to know what we're going into. But honestly, this is going to be very risky. Rutledge told me the *Achlys* shot ten of their people into space while capturing the scout ship. And they don't know it, he says they think the ship is missing."

43

Greene leaned back. "I read the report. It doesn't make things any easier on us, that much we can count on. Even if we do broker some kind of alliance with them, it will probably come out eventually."

"Is an alliance even realistic?" Evie asked. "After a hundred years of zero contact and another five hundred before that of feigned ambivalence?"

"I'm hoping," Greene said, "Once they see what our long-range telescopes picked up they'll be more open to talk. The Coalition is the only thing that stands in between them and these things coming at us. It's at least in their best interest to use us as some kind of shield."

"How sure is Coalition Central of the evidence?" Cas asked. "We can't go in there touting this information unless we're a hundred and ten percent sure." Was he the only one who didn't see the possibilities here?

"What are you thinking?" Evie asked. "It was doctored?"

"I had that thought as well," Greene said.

"Captain?" Evie asked, her mouth remaining open.

"Honestly, Commander, after everything we've learned recently about the Coalition, I wouldn't put it past them." Greene clasped his hands on his desk.

"But that was just one man," Evie protested. "He couldn't—"

"One man, his crew, and a couple of admirals," Greene said. "I always suspected things like this inside the Coalition, I had hoped they would never come to light. Not in a way that could hurt what we have here. But if the Claxians ever found out about the *Achlys*, I don't know how they'd react. It probably wouldn't be good."

Evie shook her head. "I don't believe the entire Coalition is corrupt. Some elements, yes; but to go as far as to doctor telescope footage to justify an alliance with the Sil…"

"If it were just to build a weapon, I would say it was more likely," Greene said, mirroring Cas's thoughts.

"You think because we *have* to turn to the Sil for help it's genuine," Cas said.

"They wouldn't risk it otherwise. A potential miscommunication here could send us into a full-scale war with the Sil. And Kor knows we don't have the technology to fight them, even with what the Claxians come up with. By the time the alien threat gets here, we might all be dead anyway."

Cas hung his head again. "I really wish a diplomatic team was making this run."

"Then you're in luck. We're getting a new, temporary crewmember. She'll help guide you on what you should and should not do when trying to engage with the Sil. It'll be a crash course on diplomacy, but it's better than nothing."

"Great," Cas groaned.

"How are we going to explain this to the crew?" Evie asked. "Won't it look suspicious, us heading into Sil territory with Cas on board? Especially after everything we just went through?"

"Our cover is we are initiating *second contact* due to the capture and prosecution of the criminal responsible for the antagonism between the Coalition and the Sil. Now that Rutledge is in jail, Coalition Central feels it acts as a good jumping-off point to open up formal negotiations." He turned to Cas. "With you at the lead, of course."

Cas shook his head. "Of course."

7

"Did'ja hear?" Izak whispered. "He's back on board. Strutting around like he can come and go as he pleases."

Lieutenant Jorro Page glanced up from working on the tactical station. "When?"

"Bout twenty minutes ago. While you were in the stacks."

Page glanced at the door to the command room. No doubt he was in there making up some story to the captain about why he deserved a break while the rest of them had to earn their places on this ship.

"You don't think he's coming back on board, do you?" Izak added. "That was a one-time thing, right?"

"I don't know," Page replied. "I heard the admiral lifted his warrant. Fuckin' criminal if you ask me." He turned back to the console, trying to get the connections apart. "Damn thing. Why don't we have another Engineering team up here yet? Isn't this their job?"

"We're waiting on more teams," Izak said. "They haven't started on my station either."

Page glanced over to the helm. Everything on the bridge was in pieces. And they were supposed to be ready to launch again in three days? What could be so important? They'd found the stupid ship. And the traitor had gotten his revenge by having one of the top admirals in the Coalition arrested. Wasn't that enough?

Page hunkered down and put his arms on his knees, staring at the command room door. "Is she in there too?"

Izak shrugged. "I guess so."

"Why does she defend him so much?" he asked. "I don't get it. Turn against your crew, get twenty-four of them killed. Then escape while on parole and five years later you're the new golden boy of the Coalition?" He shook his head. "Something doesn't make sense."

"I don't know," Izak replied. "If we hadn't had to go after his stupid ass Blackburn would still be here."

Page crossed himself. "It's like wherever he goes death isn't far behind." The door slid open revealing the traitor and Commander Diazal exiting together. Neither looked very happy, so that was a plus. Page realized he was staring as he watched them cross the bridge and make their way to the hypervator, but he didn't care.

"I bet they're screwing," Izak whispered.

"Hey, that's your commanding officer there," Page reminded him. "Show a little respect."

"Sorry, sir." Izak stiffened. "I need to get back to my station." Without another word he turned and made his way back across the bridge just as the traitor and the Commander stepped onto the hypervator.

Page stood and walked over to the command room's door, spanner still in his hand.

"Yes?" Greene said as soon as the door recognized he was on the other side. The doors slid open to reveal Greene sitting behind his desk, reading some reports. The wall behind him sported sparse decor, other than his medals for honor and distinguished service. The captain was a man of few possessions. "Lieutenant, what can I do for you?"

Captain Cordell Greene was one of the most respected captains in the fleet and Page had been proud when he'd been chosen for his crew last year. But this nonsense with the traitor had tainted his impression of the captain. What sort of captain would allow someone like that on their bridge? To dictate the missions even? Page had played along in the beginning, especially when he'd been assigned to the team that had to inspect that derelict drydock. But he couldn't get past the thought of a deserter having any kind of authority or clearance on board *Tempest*.

"I'm sorry, sir. I may be out of line, but I have to know. Is that—is Mr. Robeaux coming back on board?" He clasped his hands behind him.

Greene eyed him for a moment then put down the display he'd been studying and straightened himself in his chair. Page took notice of his strong, weathered hands. "Is it a problem if he is?" he challenged.

Damn. Had he not been coming back on the captain wouldn't have asked. "No, sir, I was just curious."

"I'm not at liberty to reveal anything at the moment, Lieutenant," Greene said. "But I suggest if you have a problem with Mr. Robeaux, you take care of it."

Page winced. "No problem, sir, I was just…curious. Like I said."

Greene regarded him for a moment. "How are the repairs and refit going on the bridge?"

He relaxed, relieved Greene had steered the conversation off Robeaux. "Slowly. We need at least two more teams if we're going to be ready in three days."

"I'll put in the request," Greene replied. "Anything else?"

"No, sir."

"Dismissed." Page felt Greene's eyes on his back as he left the command room. Why had he gone in there; had he needed to know that badly? Izak glanced up at him as he re-entered the bridge. Page dropped his eyes and gave a shake of his head that said, "You were right."

Izak mouthed "*fuck*" and rolled his eyes.

Page returned to his station, depressed. How much longer would they have to suffer that treacherous bastard? Why

48

couldn't they leave him here on the station? He couldn't be important for their next mission. Was he supposed to be a member of the crew now, too? One thing was for sure, when Page became captain, no one who was ever associated with the Sargan Commonwealth would ever be allowed anywhere near his ship.

No matter what.

***

The console finally lit up, all of the displays coming back online. "That's it," he said. "Looks like you got it."

"Sorry that took so long, Lieutenant," Ensign Tyler replied. "We've been having a hell of a time reconfiguring the bridge. These new Dragon class ships seem to have a mind of their own."

Page stared at the display, double-checking all of his systems were back online. It had reset to the default and he'd have to reconfigure it to his own personal preferences again. "Better than nothing," he grumbled. "How they expected the ship to be ready in such a short amount of time I'll never know."

"If there's nothing else," Tyler said, replacing his tool in the small satchel he'd brought with him from Engineering.

"Did you hear? The deserter is coming back on board," Page said, still furious at the situation. It had been all he'd been able to think about since his meeting with the captain.

"The…deserter? Oh, you mean Robeaux," Tyler said, his voice too cheerful for Page's mood. Had everyone forgotten what he'd done?

"I'm good here, you can go." He turned his attention to fixing his reconfiguration. He barely registered Tyler leave his field of vision. There had to be *someone* else not happy with the fact he was coming back.

Page glanced over his shoulder at Izak, sitting in his new helm chair, probably doing the exact same thing he was—configuring his systems. Page locked down his station and walked over, avoiding all the parts still on the ground and the teams reassembling the bridge.

"Lieutenant," Izak said. "They get you all squared away over there?"

He nodded, leaning down. "You?"

"Still working on the last few things. I can't wait to have all this cleaned up and out of the way." He indicated the mess that was the bridge.

Page leaned over, his eyes sliding to the side to make sure no one else was close enough to listen. "I need your help."

"With what?" Izak locked down his station.

"Have you ever been down underneath the undercurrent engines, on the lower decks?" Page asked.

"No, sir, I don't see—"

"Gets real hot down there. All the plasma is vented through the ducts that line the walls. It's why we don't have any critical ship systems there that require constant maintenance. Because most humans can only stand it for a few minutes. Only a Derandar could stand it long-term. The heat is unbearable."

"Sir, what does this have to do with—?"

"When you're down there," Page continued, "from the moment you step into that corridor all you want to do is leave. To go back to where it's a lot cooler and the air isn't so muggy. Some people feel like they might pass out. It's *very* uncomfortable. Do you get what I'm saying?"

Izak pulled his lips between his teeth, nodding. "I think so, sir. I don't want him here anymore than you do."

"Good. Then I need you to do something for me. And I need you to be quiet about it."

8

"Feel like anything to eat?" Evie asked as they made their way down the hallway.

Cas had intended to go back to his quarters on the station, but food sounded pretty good. Apart from a few deciliters of alcohol, he hadn't had anything since the meeting with the admiral. "You buying?" he asked.

"Ha," she said, unamused. "Very funny. You look a little pale. I think you need something in your stomach before you head back."

"It's this whole damn thing," Cas said. "I'm still trying to get used to the idea of heading off on a suicide mission."

"Hopefully," she offered as they turned the corner. "With you along it won't *be* a suicide mission. I know we don't know much about the Sil, but I can't believe they would be willing to allow a threat like this go unchallenged. If nothing else, we've been peaceful neighbors to them." Cas shot her a look. "For the most part."

"I'm not sure. All we know is they are very defensive about their territory, ever since we first tried to capture that ship. It won't take long to get their attention," Cas said. His stomach rumbled as if Evie's mention of food had ignited his senses. He glanced over to see her slip the small item Greene had given her into her pocket.

"What's that?" he asked.

"Hmm? Oh, nothing big," she replied. But he could tell there was some excitement in her voice.

"C'mon, you know you want to show me." She retrieved it from her pocket and placed it in his hand. "Commander stripes? You got promoted?"

"Yeah, I guess I did. For consistent, exceptional behavior becoming of an officer."

"That's amazing! We *have* to celebrate now. Why didn't you say anything? Why didn't the captain make an announcement?" He turned the small bars over in his hand. It was a symbolic piece, her uniform would be modified later to reflect the change.

"He will, eventually. But he wanted to congratulate me in private. I'm not big on blowing my own horn." She looked downright embarrassed if anything.

"Hey, you deserve this," Cas said. "Which I guess it means I'm buying." He handed the bars back to her.

She chuckled. "If you insist."

They entered into one of the two mess halls on the ship and made their way over to the food dispensers, each taking a tray.

"Tacos," Cas remarked, staring at Evie's tray. "You're having a taco to celebrate your promotion." He put his own tray back and took one from the other dispenser, matching what she had. "I haven't had a taco in years."

"Tacos are just about the most amazing thing in existence. What, they don't have tortilla shells in the Sargan Commonwealth?" she asked as they took their trays to one of the long tables in the room.

"Things out there are more...eclectic," he said. "There's a lot of variety. Most of the time I had to scan something before I put it in my mouth, half the stuff there will kill a human if he eats it." She made to take a bite but he held up his taco. She stopped, smiled, and held hers up as well, tapping the shells together. "Congratulations, full Commander Diazal."

"Thanks," she said, taking a bite. "It's going to be weird for a while." They chewed in silence for a moment. "You know, it was like that on Sissk too. We never knew what we were going to eat the next day, it was up to the local populations. And Sissk has more indigenous intelligent species than any other planet I've ever seen."

Cas furrowed his brow as he chewed his own taco. "That's out near Epsilon Lyre, right? Near the border?"

She nodded. "Sort of. I spent most of my childhood out there, on the fringes. The Coalition didn't have the biggest presence so when a ship came by it was a big deal."

"Is that what made you want to join the Coalition?" he asked.

"Partially. But I was tired of living on the fringes. I wanted to be in the middle of the action. Be part of the solution. Sissk was…well it wasn't the safest of places. That many species all co-mingling, half of them in the Coalition, the other half not loyal to anyone. It made for some interesting years." She took another bite.

"Is your family still there? Or did they follow you inward?"

She paused for the briefest of moments and then shook her head. "What about you?" she asked, mouth full of taco. "Where is your family?"

Cas took a deep breath and swallowed. The taco was delicious. He hadn't realized how famished he was. "Oh, it's a riveting tale. Full of heartbreak and deception. Something truly worthy of its own net drama."

She laughed. "Does Box know?"

"It was the first thing he asked me about when he first became self-aware. I think my own family's drama may have inadvertently influenced him to seek out those damn things he watches on TV all the time."

"So…" she tempted after waiting for him to continue. "Spill it. You can't give me a hook like that and not follow up."

Cas took a deep breath and cracked his knuckles. "It's not as interesting as I probably make it sound. I was born on Earth, but my mother died when I was six. She was in the Coalition, serving on the *Charybdis* when it was destroyed out near Archellia. Solar storm, there was nothing anyone could do. And it drove a wedge between me and my father. If you go back and look at my sealed records, you'll see I was a hellion in those early years. But when he forced me to join the Coalition—something I had adamantly refused—I finally straightened up. Got out of his sphere of hatred and realized there were good people in the universe. Kind people. And even though I hated him for it, it was a good thing he did for me. Even he knew he was a bad influence on me all the time."

"How did he get you to join?" Evie hadn't touched anymore of her food.

"It was either join or jail. Which, is kind of ironic if you think about it." He watched her horrified face a minute before bursting out laughing. "It's okay. Honestly, I've always felt like the universe had it in for me in one way or another. It turns out I was going to prison no matter what I did."

She smiled, but it was full of pity. He didn't want that, he didn't want her to feel sorry for him. *This* was why he never told anyone anything. "So anyway. Like I said, not that riveting."

"Have you talked to him lately?" Evie asked.

"Not since the day I was arrested. He stopped by to let me know how disappointed in me he was. Though I would have loved to have seen his face when he learned I had escaped my parole. That would have been a memory worth keeping."

"He doesn't know you're back? That your warrant has been lifted?"

"I doubt it. He's a civilian now. He used to work for the science division but hasn't for a long time. And since the details of my...*release*...aren't technically public yet, he probably assumes I'm still hiding out with the Sargans."

"You're not going to call him to let him know? Don't you think he'd like to know his son isn't a criminal anymore?" He caught the hint of some fire in her voice.

"I doubt he'd care. Or even if he did, he wouldn't show it." He sat back, pushing his tray away. "If Coalition Central decides to make it public then he'll know. But by then it won't matter." He stared out the windows that lined the side of the mess hall out into space. His thoughts drifted to the threat. They were out there, and they were coming. "So," he said, shaking himself from the thoughts. "What about you? You didn't say much about your parents, so I figured—"

"Excuse me, Lt. Commander Diazal." Cas glanced over to see Ensign Yamashita standing over his left shoulder. She had been on the mission to D'jattan when Cas had found the shipment of human slaves the Sargans were transporting. That had also been the moment Cas had almost left *Tempest* and run. It hadn't been his finest hour.

"Ensign?" Evie said, sitting up straight. "Is there a problem?" It didn't escape Cas's notice she didn't correct Yamashita as to the status of her new rank. Maybe she didn't want to embarrass the young ensign.

"They said I was supposed to talk to you about all personnel transfers? We've got a few more crew members coming over from Eight and they need your authorization." He also couldn't help but notice Yamashita's wide smile and the gleam in her eye as she spoke, something Cas would almost call amorous, but he couldn't be sure. She hadn't even bothered to acknowledge Cas.

Evie sighed and grabbed her tray. "Duty calls, I suppose. Get some rest. You look like you need it."

"I can take that," Yamashita said, taking the tray from Evie who seemed stunned at the sudden onslaught of attention.

"T-thank you," she said as Yamashita deposited the tray in the recycler. She then followed the younger officer out of the mess hall but turned at the last second and offered Cas a wave. He didn't have time to wave back before she disappeared through the doors.

***

"Caspian!"

Cas turned as he was about to enter the dock launch back to the station. Approaching was a navy velvet robe, appearing to hover as it grew closer, obscuring all but the face and hands of its wearer. Of course, they weren't actual hands or a face at all; it was nothing more than a hard-light projection used by the Untuburu to make themselves appear more humanoid. Some chose the forms of humans, others of Erustiaans, and some even made up their own designs. Cas had never seen the apparatus underneath their robes before—they were the only Coalition officers who could appear out of uniform due to their religious beliefs. He'd heard it was a mechanical suit, holding the small, crab-like Untuburu inside, protected. The suit then had projectors built inside the hands and face to display whatever kind of exterior the Untuburu wanted. Cas had long wanted to get a better look at their suits, but it was very bad manners to ask an Untuburu to remove his cloak.

"Zaal," Cas said. "I missed you on the bridge earlier."

"I'd heard you stopped by," he said. "Are the rumors true, will you be joining us on another mission?"

Cas had to adjust his expectations. He'd forgotten the Untuburu spoke in very harsh, hushed voices, so that their words came across like death on the wind. It was a by-product of the types of translators they used. Despite their threatening voices, most Untuburu were very friendly. Though he had to admit a shiver often ran down his back when he listened to them pray. "Where did you hear that?" he asked.

"It is all over the ship. People have very strong opinions about you joining us again. Currently your support is fifteen percent. Opposition seventy-five percent. Only ten percent remain undecided."

"Are you taking a poll?" Cas asked in an uncertain tone.

"I am the operations officer. People trust me with information."

Cas ran his hand down his face. "You might as well know. I have been asked to accompany you."

"Excellent," Zaal said, though it came across like a threat. Had a human said it in that way Cas would have feared for his life. "I was so disappointed we didn't get to know each other more during our previous time together. I find you a fascinating specimen of the human race, and look forward to speaking with you further. May I ask, do you have any food allergies I should be aware of?"

"Umm..." Cas stumbled. "Nothing...out of the ordinary."

"Very good," Zaal whispered. "I would like to invite you for a meal once we are underway. Look for my communique." His artificial face produced a smile and Zaal floated back the way he came.

Cas shivered anyway. He'd never been to Untu and had no intention to. From all reports it was a hellish world, constantly under the cover of darkness or storms and most of its population lived underground. The surface was said to be like an asteroid, sharp peaks of ice and rock, constantly changing and eroding as the planet spun on its axis three times as fast as most inhabitable planets. And if that was their homeworld, what would Zaal's quarters look like? Cas figured he'd find out. At least there were a few people on board who didn't mind him coming along. And based on his observations on the last mission, his popularity seemed to be increasing.

Cas made his way back through the launch and into the station, taking his time getting back to his quarters. The food had provided some much-needed nourishment and he felt like he could sleep for a couple hours. His mind produced the idea of a nightcap but he pushed the image away, not wanting to make a bad situation worse.

Being the point-man to broker any kind of alliance with a dangerous and deadly species hadn't been his idea of a career, but here he was. Sure, if he failed all it meant was the probable destruction of the entire Coalition. No big deal, right? Even if he did manage to make some kind of deal with them, what then? Were the Sil going to give *Tempest* the plans to build weapons which the Coalition could one day use to combat the Sil? Doubtful. The only thing that had kept the peace this long was the Coalition's total inability to match the Sil militarily, combined with the Sil's total disinterest in the Coalition as a whole. If the power balance were to change in some way, there would be no telling what it would do to all of known space. And he was highly doubtful the Sil would hand over that sort of technology.

The other option, then, would be that the Sil would send their own ships to fight off the advancing threat. Either by invading the Coalition, or by waiting for the Coalition to be destroyed before taking any action. Either way it was a lose-lose. Cas understood why the admirals wanted to take the risk, but he could see no good way in which this played out. They were stuck between a rock and an even bigger rock with nowhere to go. The Sargans could sit back and watch, though they would be as outmatched against the Sil or any other threat, especially due to the disorganization within the Commonwealth. They were more likely to tear each other apart than wait for some outside influence to do it. Cas had often dreamed of the Sargan hierarchy collapsing in on itself, leaving all its employees—including him and Box—to their own devices. Had that happened Cas could have found parts for his ship and they could have taken off into the deep black ocean of stars, getting far away from any impending doom facing the Coalition.

He stared at the door to his quarters for a few minutes before going in. When he finally entered Box looked up from the screen he'd projected against the far wall, pausing the unit. "Have a nice lunch?"

"Were you monitoring me?" Cas asked, pushing past him to the bed.

"I was given direct instructions not to let you near the bar again. So yes, I was monitoring you."

Cas flopped down, face first into the mattress. "Thanks."

"I'm happy to babysit anytime," Box replied, resuming his show.

"Could you turn that down some? I need to get some sleep."

Box paused the show again. "That's right, walk right in here like you own the place—"

"Box."

"—no consideration for *anybody*. Just strutting around." His voice raised two octaves. "Look at me, I'm a human. My needs are more important than anyone else's."

"Box!"

The machine fell silent.

Cas turned on his side and sat up. "Is rejoining the crew on their mission really what you want to do? Because no one ordered you. You could stay here if you wanted to, do what you want."

"Oh, so now you're interested in the mission?" Box crossed his metal arms.

"No. But I don't see much of a choice. It's either try to make this work, or don't and wait for the inevitable. What I'm saying is where I don't have a choice, *you do*."

He uncrossed his arms. "You'd let me choose?"

"Look, I'm sorry if I've come across as someone who thinks of you as their property. I don't. We've been together so long I thought—what I'm saying is you *should* choose. I won't make you do one or the other. But keep in mind if you come on the ship you're going to have to put up with a lot of bullshit. They already don't like me over there."

"Good thing I'm not you then." His eyes blinked rapidly. "Maybe I could convince the captain to give me a position on the bridge. Do you think Lieutenant Commander Diazal would put in a good word for me?" He paused. "Technically I don't have any rights."

"You're a sentient being. You have as many rights as anyone else. We'll just have to remind people of that." Cas paused. "Oh and by the way, Evie got promoted. Make sure you congratulate her next time you see her."

"Uh oh. That means she's ranked higher than you now," Box replied.

"I don't have a rank. And I don't ever plan to, so it really doesn't matter."

"Whatever you say boss." Box turned his head by an almost imperceptible amount.

"What do you want to do on the ship? Surely not watch net dramas all day."

Box's eyes remained steady. "Autonomous robot liaison. I could do the first contact thing if we come upon a planet of robots. Or I could be the entertainment officer. Host movie nights. I doubt they need a pilot."

Cas laughed. "That's a shame because you're such a good one." That seemed to put him in a better mood. "Wake me in six hours."

"If I haven't already moved into my new quarters by then you mean?" His voice was more animated than normal.

"Sure, whatever."

"Thanks, boss!" Box said, resuming his program.

Cas sighed, grabbed a pillow and shoved it over his head.

<u>2</u>

"Home, sweet home," Box said as they traversed the long docking ramp back into *Tempest*. He carried most of the cargo, whereas Cas had one measly bag and a small container. Who cared if he could carry three times his own body weight? Did that mean he was resigned to *always* carry everything around here?

"Why are you so chipper?" Cas rubbed his temple and winced. He'd woken up from his "nap" in an even worse mood than when he went down. Served him right for getting into a rumble in the station's bar.

"New day, new me." Box hauled the cargo crates over the threshold.

"You! Hold!"

Box peered around the boxes, staring at the person who'd shouted at them. He searched his databanks. Crewman Wallace. A junior *junior* officer. Not worth Box's time. He proceeded to march right past the human, paying him no attention.

"Hey, 'bot, you need to check those!" Wallace said again as Box passed. Box continued forward, ignoring the human. What could he do, he was small and squishy while Box was—at the moment—able to crush a human's skull with one hand.

"Box, you have to listen to him," Cas said, already sounding tired again.

"Do I? Do I *really*?" He stopped in place, debating on how far he could push it. They just wanted to inspect the crates because *he* was carrying them. If Cas had been hauling them they would have let him pass right by.

Wallace jogged up behind him. "Open those containers," he ordered.

Box regarded him; a small, wiry human, not even one and a half meters tall. He had the look of someone who needed to jog a lot in order to stay healthy. Sweat coated on his forehead, despite the temperature in the corridor being quite comfortable according to human standards.

Box set the containers down, stepping back. "You want to know what is in them so bad, you open them."

Wallace turned to Cas. "What is your bot's problem? Is it malfunctioning?"

"*It* doesn't have a problem," Box said before Cas could open his mouth. "*It* doesn't appreciate being called *it* by a small-minded, weak little man."

Wallace backed up a step, the manifest device in his hand slipping from his grip and clanging to the floor.

"Box, come *on*," Cas said. He walked over to the junior officer. "He's not like other machines. And he's not programmed to follow orders."

"That—that doesn't matter," Wallace stammered. "I still need to scan the manifest. Yours too."

"We were on this ship not more than a week ago. It's all the same stuff!" Box exclaimed. "If I wanted to bring something aboard that would threaten this ship, do you think I'd be stupid enough to hide it in the containers I'm carrying? No, I'd hide it right *here*." He pointed to his crotch area, where he had a small compartment for spare parts, though he rarely used it. The look on Wallace's face told him his message had gotten across.

Cas groaned. If Box could have smiled, he would have.

"Caspian?" Cas's comm chirped.

He tapped the device on his arm. "Here."

"Are you on board yet?" It was Evie. "The captain wants a debrief. We're set to launch in twelve hours."

"I'll be there in a minute." Cas dropped the rest of his gear, turning off the comm. "Can you get all of this to our quarters?"

Box made a noise deep in his processor indicating his displeasure. "Yes."

Cas pointed at Wallace but kept his eyes on Box. "And cooperate with this man. Don't make things here harder than they already are. Let me know as soon as you've got everything set up."

Box raised his hand to the brim of his head. "Yes, sir!" he said in a mocking tone. Cas rolled his eyes and left them standing there, making his way down the corridor to the closest hypervator.

Box moved to pick up the containers.

"I-I still need to scan those," Wallace said, having retrieved his manifest.

Box stepped back. "Be my guest." Wallace used his manifest—which doubled as a scanner—to retrieve a list of everything in the containers. It wouldn't take him long, but it was longer than Box was willing to wait. "You have drones on this ship, right? Auto-drones?"

Wallace glanced at him. "Yes, we use them for the dangerous—"

"Great. When you're done have them deliver all these to my quarters. I have an important meeting to get to."

"But we don't use them for—" Wallace protested.

"And make sure they don't break anything," Box cut him off. "I know some of those autos can be clumsy. I have valuable things in here."

"I'll be done in just a moment, then you can—"

"Thanks. And keep up the good work." Box walked off and shot Wallace a quick wave as he made his way through the ship.

"Hey. *Hey!*" Wallace called but Box paid him no attention. He wanted to know what was in those crates so badly he could deal with them. Though he better not mess up Box's media collection. He'd been back to visit the shop on the promenade a couple more times, each time with his database purged and ready for more uploads. This place was so much better than the Sargan Commonwealth. People weren't trying to kill each other and media was readily available. He wasn't sure how many more times he could watch *Gleeph Station Party 7* before ripping his own optics from his eyes.

Box stopped at the end of the corridor and turned left. Did he want to head down to the shuttle bays? It was where he and Cas had kept their ship before Cas had single-handedly decided to destroy it. That had been his home too, and Box would have at least liked to have been consulted before losing his only place of residence.

He turned to the right. That led to some maintenance areas as well as the entertainment level where they kept the ship's library. It seemed like an easy choice. Just as he turned right someone called out behind him, "Excuse me," a male voice said.

Box turned, expecting to see Wallace running up behind him to complain but instead it was Lieutenant Ronde, the helmsman. What was he doing down here?

"You're the robot, Box, right?" he asked, a smile plastered on his face.

"Yes," Box replied. He hadn't had a chance to meet the lieutenant as the only time he'd seen him was when he was on the bridge, helping clean up the mess from the battle with the Sargans.

"Sorry, I never got to introduce myself," he said, holding out his hand. "Lieutenant Izak Ronde."

"I know." Box took the hand and shook it. Technically Ronde was a Lieutenant, Junior Grade. But regardless of his rank, it was rare for a human to give him any kind of acknowledgment, much less offer to shake his hand. Box had always thought that was something they kept to themselves. "Your service record and your piloting skills are impressive for a human."

"I hear you're not a bad pilot yourself," Izak said.

"I am a better pilot than most humans, but I sometimes lack the nuance required in high-stress situations. It can lead me to make mistakes where a human might have an intuition about a situation and be able to avoid it." He wasn't used to being confronted, much less engaged, by humans and felt uncomfortable. Off his game.

"Oh yeah? That's kind of interesting. Hey, I was wondering if I could get your help with something. I saw you'd just come on board and if you're not doing anything else..."

Box had to mentally take a step back. A human wanted his *help*? When in the time of Kor had this ever happened? Other than Cas barking orders or Evie telling him to come save Cas, Box couldn't recall a time when he'd been asked for help where it hadn't been ordered. And Lieutenant Ronde was even giving him the option. *If you're not busy.*

He should say he's busy. What would it be like to be able to say, "Sorry, I have something else I have to do right now. But I'll catch up with you later."? His processors drew out the moment, weighing the decision. But in the end, his curiosity was too great.

"I can help. What do you need?"

"Here, come with me. It's down in the cargo bays," Izak said.

"The cargo bays? Do you need me to lift something because if that's—"

"No, no. Nothing like that. We need help identifying some material that the ship's computer can't pinpoint. I was thinking with your wide array of experience you'd be able to figure it out."

Box couldn't help but feel a surge of pride and he may have pushed his metal chest out in front of him a little more. "I'd be happy to," he said.

Izak led him down the corridor to the hypervator. "So, let me ask you a question, and this has been bugging me."

"Okay," Box replied.

"If I were to tell you I was lying, would you believe me?"

Box stopped and turned to him, stunned. "What?"

"I said, if I were to say to you, *I am lying*, would you believe me?"

It *had* been too good to be true. *Smarmy human bastard.* He should have known. Box moved to leave. "I just remembered, I have something else I need to take care of."

Izak turned to him, tightening his posture. "What? What did I say?"

"Your meaning is clear, *Lieutenant*. You think I'm some simple program that can be tricked with a logic test."

"Wait, that's not—"

"What," Box interrupted. "Did you think you'd be able to make me overload or shutdown if I couldn't figure out a way of your silly little riddle?" He leaned over Izak. "Let me tell you, I've calculated more variables of the universe than your tiny mind can even comprehend, so don't treat me like I'm some simple machine. Otherwise I'll make you sorry the thought even entered your brain when I drill inside and pluck it from your tiny, human skull."

Izak scoffed, his demeanor changing. "You won't do anything to me. You're a machine, programmed not to harm humans."

Box slammed his fist into the wall behind Izak's head, centimeters from his ear. Izak ducked down, covering his face. "I'm also programmed not to take any bullshit. So don't test me. Go identify that material yourself. And be glad I'm in a charitable mood." He left Izak cowering, not turning back to see if he would say anything else. Frankly, Box didn't care if he screamed himself hoarse. He should have known it was a trick. And then for him to try and get Box stuck in a logic loop? What a dickhead.

Box headed back down toward the library like he should have done in the first place; his rage at Izak stewing in the back of his mind.

10

Was it just him or were the corridors on Eight brighter than the ones on the ship? They were standard Coalition architecture, all gray and white with rounded edges and soothing forms but for some reason things seemed brighter over here. Cas wasn't sure what it was, but it had distracted him long enough to get to Admiral Sanghvi's office. He pressed the small button beside the door.

"Enter," the admiral's voice said through the speaker embedded in the wall. The doors slid open to reveal the same room he'd been in only a few days before, watching his future slip away from him. "Mr. Robeaux." Admiral Sanghvi stood and stuck out his hand, taking Cas's with some force. Sanghvi was a large man, and very strong. He looked like the kind of man who could pick up a flag on a battlefield and lead troops into battle. He'd never taken the time to research Sanghvi's service record, but it was a good bet there was come combat in there somewhere. "I understand you had a run-in with some of the crew of the *Persephone.*"

Cas took a seat and scoffed. "Word of my pardon didn't spread very fast."

Sanghvi ignored the jab if he'd even caught it at all, which Cas bet he had. "That was by design. I'm sorry but I didn't want the media nets to catch wind of it, not when we're about to ship you off on another mission. And frankly, I'd like to keep it that way. The less people know you're back in Coalition space the better. For the time being."

"Then you better get a hold of those three guys who jumped me; they heard the news from somewhere and I bet they can't wait to tell their friends about the traitor they beat up."

"It's already been taken care of," Sanghvi said, making a dismissive wave with his hand. Cas was nonplussed. "You look like you're not used to people standing up for you."

"Can you blame me? After what Rutledge did?"

Sanghvi tapped a few panels on his desk. "I see you paid him a visit as well."

"I needed to know what kind of hornet's nest I was about to get myself into. Sir, I don't know how many times I can say this, but this is a suicide mission. Even if we manage not to die out there contacting the Sil. They will either wait for the threat to destroy us and deal with it on their own, or they'll send an invasion force into Coalition space and occupy the territory. But more than likely, they'll take one look at *Tempest* and blow it out of the sky."

Sanghvi regarded him a moment. "I appreciate your candor, but we are low on choices at the moment. And it is your job to make sure none of those things happens. We want the Sil to join forces with us, not conquer us and not wait for us to be annihilated. And I know it's a lot to ask, but my hope is the compassion you showed them—"

"Yeah, yeah," Cas said. "I know the reasons. I don't agree with them."

Sanghvi leaned forward. "Does that mean you're rejecting the mission?"

Cas pursed his lips, working his jaw. "And if I did? You'd make me go anyway. I'm not stupid, I know I don't have a choice here. But at least you're being courteous enough to give me the *illusion* of choice. It's what the Coalition is best at."

"I'm sorry your time in the Coalition wasn't what you expected. But we can't allow assets to go unused, and right now, you are an asset. The moment you start to become a liability again I'll be happy to send you off into the sunset."

Cas wasn't sure if he meant letting him go or killing him. But he didn't want to press to find out.

Sanghvi sat back in his chair again. "The reason I asked you here is I wanted to offer to reinstate your commission. Back to your original rank. I'd need you to pass a competency test, but none of the other requirements. Your rank was unfairly stripped from you and I'd like to right that wrong."

Cas dropped his gaze, staring at the floor a moment. He hadn't expected this, but on some level he'd known it was coming. Hadn't this been what he'd wanted ever since he'd been thrown in that prison seven years ago? Wasn't this the retribution he'd been seeking? And it would probably make life on the *Tempest* more bearable. The rest of the crew would have to be much more careful insulting him and he'd be able to shut down anything he didn't like with a simple order.

"Thank you, admiral, but I have to decline."

Sanghvi arched an eyebrow but otherwise remained still as stone.

"I'm not sure you'd understand, sir. But that rank, this job, everything I left behind, that was a different person. That person believed in the purity of the Coalition. And that person died in prison. The one who sits before you today isn't the same man. And he didn't earn that rank."

"I see," Sanghvi said softly.

"But I appreciate the offer." Cas stood, flattening the front of his shirt as he did. "If there's nothing else?"

"I've been getting reports your robot is out of control over on *Tempest*. I'm not sure it's a good idea to take it with you. Perhaps just leave it on the station, I can have some techs take a look and fix any kind of malfunction it might be experiencing."

"Um." Cas couldn't say he was surprised. He'd left Box over there alone and without a chaperone. Last time it had been different because Box could stay on their ship and keep himself occupied and out of the way. But now it was like he'd been untethered. Cas wasn't sure if it was all part of this identity crisis Box had been talking about or if it was his usual nature and this was what he did when he was bored. "What kind of reports?"

"It's threatened some of the crew with physical violence, and I have to tell you, that doesn't instill a lot of confidence in me. One hit and that thing could kill a person. All it takes is a minor malfunction." Sanghvi spread his arms out so his fists rested in the middle of the table.

I could say the same thing about humans. "I'll take care of it, sir. He's just bored."

"Where did you find it anyway? I've never seen another machine quite like it," the admiral asked.

"I...uh found him after I reached Sargan space. After the...parole incident," Cas lied. Sanghvi didn't need to know Box's origins, and Cas wasn't about to spill them. "I spent a couple of years tinkering with him, making him better, more efficient." *And more alive, but that was a complete accident.*

"Before you leave, I want it evaluated. Have Commander Diazal administer the tests. I'll need her to sign off on its condition before you depart."

Cas sighed, staring at the space next to the admiral's ear, unable to look him in the eye. Box didn't need an evaluation, he needed a job; something to keep him occupied. But he certainly wasn't about to leave him on Starbase Eight unattended. More than likely he'd come back (if they came back at all) to a crate full of spare parts and a "Sorry, we tried."

"I'll take care of it," Cas said, the sliding doors opening for him.

"See that you do. And good luck."

***

"You have to be kidding me," Cas said, stepping into the room. Though stepping was a generous term, *squeezing* would be more accurate.

"Not kidding." Box stood in the corner, his display projected against the wall less than a meter in front of him showing a new net drama. "What's wrong, different from the size you ordered?"

Cas took the room in. It couldn't be more than three meters square in any direction. The crates he'd left with Box stood stacked beside the door, shoved against the wall. A small bed occupied most of the room, but there was no way it could fit a human adult, much less provide any kind of comfort. "There has to be a mistake. I'll talk to Evie, or the requisitions officer. They can't honestly expect us to both stay in this room. It's a quarter of the size of my quarters on the *Reasonable Excuse!*"

"Some of us didn't even *have* quarters," Box mumbled.

"Where is the lavatory? Or the kitchen? Or the windows! It's like someone took a closet and shoved a bed in here."

"According to the ship schematics this *was* a storage unit. Up until about a day ago when the updated plans for the ship were released. You know they performed some updates, right?" Box asked, absently watching his program.

"Yeah, I saw the work on the bridge," Cas replied. "But are they really so hard up for space they had to put us in here?" He tried squeezing around the crates to the bed.

Box raised and lowered his shoulders, not breaking his attention span. "Not my problem, I'm perfectly comfortable over here."

"Oh, and that's another thing," Cas said. "You're about one misstep away from being kicked off this ship."

Box shut the show down and stared at him, his yellow eyes blinking rapidly. "He provoked me!"

"Who?"

"Lieutenant Ronde. He tried to trick me with a logic test. He thought it would make me malfunction," Box protested, scooting forward. "But he's never met a class 117 autonomous mining robot before; we're not like a drone otherwise he'd know even the simplest of us are designed to ignore logic fallacies. I can't believe he'd think I was so stupid I—"

"How do you know it wasn't a mistake? Or a joke?" Cas asked, cutting off Box's rant. Though Ronde had been ambivalent toward him as well from the very start. That first day on the bridge had been particularly uncomfortable.

"Ohhh, I know," Box replied. "You were right. I *do* have to put up with a lot of bullshit here. And my bullshit meter is already *this* full." He held up his hand above his head.

"Stick a dampener on whatever you're doing because it got reported to the admiral. And now I have to get Evie to administer and sign off on an evaluation because of your behavior." Cas gave up trying to get to the bed and made his way back toward the door.

"Evaluation for what?" Box asked.

"To make sure you're not a threat to the crew."

Box made a buzzing noise deep within, a sign of frustration. He leaned back against the wall again and turned on his device, resuming his net drama.

Cas placed his hands on his hips, staring at the tiny space a moment. Even though he didn't have it on him, he still wore the holster under his jacket for the boomcannon. If this had been a Sargan ship all he'd have to do was go to the nearest officer, threaten their life and get them to move them to better quarters. But here in the Coalition it was a lot different. He had to make a complaint, fill out requisition forms, wait the pre-determined amount of time, et cetera, et cetera. The Sargans might have been a hotbed of crime and death, but it was a hell of a lot easier to get things done over there.

"I'll be back," he said, leaving through the doors. "I need to fix this."

ERIC WARREN

11

The hypervator doors opened on the brand-new bridge, giving Cas pause. He'd been so accustomed to the old bridge layout it took him a moment to adjust to this new one. Gone was the center 3-D display, replaced by a more traditional 2-D display on the far wall opposite the hypervator where the Master Systems Display used to be. The MSD had been relegated to the left side of the new display while the helm and navigation stations had been positioned closest to the viewscreen with the operations and tactical stations situated behind them at a slight angle. Closest to him was the bridge Engineering and the specialist stations, positioned furthest away from the screen as they were least crucial posts on the bridge. Technically both could be empty, and the bridge wouldn't lose any functionality.

In the center of the room, right where the impressive 3-D display once stood were the captain and executive officer's chairs, facing the new display. Cas glanced down, even the floors had been changed to reflect the changes, with the floorplates having been coated with new colors to help navigate the area.

Evie turned in her chair as he entered, giving him a supportive smile and returned her attention to the front.

"Prepare to depart," Greene ordered. Each person focused on the work at their respective stations.

"Moorings have been cleared," Zaal said. "Ready, Captain."

"Lieutenant, at your leisure," Greene said. Ronde nodded without glancing back and worked his controls. The view through the viewscreen rotated around, indicating Ronde was turning the ship in a counter-clockwise direction. As soon as the ship was straight again it drove forward to the giant hatch in the side of Starbase Eight. Cas couldn't help but feel a pang of longing as the ship left its moorings and began its departure. In another life it would have been him on the bridge giving the orders, preparing to explore the great unknown.

"Approaching terminus," Ensign River announced. She had taken over for Blackburn at the navigation station and Cas noticed her hands were cybernetic replacements. She also had a small augmentation close to her eye which was mostly obscured by her short, neon green hair. She seemed anxious in her new role. It was never easy taking over for a fallen comrade, especially when the death had happened right here on the bridge.

The opening approached, the starfield beyond nothing but white specks in a sea of night. As they passed through the force barrier to open space Cas couldn't help but feel a sinking sensation in the pit of his stomach. He wasn't sad about leaving Eight, far from it. But rather it felt more like leaving another life behind, the one that he'd crafted for himself after being ejected from the Coalition. Here he was, on a Coalition ship for the second time in as many weeks, preparing to engage in a dangerous mission. He'd sworn he'd never find himself here again, but life never tended to go the way he'd expected.

"We're clear, Captain," Ronde said. He turned to look back and caught sight of Cas. Something flashed over his face, but it was gone before Cas could discern what it had been.

"Set course for Quaval," Greene's voice reflected the seriousness of the coordinates. Quaval was one of the few charted systems in Sil space, and the closest to their current position. It had been where Rutledge had first taken them on the *Achlys*. No doubt it was Greene's plan to use Cas's familiarity with the area to give them any kind of advantage. "Find the nearest undercurrent and send us through as soon as we're within range."

"Aye," Ronde and River said in unison, sharing a brief glance.

Greene stood. "Now that we are underway I can reveal more about our mission, though this information is classified to officer-level clearance only. If I hear any of the crew talking about this, I *will* find who decided to leak the information."

"There's only one person on this bridge who's a known traitor, start there," Page said, staring at Cas.

Greene ignored him. "Our mission is to reach and make contact with the Sil." There was a gasp in the room, though Cas couldn't tell where it had originated. "Mr. Robeaux will be our point-man. He is the only human who has ever assisted the Sil in any way and Coalition Central thinks he is our way in."

"But why?" Blohm asked. "What do we need the Sil for?"

"That's classified," Greene replied. "Just know that we wouldn't be taking these steps were they not absolutely necessary." Page scoffed. "We will be using the same route taken by the *Achlys* seven years ago," Greene continued, "Hopefully that will give us a small advantage as we are—for lack of a better word—flying into their space blind. But the hope is they will recognize and appreciate what Mr. Robeaux did for them and agree to talk."

"Captain, what is the endgame?" Zaal asked, his voice deep and heavy. "What does Coalition Central think we can accomplish?"

"We would like to broker a peace and opportunity to share information," Greene said. "I can't say more than that. But any situation in which we leave in one piece I will consider a win."

The rest of the bridge officers exchanged looks, many of them turning to Cas then turning back to the Captain again. Evie remained stone-faced.

Greene turned to Evie. "Commander, the bridge is yours. Notify me of any problems."

"Yes, Captain," Evie said, staying in her seat. Greene made his way to his command room, motioning for Cas to follow him. Once inside Greene indicated Cas take a seat.

"I assume you didn't ask me here to parade me in front of the bridge," Cas said.

Greene raised his eyebrows. "No. But having you there helped. I'm not a fool; I know there is a lot of animosity toward you from this crew. There would be on any ship. But we don't have the luxury of making the crew love you. We have a job to do and I am going to see it gets done, one way or another." He paused. "Since it will take us between thirty and thirty-five days to reach Sil space I wanted to get your thoughts on a strategy and spend some time going over it with you and the new negotiator. Have you met her yet?"

Cas shook his head. His last twelve hours had been spent shuffling from requisitions officer to requisitions officer, having little to no luck on procuring a new room. He couldn't help but think someone was deliberately blocking him but he didn't have the proof yet.

"When you get a chance, take some time to see her. She's one of the best in the Coalition and will help guide you through this process. I expect by the time we reach Sil space you to be well versed in diplomatic protocol. We have one chance at this and can't afford to screw it up."

"I'm aware," Cas said, an edge in his voice. He didn't need anyone telling him how important his role here was. All this had taken its toll and he felt like he could sleep for about a week. But there was little chance of it with that tiny bed in his room.

Greene regarded him. "Are you alright, Robeaux? You look tired."

"I'm just—it's nothing. I'm not used to not being on my own ship."

"Then see you get some rest. But I want you to be on the bridge for the second shift change each day. We'll be passing through an area of space not often traversed and I want you to be caught up on everything we're encountering. Consider yourself a temporary bridge crew member."

Cas sat back, having not expected this. "Captain, I'm not sure I'm the person you want—"

"Are you trying to tell me how to run my own ship, Mr. Robeaux?" Greene asked, challenging him. "The fact is you need to be apprised on what is happening every day. Whether you want to or not. I had one last thing I wanted to discuss with you." Cas glared at him, wondering how much worse this could get. "Have you considered wearing a Coalition uniform again?"

By his sides, Cas's hands flexed into fists and back, clawing at the material of the chair. "I haven't but I'll…take it under advisement."

"Excellent," Greene replied. "I believe it would be helpful to present a united front to the Sil, show them we're professional, organized, and serious."

"Was there anything else?" he asked.

"No. But make sure you take the time to meet with Negotiator Laska, today if possible. Thirty days may seem like a long time, but we'll be there before we know it."

Cas nodded and stood, still fuming over the suggestion he wear a uniform. If he had any say in the matter he'd never put that piece of cloth on again. He'd come on their ship, he'd even help them in their negotiation. He'd sit on the bridge for a daily briefing for as long as the captain wanted him there. But one thing he would never do would be to put that uniform on again. Not after everything they had done to him. It represented something tainted and treacherous. And Cas wouldn't have it.

He exited through the sliding doors without another look at Greene, doing his best to keep his cool. As he turned to head back toward the hypervator he locked eyes with Jorro Page, who wore a sinister sneer on his face. His lip was curled so Cas could even see his teeth underneath and yet it was twisted in a way that if he looked at it right it could resemble a smile. Cas narrowed his eyes and made a detour over to Evie.

"Do you have a second?" he asked. When he glanced back Page still hadn't taken his eyes off him.

"Sure." She tapped a button on her chair. "Lieutenant, notify me when we reach the undercurrent," she said to Zaal, whose robed head bobbed in response. She stood and escorted Cas to the hypervator doors. "What's going on?" she asked.

"I've been trying for the past twelve hours to find out who assigned me and Box a closet for quarters. But I keep getting the runaround. I can't believe every available space on this ship is full."

Evie furrowed her brow. "It's not. We have plenty of rooms available. Did you say you were in a *closet*?"

"Up on seven. We're in what seems to be a maintenance storage room."

Evie glanced over her shoulder then back at Cas again. "I'll take care of it. I think I know what's going on."

"It's Page, isn't it?" he asked.

"I'll tell you later. But you might wish you still had your old commission before this mission is over," she said, frustration in her voice.

"The admiral offered, but I refused," he said. He wanted to get off the bridge, get back down to his "quarters". Now that he'd hopefully taken care of his housing problem he didn't need to be here anymore.

"What?" she said. "Why? You would have been the third-highest ranked person on this ship if you had."

"It wouldn't be right," he replied. "I'm not the same person I was when I earned that rank. A lot has happened since then. Plus, I would have had to wear—" He gestured to her uniform.

"You don't want to take a downgrade, *Captain*." She smirked. "Who would want to go back to being a commander after running his own ship for so long?"

He forced a smile. "Yeah. Thanks for your help on the room, I'm going to pack what little we unpacked."

"You got it. Lunch tomorrow?" she asked.

The weight on his back seemed to lift briefly. As if a pulley had raised it up slightly so he wasn't holding so much all at once. "Sounds great."

She nodded then returned to her station. "Mr. Zaal, how close?" she asked as the hypervator doors opened for Cas.

"Another hundred-thousand kilometers," he replied in that heavy voice of his. Cas sighed. As the doors closed, he caught one last look at Page who appeared to be laughing to himself.

12

"Former Commander Robeaux, please report to meeting room Epsilon immediately," Cas's comm chirped. It happened to come on as he passed another crewmember in the hallway who glanced over at him with disgust. He needed to change his settings, so it only notified him of a comm and didn't blurt it out for everyone around him to hear.

Meeting room Epsilon? What could be down there? The voice had been a woman's, but it had been shrill and serious.

"Former Commander, do you read me?" the comm chirped again.

Cas grabbed it and tapped it. "This is Robeaux," he said. "Who is this?"

"Negotiator Laska. Captain Greene notified me you were ready to meet. I would like to begin as soon as possible." From the sound of it she wasn't a woman to be trifled with, but also thought a lot of herself. What if he was in the middle of a job, or a shower? It was best to get this over with.

"Fine. I'll be there momentarily," Cas replied.

The comm chirped again. "And make sure you bring a better attitude than the one I'm hearing. I'm not about to waste my time on someone who will not take these negotiations seriously."

There won't be any negotiations at all if we're not careful.

"I'll be there in a few minutes," Cas replied, turning off his comm. Every time the stupid thing beeped now it sent a shock of anxiety through his system. He wasn't used to having all these people around who could contact him. He'd hoped falling back into his old routines would be easy; making jokes with the crew, performing his daily duties. A structured routine. But it hadn't been like that at all. He was miserable and he knew it. Before, when he'd still had his ship and the promise of leaving the Coalition forever he'd been much more hopeful. Now everything seemed like it was falling apart.

He took the closest hypervator down to meeting room Epsilon, expecting to meet a someone who reminded him of his professors back at the academy. There had been one, Professor Arxa—xenobiology. She'd been the strictest person he'd ever met, requiring the students to be perfect in their knowledge of alien species, their traits, and their histories. She had said the entire back of the Coalition was made up of each person understanding where someone else came from, even if they didn't come from the same planet as you. Cas had hated her with a passion, but she was the professor he remembered the clearest, and some of her lessons had even helped him back when he'd been in the Sargan Commonwealth. It turned out when you knew a little bit about a person's planetary history they were much more likely to buy you a couple more rounds rather than punch your face in.

The door to the room slid open revealing what Cas thought at first was a child. But as he stood in the doorway, he realized she was in fact a full-grown person, she happened to be a little over a meter tall. Her dark black hair was swept back and pinned to her head, the back of it done up in an ornate, but classy bun. Her dark eyes seemed to pierce his very soul and she held a long, black stick of some sort, to Cas it looked to be made of a polymer carbonite? He couldn't be sure.

"Former Commander Robeaux, I presume," she announced, somehow managing to look down on him despite the fact he was a good half meter taller than her.

He stuck out his hand awkwardly as he entered, trying his best not to be rude. "Yes, and you must be—"

SMACK!

Cas retracted his hand, the back of it welting up with a red mark. He hadn't even seen her move the stick. "Goddammit! Ow!" he yelled.

"You are not to initiate physical contact with any being without first gaining their consent. Improper physical relations led to the twelve years war between the Maxians and the Ornagothi. We will not be making the same mistake in this classroom."

"Classroom?" Cas asked. He glanced around. There was one small chair with a desk facing a larger desk at the end of the room. And on the far wall an interactive board. "Am I…going to school?"

SMACK!

"Dammit, stop hitting me!"

"We will not be speaking out of turn in this classroom. Improper adherence to verbal contracts caused a three-fold rift in the Lek-Makal Empire, leading to two hundred years of famine for its people. We do not want to be unleashing any plagues in here, do we, Former Commander?"

Cas held his hand, rubbing the back of it, afraid to respond or move. She was quick as a whip with that thing. He had an urge to tackle her and wrench it from her grasp. She was small, what were the odds he'd get it before she beat him to death?

"Very good, Former Commander," she replied, turning to her right with the practiced motion of someone who had run military drills. "You didn't speak out of turn a second time. It seems you can learn after all. You may answer the question."

"I have to have permission...to answer a question you've asked me? Isn't an answer implied within the question itself?" he asked.

"Not if you're dealing with the Rummstäd." She walked to the front of the room and around the large desk, stepping up on something behind it so she was visible over the edge. She placed the stick in the middle of the empty desk.

"Am I dealing with the Rummstäd?" Cas asked, attempting to duplicate the inflection the woman had used.

She sighed, drawing her brows together. "No, I am Val. I'm surprised you didn't know. They told me you were well versed in other cultures, but I see I have my work cut out for me."

Cas approached slowly. "You'll have to forgive me, it's been a long time since I've met one of your people. And they weren't the...friendliest of people."

"That's a diplomatic way of saying we're hermits," she announced. For all intents and purposes she appeared human, just more diminutive in stature. Sturdier, like a piece of unbreakable stone. "You've never paid a visit to Valus, have you?"

He shook his head.

"I might have figured. Do yourself a favor, take the time to visit sometime. You might be surprised if you're willing to open your eyes to another culture."

"I've visited plenty of worlds," Cas said, still rubbing his hand. "I think I'm well versed in cultures ranging from both inside and out of the Coalition."

She picked up the stick again and smacked it hard against the table, producing the audible sound of a whip as it hits bare skin. "That is what we are here to find out!" she announced. "Now. I am Negotiator Xerxes Laska. I have negotiated over four hundred treaties in the past seventy years and am single-handedly credited with saving billions of lives. However, they have told me only *you* can negotiate with the Sil, so I am to

85

impart my knowledge on to you. I hope you are a quick study because we will need you to absorb seventy years' worth of experience in only thirty days."

Seventy years? The woman didn't look a day over forty. Maybe time worked differently on Valus. "Pleasure to meet you," Cas said, doing his best to keep the sarcasm out of his voice and failing miserably.

"I know," she said, looking down on him across the bridge of her nose. "I do not need to hear your qualifications or your experience. I have already extensively studied your records and have concluded you are a poor choice to make this contact. However, since I am only a negotiator and not an admiral we will be abiding by their orders. Are you prepared?"

"Prepared for what?" he asked.

SMACK!

Cas withdrew his hand again, seething while sucking in air through his teeth. "To learn!" she snapped.

***

Box stared at the door to their quarters. Six days. Six days of the exact same thing: waiting. Waiting for what? For the ship to explode? For Cas to finally give him permission to leave their quarters? Neither was very likely at the moment.

True to his word Cas had found them better accommodations; this room was much more the size he assumed humans were accustomed to. Box had spent the first day moping after Cas told him he shouldn't leave their quarters until things had calmed down. Evie had filled out a quick evaluation on him without even asking him any questions and sent it off to the admiral before they departed, ensuring Box could remain onboard, but she apparently agreed with Cas it was better if Box laid low for a while. Tensions about Cas being on the ship were high, and for some reason Box had to suffer right along with him. Death by association, he supposed. Over the next three days Box appeared not to have moved an inch in protest, not speaking or responding to anyone when he was addressed. At first it had annoyed the hell out of Cas as intended, but he'd seemed to have become used to it, even commenting the silence was a nice change of pace for once.

Except Cas didn't know what Box did when he was gone. He was off with some negotiator for at least three hours out of the day and now he also had a bridge shift he had to show up to which gave Box a *lot* of spare time. And despite having years' worth of net dramas to watch, they'd lost their luster. Without the comfort of the *Excuse* he needed more. So far Box had managed to explore twelve percent of the ship on his own without tripping any alarms or arousing any suspicion. He treated it as a challenge, much like he had when he'd been piloting the *Excuse.* If something looked challenging it made him want to do it more, like sliding the ship into a spot that had less than a centimeter clearance on either side. He chuckled; Cas had hated that.

Two open doorways down the shower stopped and Cas appeared in the opening a moment later, drawing Box from his thoughts. "That woman is a menace!" he yelled. "Look at this! Look at my hands!" He shoved the backs of his hands toward Box. Red marks covered all of his skin, inflamed from the hot shower. "I have got to figure out how to get that stick away from her, this can't be legal!"

"Why don't you haggle it away from her? Aren't you supposed to be becoming a master negotiator?" Box's voice was devoid of emotion. He'd tried the silent treatment which hadn't worked. Now he'd moved on to the emotionless machine treatment. Perhaps that would annoy Cas enough to formally lift his temporary "imprisonment".

"Maybe she needs to *lighten up.*" He headed back to the bathroom. "I've never met anyone who is so…strict regarding the rules. And let me tell you there are *a lot* of rules. Rules like you wouldn't believe." He returned to Box. "Did you know, when you're in the presence of the Husmus-riza you are supposed to pass gas as a sign of respect?"

Box was intrigued and couldn't help a bit of curiosity prompting his response. "Are you finding that helpful in preparation for negotiations with the Sil?" he asked.

"No!" Cas roared, oblivious to the fact Box had shown the first emotion in days. "Nothing has helped so far. It's because no one knows anything about the Sil except how destructive their weapons are. The net result of all these 'classes'," (he used the air quotes) "serves no purpose other than to keep me busy and out of everyone's way on this ship. How much trouble can I get into when I can barely use my hands? It's a conspiracy," he said.

"Like our quarters situation?" Box asked.

"Yes! Evie told me she is sure Page was the one who assigned us the closet, but she doesn't have any direct evidence. Which I should have guessed, had I known he was good enough to break into the requisitions database and change our assignments."

"Or find someone else who hates you as much as he does. It's much simpler," Box replied.

"I don't know," Cas said, dropping his arms. He returned to the bathroom, taking off his towel as he did and giving Box a perfect view of his ass. Box was about to make a remark but refrained. He had to remember: emotionless machine. That's how the people on this ship wanted to treat him so that's how he would act.

"I'm off to the ursanomium mines again," Cas announced after a few moments, having slipped on a clean set of clothes and boots. A Coalition uniform had been delivered to their quarters two days prior when Box had just returned from a jaunt—a lucky coincidence he'd been inside when the delivery arrived otherwise they would have no doubt asked Cas why he'd scheduled a delivery when no one was inside.

But that uniform had remained untouched ever since, hanging in the back of the closet. Box wasn't about to open that can of wasps, but instead admired Cas for not conforming to what was expected of him.

Box made no motion to indicate he'd heard Cas other than raising his right hand ten centimeters before lowering it again.

"Have fun...uh...doing whatever it is you're doing today," Cas added. "I'll talk to Evie again after I'm done with my bridge shift to see if she thinks it's okay for you to move around the ship again."

Box couldn't help but feel some guilt at his deception. But he wasn't about to tell Cas now, not when he still had eighty-eight percent of the ship to explore. Some areas would be much more challenging than others, but he welcomed the risk. "Thank you," was all he said in that same, emotionless tone.

Cas stood in the doorway, staring at him a moment longer than made Box comfortable then he turned, and the doors slipped closed. Box stood, walking over to the closet holding the uniform. He stared at it long enough until he was sure Cas would be far enough away not to spot him leaving the room. Box turned and walked right out the door.

13

The halls were quiet this morning; it seemed most people were on duty. Box hadn't experienced a full week on the ship yet so some of the schedules were still foreign to him, but he had plenty of time to learn. According to the most recent estimates they were a good twenty-five days from Sil space. And twenty-five days was an eternity for exploration. Though he was still figuring out how he'd get into the weapons lab. He'd be noticed there, or any sensitive area of the ship really, but he was determined to see all of it. Box'd known the *Reasonable Excuse* inside and out and hoped to form a similar bond with *Tempest*.

Perhaps today would be a good day to visit Engineering. During their last mission, Cas had spoken of the Claxian stationed onboard who worked down there, which was what helped *Tempest* generate its tremendous speed. Yes, that was something Box would like to see for himself, despite the risk. The weapons lab could wait, perhaps on the return trip.

Box took the hypervator down seven more levels to fourteen, stepping out into another empty hallway. His luck held. A few times he'd had to make up some excuse about running an errand for someone or having programmed in the wrong coordinates for his destination. Usually no one paid him any mind, though a few regarded him with skepticism. He'd filed their names for later.

As he turned the corner, he caught the movement of someone down the hall to his left, speaking in a loud and jovial manner. He pulled back, shuffling across the intersection into the far side while listening to the voice grow closer.

"—sn't a big deal. I told Greene I'd be happy to pilot but he didn't want to lose one of his best." Box recognized that voice. It was Ronde again, no doubt bragging about his piloting skills. Maybe if he'd challenged Box to a flying competition instead of trying to best him with a logic test he might have learned something. As it was, Box didn't want Ronde to catch him down here. The Lieutenant would know something was wrong immediately and report him.

"He didn't say that? Did he? You're embellishing," the other voice—female—said. Box didn't recognize her from his copy of the crew manifest.

"He might have hinted at it. I'm just telling you what I heard." Ronde chuckled. Box took off down the hall, his metal feet loud against the floor panels. He couldn't stay out here, Ronde would find him for sure. Box turned to the right and entered the first door that opened for him.

Inside was a large room full of beds, equipment, and people moving all about. He'd accidentally entered sickbay. One of the nurses glanced up, did a double-take, then returned to her duties, apparently sure robots couldn't need any services they would provide. Box couldn't stay here; someone would report him for sure. As he turned to leave someone came up beside him.

"May I help you?" a new voice asked.

Box turned to find himself face to face with the ship's doctor, Xax. "I believe I am lost," Box replied in his monotone, doing his best to conceal his panic.

"You're Mr. Robeaux's artificial life form, correct?" Xax asked.

Box had to do everything he could to tamp down his fury. "Yes," he said in the same monotone.

"I was told you are more than most other machines. You have—what the humans call—a soul? Would you say that's accurate?"

Conflicted, he remained silent. How was he supposed to respond? *Yes, I'm an autonomous being. Cut me open and study me, please?* Or *No, I am like everyone else. Nothing special at all.* The tension of it was killing him.

"I am...just a machine," he eventually said.

Xax stared at him through six black eyes positioned in two columns running down Xax's face, each with an aquamarine center that could rival even the most beautiful of galaxies. "I don't believe that is true," she whispered, "but if it's what you want to believe who am I to tell you any different?"

Box regarded the doctor, unsure of what to make of the Yax-Inax. He'd met a few before in the Sargan Commonwealth, though they were usually trading information or working off a debt. Poor souls who—like Cas—had been ejected or otherwise found themselves outside the protection of the Coalition. The one thing all Yax-Inax had in common though, was that they had complex mating structures; a prospect that had only increased Box's fascination with biological reproduction. This might be his one chance to learn more from an actual source instead of second-hand knowledge from the ship's library or even worse...hearsay.

"Would you like a tour of our facility?" Xax offered. "Perhaps it will add to your knowledge base in a significant or meaningful way."

"Uhh..." Box stammered, unsure why the doctor was being so accommodating. "Yes, please."

Xax's small mouth stretched into a smile.

"I understand Yax-Inax do not have genders," Box said. "At least not binary ones."

"This is true. My species has developed, over many thousands of years, the ability to reproduce with one or many partners. Any of the involved parties can carry the child or children and in some cases each member of the bonded unit will carry a fetus to term. However, I realize being on a Coalition ship filled with species that are binary, this is out of the norm. If you need to refer to me, it is easiest to use she pronouns."

"Thank you," Box said, losing even more of the monotone. He was already fascinated by Xax and only wanted to know more. It was as if he had stumbled on a gold mine, not to mention with a tour he could check off all of sickbay on his exploration chart.

"Follow me this way," Xax said, her long, slender body moving through the space effortlessly. "Here we have the examination beds and tables for minor injuries." Along the wall were twelve different tables that could fold into a chair or flat into a bed if necessary. "All of our scanning equipment is the best in the Coalition. I made sure of that when I came aboard as chief medical officer."

Xax led Box to another section while the nurses moved around them, paying neither of them any attention. "And here we have the surgical bay. My team and I can perform up to seven surgical procedures at once if necessary. And on a starship you never know what you will need to *repair*. I'm sure you've seen your fair share of scrapes and bruises, if you'll pardon the term."

"I have been injured in the past," Box replied, thinking of the time he and Cas had to chase down a Sargan defector who happened to be an excellent bomb maker. Box had lost half his appendages that day, though Cas had him back up and working in perfect order not more than sixty hours later.

"Despite the fact it doesn't technically fall under the prevue of medical science, I have also studied a fair bit of mechanics to tend to your or any of the drones' needs, should the occasion arrive." She leaned in close. "Personally, I don't always trust the engineers to get it right." Three of her eyes winked at once.

Box blinked rapidly, staring at the doctor in disbelief. "You...studied for me?"

Xax smiled and lifted two of her four arms up as if to say "it was no trouble". "Yax-Inax are curious and we can retain great volumes of information," she said. "I figured I had some extra space in my head so why not? You are a member of the crew after all."

"That's debatable," Box said, losing any last remnants of camouflage. Perhaps Xax was someone he could trust after all.

"Not to me." She turned to continue the tour. "Back here we have our morgue." Xax pointed to the far wall in the adjacent room. "Which has remained mostly empty so far. Thankfully. It means my team and I are doing our jobs."

Box had a flash of memory of the ensign on the bridge who'd been impaled by a large piece of the bulkhead that had buckled in their battle with the Sargans. He didn't want to bring it up to Xax, but an image of the ensign's slack face kept replaying in his mind. Her dead, empty eyes staring into space.

"And here is our science division where we research, cultivate and study new and interesting ways to help people." Xax held one of her arms out to the people in the next room. It was stark white, and each member of the staff wore dust-repellent garments. A low-level force barrier separated the clean room from the rest of sickbay. "And finally, we have our disease storage unit. In here we keep over five hundred-thousand diseases from three hundred different planets."

Box, despite not being able to catch a biological virus, stepped back. "Why would you keep those?"

"Because most often the best cure for a disease is the mutation of a similar disease. Most Coalition ships don't have a collection this large but that's because many of these are from my personal stores. It never hurts to be prepared."

"And what happens if one of those containers breaks?" Box asked, staring at the wall of vials.

"The system locks down and incinerates the vial at over five thousand kelvins. In the unlikely event the entire set is in danger it will all be destroyed. Which would be such a shame."

Box, intrigued, leaned in closer. "I never knew Coalition ships had these on board."

"It isn't a secret," Xax said. "But it's also not common knowledge. Most people don't *want* to know about it. But as long as the captain knows, we're fine. We're not violating any Coalition laws here. And I have to admit I really hope this encounter with the Sil goes well. I'm hoping to add some Sil diseases to my collection." She turned back to Box. "Your friend, Caspian. He's the one who is supposed to make contact?"

Box nodded. "He doesn't think it will go well." Xax pursed her tiny lips and led Box back into the main sickbay. Box found it soothing; a soft, blueish light filled the room. He wouldn't mind spending more time here if he could. "Thank you for the tour," he said, for once genuinely grateful to someone.

"Why don't you come back tomorrow?" she said. "There's always plenty to learn here and we have the most extensive database in the Coalition on biological processes. I'd be happy to show you. That is, assuming we're not under attack or finding our way out of a wormhole or whatever it is they do up there on the bridge."

If Box could have smiled he would have, as it was he just blinked his eyes rapidly. Did that mean he wouldn't be reported after all? "It's not a...problem?" he asked.

Xax shook her head. "Absolutely not. I think you'll find medical personnel some of the most empathetic and caring people on this ship. You have nothing to worry about."

It was as if she could read his mind. Box couldn't help all his processors from firing at once. "Yes...I'd like that," he said with as little enthusiasm as he could muster. Though a lot still came through in his words.

Xax smiled in response and Box decided he liked her smile.

He liked it a lot.

14

The doors to the main bridge hypervator slid open, revealing third shift. Cas muttered a silent *thank Kor* into the ether as he stood from his specialists' station—which still had only been given the barest of functionality for his access codes—and made his way past his counterpart who would take over for the next shift. Along with third shift came Jorro Page, whose shoulder collided with Cas's as they passed each other. Cas thought to shove the man, beat his face in until it was pulp and laugh over his unconscious body. Instead, he didn't even give him the satisfaction of having been inconvenienced, only made his way to the hypervator with the rest of the shift.

Inside the crowded hypervator Zaal moved next to him, the hard-light face smiling its somewhat unnatural grin. "Exciting day today, don't you think?" he asked.

"If you call a stellar nursery five hundred million kilometers away exciting, then yeah." Cas wanted to do nothing more than to sleep for the next fourteen hours. On an average day he would have been more than interested in the nursery, but class with Laska this morning had been rough. The backs of his hands had throbbed all day. He had half a mind to go down to sickbay for some ointment except Laska would know he would have done it and he didn't want to give the witch the satisfaction. He noticed how she eyed his swollen hands each morning as if they were a rite of passage for him.

"I do, though I wish we could have stopped to take a look. I'm sure the Coalition will send a research or survey ship to come and study the phenomenon." Zaal turned back to the front. "We are still on for dinner this evening?"

Fuck. He'd forgotten all about the dinner he'd agreed to weeks ago. What he really wanted was a good, stiff drink but Laska had put an end to that when he'd shown up to her class hungover last week. She'd had all his bar privileges revoked until after the mission was over. But after it wouldn't matter, because they'd all be a bunch of corpses floating in space.

Cas felt the eyes of the rest of second shift on them in the small space. Did these people not have lives of their own? "Uh…tonight? I thought…"

"I am making a human delicacy. Smoked brisket of yaarn. Smothered in a whiskey glaze."

Cas's mouth watered at the very prospect. He'd been eating nothing but the mess hall food for weeks now. How could he say no to that? No matter how weird Zaal's quarters were. "Yes, I'll be there." The hypervator stopped, letting three of the crew off. Zaal, Cas and two others remained.

"Excellent," Zaal said in his most-threatening voice. "I very much look forward to it. And learning more about you." The hypervator stopped again and Zaal stepped off. "Don't forget, fifteen hundred hours."

"I won't," Cas replied. The doors slid closed again and Cas caught one of the ensigns staring. The ensign's eyes found the floor as soon as he was caught. "Something you want to say?"

"No," the ensign replied. "Nothing at all."

Evie was right, maybe he should have kept his commission.

***

"How are things for you these days?" Cas asked, buttoning his shirt.

"Asking out of guilt or genuine concern?" Box replied, his attention seemed like it wasn't all there.

"What kind of a question is that? Of course I'm concerned. You sit in this room all day despite having all your privileges returned; you can go to any non-secure part of the ship if you want."

"Why would I want that? My home is right here, in my *chair*," Box replied, his face not moving.

"Fine, be an asshole. I'm just trying to make sure you're doing okay. I noticed you haven't asked the same of me." He finished the buttons and smoothed the wrinkles on the front. It would have to do.

"That's because I don't care," Box replied. "I'll sit here like a good little bot and keep to myself. Like I'm *supposed* to."

"Hey," Cas replied, suddenly hot. "It isn't my fault on our *first day* on this ship you nearly took the head off one of the lieutenants. There are consequences for your actions. I didn't impose them, but we're not in the Commonwealth anymore. We can't go around doing what we like."

"You seem to be doing what you like just fine," he replied.

"You call getting beaten every morning and falling asleep at a bridge station every afternoon doing what I like? All the while we're only getting closer to what I know will not end well."

"You're such a baby. At least you get to be on the bridge," Box said. "And you get to go to fancy dinners."

Cas sighed, exasperated. "You want to go? No one's stopping you. Why don't you come along if you want to talk to someone from the bridge so badly?" Box hesitated. What was going on behind those blinking yellow eyes? He'd been acting strange ever since they'd come on board and Cas couldn't help but think there might be something seriously wrong with him.

"I'm fine here. If you're lonely take Commander Diazal," he said.

Cas's mouth turned into a frown. Why hadn't he thought of that? Because of their schedules they hadn't seen much of each other the past few weeks. He tapped the comm on his arm. "Zaal?"

"Yes, Caspian?" the Untuburu's voice came over the comm, heavy as ever.

"Would you mind if I brought a…guest?"

"Please, bring whomever you wish," he replied. "I have more than enough for everyone."

"Thanks. I'll be there soon." Cas cut the comm and let out a breath. He felt better already.

"Does the commander know she's going or are you just going to show up on her doorstep with flowers?" Box asked.

"Shut up," Cas replied, tapping his comm again. "Evie?"

"Cas? Is everything okay?" she asked over the comm, her voice wavering.

"Yes, it's just I have this…invitation by Zaal to eat and I need a wing woman."

She chuckled on the other end. "Zaal's famous dinners. He only does it for people he really likes. When is it?"

"Fifteen minutes," Cas said sheepishly. He could imagine her shaking her head at him.

"It beats the dinner I had planned for myself," she said. "I'll meet you over there."

"Wow, that was easy," Cas said after he'd cut the comm.

"I can't wait to see what your kids look like," Box replied, his eyes blinking in a slow rhythm. That meant he was focused on something important, but whatever it was must be in his databanks. He stared into space, seeing something Cas couldn't.

"For the thousandth time, it's not like that," he replied.

"So you say. But I'm becoming an expert on biological relationships," Box stated. "I know what I'm talking about."

Cas shook his head, inspecting himself one last time in the mirror. Box was about as good at predicting relationships as he was at small talk. "Thoughts?"

"I would say you look like shit but even shit has its good days," Box replied, his eyes laughing for him.

"Whatever, enjoy your evening." Cas stepped out into the hallway. Normally Box wasn't so combative and edgy. Cas had thought it had been the confinement but as soon as it had been lifted Box had still refused to leave the room. Instead, he seemed to pass the time analyzing...what? Should he have insisted Box stay back on Eight, where he wouldn't be under as much scrutiny and where he had greater autonomy? No, at some point someone would have said the wrong thing and set him off. But that one room was too cramped for him. What he really needed was his own place. Evie had said there was plenty of room...so why was he still staying with Cas? It wasn't like he needed a babysitter. He'd bring it up to Evie after dinner.

After taking the hypervator to Zaal's floor Cas turned the corner to see Evie already outside the door, leaning up against the wall in much the same way she had when he'd spotted her that day at Devil's Gate. "Not going to shove a blade up under my neck today, are you?" He smiled as he approached.

"What?" It took her a moment to remember. "Oh, no." She chuckled and glanced at his hands. "She's a taskmaster, huh?" She motioned to the welts.

"Don't even get me started. I think she's pissed I'm the one to talk to the Sil and not her. But I can't prove it yet. If nothing else, my long-term goal is to get that stick from her and toss it out an airlock."

Evie suppressed a laugh as Cas pushed the small button beside Zaal's door.

"Enter," his ominous voice said. Cas exchanged a smile with Evie. Zaal could make a killing shooting propaganda commercials.

He'd been expecting…what, exactly? That Zaal would transform his quarters into a replica of his own home planet? That it would be hot and dark and full of smoke and soot? However, when Cas stepped into the otherwise normal room he felt somewhat silly. It was no different than his own quarters, with the only exception being that what looked like a track suspended from the ceiling skirted the walls until it made a complete loop.

"Welcome," Zaal said, setting some plates on the wide table in the middle of his "dining room" which was off to the side of the kitchen. Along the back wall were a series of windows that showed the field of stars blurring by in the distance. "Commander, nice to see you again."

"Lieutenant," Evie replied. "Thanks for allowing me to crash. You know I can't resist your meals." She turned to Cas. "Zaal is known to be better than some of the cooks down in the mess hall. Half the crew would love to be sitting in your shoes at the moment."

Cas turned to Zaal. "I didn't realize…thank you for inviting me."

Zaal's hard-light avatar smiled. "You're welcome. The cooks only need to take the time to learn more about the cultures they serve food to. Once they understand how they can work in conjunction with each other, it makes the dining experience much more pleasant."

"Will you be…I mean I know…" Cas wasn't sure how to finish the sentence he'd started. The last thing he wanted was to be rude to his host. Then he'd be known as the man who'd screwed up one of the most coveted dinners on the ship. Like he needed something else on his plate.

"This apparatus allows me to consume foods through the hands," Zaal replied. "Though they have to be in a…less than solid state when they reach 'me'. Please, make yourselves at home while I finish."

Evie took a seat and tapped her comm, bringing up a 3D display emanating from the device. "If you'll excuse me a moment I need to finish some work. I won't be a minute."

Cas, meanwhile, took a short stroll around the space. An open doorway led to the next room over, which instead of a bed, sat a large pile of obsidian and volcanic rocks, all arranged in the shape of a small mountain.

"My altar," Zaal said. "For when I disengage from my apparatus."

"How often do you…you know?" Cas asked, doing his best not to trip over his words.

"I can stay inside for over three weeks if necessary, but I take it off every evening to relax. I will go to my altar and pray, then take my respite."

It didn't look like any altar Cas had ever seen, but then again, the Untuburu had their own specific customs regarding religion, many of which were followed to the letter. Laska had drilled that into his head last week, despite Cas already knowing much about the Untuburu culture. He pointed up. "What's the track?"

"Because I spend so much time in the apparatus, my body can grow weak. Once a week I will disengage and spend hours doing laps to keep up my stamina. It provides for most of my exercise needs."

"Why not use the gym down on level twelve?" he asked.

"Most humanoid species aren't comfortable with my natural form. Especially not as I scurry around the gym." He finished setting the places at the table. "But we're here to talk about you. If you'll please take your seat we'll pray before we begin."

Cas couldn't help keep that shiver creeping up his spine. Zaal made it sound like he was sitting down to a sacrifice, not dinner. But he took his seat anyway as Evie shut off her comm.

"If you will please raise your hands," Zaal said, raising his own high above his head. The sleeves of the velvet robe fell back, revealing the metallic musculature of the apparatus he wore. He bent his head back toward the ceiling and closed his eyes. Cas and Evie followed suit. This really *was* a sacrifice.

"Great Kor, the all-knowing. You bless us with life. You bless us with death. May this meal assist us on our journey to your open embrace. Help us seek balance and unity with the universe."

Never a religious person, Cas couldn't help but reflect on the simplicity of the prayer. He cracked an eyelid to see Zaal lowering his hands, which he and Evie mimicked. Once his hands were on the table Zaal reached out to Evie and Cas. They each took a hand and took each other's. Cas couldn't help but think about how cold Zaal's hand was.

"All things in balance, thank you, Kor," Zaal said.

"All things in balance," Evie repeated.

"All things in balance," Cas said, assuming it was the right thing to do. Zaal released their hands.

"Thank you for indulging me. I know it isn't for everyone."

"It was beautiful," Evie replied. Cas couldn't agree more.

"Please." Zaal said. "Eat."

15

"So, you believe the Coalition is inherently flawed, like a diamond with a crack embedded somewhere inside. It still looks beautiful, but one day that crack will tear the jewel in two," Zaal said.

"I don't know if I'd call it a diamond," Cas said, exchanging looks with Evie. "But it certainly has cracks."

"This is absolutely fascinating," Zaal said. "I can't decide if your prejudice against the Coalition is because of their unfair treatment of you, or if you believe there are problems within the system itself that need to be corrected."

"Trust me," Cas said, taking a mouthful of yaarn. "It's not prejudice." Though it came out as *is n't pr'jdce.*

"Oh, for the love of…chew with your mouth closed," Evie said, her nose upturned.

"I'll have to challenge you on that," Zaal said. "Because of your treatment, by its very nature invites you to be biased. How can we know you are thinking with a clear head?"

Cas swallowed. "Because now I'm no longer under the brainwashing of the system, I can see it for what it really is."

"Then are you saying the commander and I are 'brainwashed'? That we do not see what is obvious to you?" Zaal asked. Evie only shook her head.

"Evie knows what's going on. But before, yeah, she was. Before she knew Rutledge had betrayed me and covered up a crime. A crime, which mind you, is outlawed in the Coalition's laws of governance."

"Cas, maybe we shouldn't be talking about classified—" she offered.

"Oh no, we've opened this can and we're getting to the bottom of it," Cas said. He was treading on shaky ground. The real story behind what had happened with the *Achlys* and Rutledge wasn't generally known. Rutledge had been arrested on charges other than conspiracy and the tragedy of the *Achlys* had been framed as the Coalition making a sacrifice to keep the ship out of Sargan hands. And while that was true, the real reason it had been destroyed was Cas. If that weapon had gotten out in any way there would have been no telling how it would have changed the balance of power.

Zaal only stared at him with a serene smile plastered on his face. And maybe the Untuburu wine was loosening his lips but Cas wasn't about to let this opportunity go. He pointed at Zaal with his utensil. "I can tell you right now the corruption goes to the very top."

Zaal turned to Evie. "Commander, has this been your experience as well?" he asked. "Do you find the Coalition rife with corruption?"

"No," she said, sneering at Cas. "I'll admit what Cas went through was unfair and horrific, but outside the norm of standard Coalition operating procedure. You can't condemn the entire Coalition for the actions of a few individuals."

"Oh, come on, Evie," Cas said, leaning his elbow on the table and staring at her. "You can't tell me you really think it began and ended with Rutledge. Someone had to authorize his missions, procure resources, make allotments."

"Yes," she said. "Admiral Sanghvi, the ranking officer in this quadrant. He told us as much." Her eyes flicked to Zaal and it didn't escape Cas's notice her hand had balled into a fist.

"Then doesn't it follow that Rutledge's orders to complete the mission no matter what would have also come from Sanghvi? Or someone else even higher up? Say the head of Coalition security? Someone else gave him clearance, otherwise he never would have taken the risk."

Evie shot him a stern look that said *shut up or I'm going to retrieve my sword and impale you.* Maybe he shouldn't press his luck.

"I was under the impression Admiral Rutledge had been arrested because he'd disobeyed a direct order. But this wouldn't have anything to do with our current mission, would it?" Zaal asked. "I've heard rumors Rutledge was arrested and imprisoned for charges unrelated to his actual conduct."

Evie's utensil clattered to the plate. "Where did you hear that?"

"So, then it *is* true," Zaal replied. "I got the information from one of the security officers on Starbase Eight. He heard it from the prosecutor."

"Hearsay," Evie said. "And you're under strict orders not to discuss what you know with anyone."

"Of course, Commander," Zaal said. He reached out and the flesh of the hard-light disappeared, replaced instead by a metal skeleton. In the center was a port that opened, to which Zaal placed over the yaarn as it sucked it up. Cas could see the food move through a semi-transparent tube embedded inside the exoskeleton which disappeared under his robe. "I have to admit, I am as good a cook as everyone says."

"Is that how you eat everything?" Cas asked.

"When I have company or am in the presence of others, yes," Zaal replied.

Evie pushed back from the table. "Thank you for the meal, Zaal. But Cas and I have some duties to attend to." She yanked his chair back, pulling him away from the table.

"I at least hope you enjoyed the food," Zaal said, standing just as Cas did. "I look forward to another meeting in the future. Mr. Robeaux, you have been fascinating."

"Thank you," Cas said, unsure of what was happening. He hadn't even finished his yaarn yet.

Evie led him to the door and gave him a little shove to the other side before turning back to Zaal. "Next time I'll host," she said. "Goodnight, Lieutenant."

"Good night, Commander," Zaal said as the doors shut.

"Are you insane?" Evie whispered to Cas as they made their way down the hall.

Cas wobbled. "What?" he asked.

"I dunno, maybe all the classified information you spilled in there? No one is supposed to know about Rutledge, certainly not a non-human species. What if he mentions it to someone on his home planet? And they happen to be a member of the fleet or the infantry. Then they start investigating why they haven't heard about this from Coalition brass. You can't just go around spouting whatever you want, there are conse—"

"But it happened…to me," Cas replied. "Shouldn't people know? Or is the Coalition going to cover it up forever? What happens when these aliens show up and we have superweapons to fight them? Don't you think people will start questioning that?"

"That's not our problem or our priority right now. Our orders are to keep quiet about Rutledge and the *Achlys*." She held up her hands in defense. "I know he wronged you, but you're going to have to keep that close to the chest. At least for now; there's no other way."

He wasn't sure if she was being intentionally obtuse or if she really did believe Rutledge had been working alone. Regardless, he couldn't keep quiet about this forever, not if the Coalition had any hope of surviving.

***

THWACK!

Cas jerked up, his eyes going wide.

"No daydreaming," Laska ordered, "Or next time it's the knuckles."

"I think I've evolved an immunity," Cas said, staring at his hands. He'd managed to cut down on the smacking, though he'd needed to be vigilant. And today he wasn't at the top of his game.

"That's not how evolution works," Laska said, returning to the desk and climbing a step she'd placed behind it to stare down on him. "We are due to reach Sil space tomorrow. Give me the eight tenets of diplomacy."

Cas sighed, knowing none of this would do them any good. The Sil weren't interested in talking. "Be patient, understand the other side, leave avenues open to retreat, seek united ground, be realistic, protect your interests, don't force the issue...ummm..."

Laska narrowed her eyes, stepping down from her perch and approaching Cas, her stick bobbing up and down as she walked. His eyes went to the instrument of pain as he racked his memory for the last one.

"Serve the common interest!" he said louder than he meant to.

"Very good," Laska purred. "What is your strategy for initiating first contact?"

"Establish myself and my connection to the Sil. Inform them of my intentions and invite them to a dialogue."

"And if that fails?" The weapon bobbed even quicker behind her back.

"Gauge their response, adjust my strategy accordingly." His knuckles were white under the small table. The few times he'd tried to hide his hands he'd been rewarded with a smack above the ear instead which hurt infinitely more. He replaced his hands on the desk despite knowing he was right.

"I suppose it will do," Laska said, her small eyes dropping. "I had hoped you'd lean into this better, but I can only do so much with the raw material. There has to be some potential there to begin with."

"I appreciate the vote of confidence," Cas replied.

SMACK!

"Dammit!" he yelled, pulling his hand back and rubbing the knuckles.

"No backtalk," Laska said. "I will accompany you to the bridge tomorrow, to ensure you are performing to your best ability."

Oh, hell no. Even if she put in the request Cas would make sure Evie quashed it.

"Negotiator—Xerxes," he said, using her name for the first time. She stiffened and looked as though she might give him another smack for good measure. "I need you to level with me. If you were in my position do you think this negotiation would have a chance? Far better people than me have tried to build a relationship with the Sil and every single one of them has failed."

Her eyes softened. "I believe dialogue is possible between all civilized species. Whether the Sil *are* civilized remains to be seen. But often diplomacy is more about what isn't said than what is. They have to know you understand their beliefs and fears and you must trust they understand the same. It's always a two-way street, which means there are twice as many opportunities for someone to veer off the road and wreck."

He took a deep breath, rubbing the back of his hand.

"You aren't the best I have ever worked with, but you aren't the worst either," she added. He wasn't sure if that was supposed to make him feel better or not. She pulled out a datapad and checked the front. "But now it's time to adjourn. We have a meeting with the captain to go over our strategy."

16

"All hands to battle stations; we are approaching Sil space. Captain to the bridge," Evie announced, watching her indicator on the arm of the chair while at the same time keeping an eye on the viewscreen. They approached the invisible barrier separating non-aligned space from Sil territory and her heart threatened to burst from her chest. Not that she let it show. She'd always had a calm and practiced demeanor which was even more important on a Coalition ship for times just like this. If the younger officers saw her sweat then they might be apt to make a mistake. Both she and the Captain needed to project calm, but with authority.

The command room door slid open revealing Greene, who took his seat beside her as the rest of first shift came on board to replace the more inexperienced officers. Among them was Cas who remained at the back of the bridge, watching without taking the specialist's seat.

"Mr. Robeaux, what can we expect in there?" Greene indicated the screen ahead of them.

"I expect we'll be stopped quickly. They'll have proximity sensors on their border letting them know when it has been crossed. The sensors weren't always there, but were installed after the war. They learned they couldn't trust the Coalition wouldn't just come barging in one day."

Evie watched him. His eyes were sunken in and he hadn't shaved in days, despite the fact he had assured her he was getting plenty of sleep. He wasn't used to a Coalition schedule. It took some getting used to; what with the days being twenty hours. The Sargans maintained a twenty-four-hour day and living among them for five years he'd undoubtedly become accustomed to it. She'd heard long ago humans were born with a natural twenty-five-hour cycle as babies and adjusting took some getting used to. He also couldn't take a nap whenever he wanted to either. She should have ordered Laska to go easier on him; to allow him to rest more since the entire mission hinged on his ability to perform under pressure. It wasn't good he was starting out tired.

"Six minutes to the border," Ensign River announced from the navigation position. She'd done a good job taking over for Ensign Blackburn. These last few weeks of relative calm had given her some good experience. Evie hoped it was enough because from here on out there was no telling what they would be encountering.

"Raise the armor and prepare all weapons," Greene said. "But I want them set on non-lethal shots only." He turned to Evie. "As if they could do any damage anyway."

"Aye, sir," Page said from tactical.

"Captain," Cas said, stepping forward. "Keep the armor but lose the weapons. They won't like that."

"Are you sure?" Greene asked. "I don't like going in there defenseless."

"It wouldn't matter anyway. Our weapons do nothing to their shield systems and flying in with our guns up and asses out is a good way to send the wrong message."

Evie caught a sneer from Page but he kept his eyes on his own station. It had only taken running a few reports to figure out it *had* been Page who'd arranged for Cas to live in a closet for his re-introduction to the ship. Some kind of practical joke though she hadn't confronted him about it yet. She wanted to wait until they were on the back end of this mission. But he acted like he didn't even care if he got caught. Evie couldn't figure out why he was more ambivalent toward Cas than anyone else. Though she'd also seen Ronde exhibiting some odd behavior around him. And of course Ronde had been the one who had reported Box to the admiral.

"Lieutenant, disarm all weapons. If they scan us, I don't want them to get the wrong impression," Greene said.

Page swiveled in his seat. "But that will leave us completely unprepared if they decide to attack," he protested. "How can we—?"

"Lieutenant," Greene said, his voice a low rumble. Page turned back to his console and dropped the weapons.

"Three minutes to the border," River announced.

"Any sign of Sil ships patrolling on scanners?" Greene asked, watching the screen. There was nothing out there but stars as far as Evie could see.

"Nothing yet, Captain," Zaal replied. "I have the scanners extended to full range."

"Ship readiness report," Evie asked, running down her mental checklist before heading into a potentially dangerous situation.

"All stations report ready. The crew is prepped and the Spacewings are on standby," Zaal said. They wouldn't have the short-range fighters set to launch on a "diplomatic" mission, but this was anything but ordinary.

"Should we drop out of the undercurrent?" Blohm asked.

Greene turned to Cas. "Thoughts?"

Cas exchanged glances with Evie. "I don't see any reason to drop out until it's necessary."

"Helm, adjust our heading to skirt the edge of Sil territory. If we get into trouble out here, I want to get out of their space as quickly as possible," Greene said.

"Two minutes."

Cas took a seat in the specialist station as the inky blackness of Sil space stretched before them. "There's a system before we get to Quaval," Cas said. "Inside Sil territory. It's full of super heavy gas giants and could make a good place for refuge if we need it."

"Send the coordinates to the helm, we'll keep that in our back pocket," Greene said.

Evie kept her eyes trained on her own display, showing summary readouts from each station. She took three deep breaths in succession. "Here we go."

"Crossing the barrier now, Captain," River said. The rest of the bridge was silent except for the constant hum of the engines. Evie couldn't even hear anyone else breathing. It had all come down to this.

"Steady, helm," Greene said.

Evie thought she saw Ronde's hand shake as he held the ship in a straight line. She stood and went over to his station. "You've got this, Izak," she whispered. He nodded but he kept his focus on his job. Evie turned to watch the rest of the crew. They may have their flaws, but they were a good crew. And they worked well together. The only one who seemed unperturbed by the intensity of the situation was Zaal, who wore the same smile he'd had the night they'd had dinner. It was hard to believe that had been over a week sinc—

The ship rocked as if it had been hit by an earthquake, throwing Evie from where she'd been standing clear across the bridge where she collided with the bulkhead. She put her arms up in time to keep her head from smashing into the metal. Her left arm snapped with astonishingly little pain. She could still function.

"Evasive action! Restraints!" Greene shouted.

"We've been thrown from the undercurrent," River called out as the auto-restraints pulled her back into her chair, as they did for each crew member save Evie. "They hit us from inside!"

Evie could feel the dampeners straining as the ship spun out from the undercurrent into normal space. She could only pray they didn't have the terrible luck to come out next to a star or other heavenly body. But thankfully most of space was empty, which gave them good odds. She pushed against the bulkhead, struggling to stand up.

"Open the comm!" Greene yelled, staring at the screen ahead of them. Evie froze. Two large Sil vessels—which to her resembled sharp claws hanging in space—faced them. Though it was hard to tell which side was the front; she could only assume they were facing them. She'd seen long-range scans of ships like these, but seeing them in person drove a fear through her she didn't think possible. She held her arm tighter, willing the sensation to return as it had gone numb.

"Open," Zaal replied, the smile having turned into a frown on his face.

"Sil vessels. Halt your attack, we are a peace-seeking vessel from the Sovereign Coalition of Aligned Systems."

The ship shook again, sending a rumble through the room. Though as far as she could tell they hadn't fired any kind of weapon, energy or otherwise. Evie finally got to her feet in time to see Cas making his way over to her.

"We're getting no response, Captain," Zaal replied.

"Keep the channel open," Cas yelled, supporting himself against the wall. Zaal nodded. "Sil vessel. Seven years ago—" The ship shook again, sending Cas to the floor and cutting him off.

"We have a breach on deck four," Zaal said. The room shook again producing a loud bang from somewhere and Evie had only the briefest thought to hope it wasn't an overload in the power systems.

"Engineering is reporting the drive is becoming unstable," Blohm said.

"Another hit or two and we'll be gone," Page added. "Captain, we have to retreat."

Greene turned to Blohm. "Get the engines back and open up an undercurrent. Helm, about-face, get us out of here as quickly as possible."

"Captain?" Cas called, trying to stand again.

"Cas." Evie shook her head. There was nothing they could do unless they wanted to be destroyed.

"Undercurrent charted," River announced, her voice shaky.

"Helm, go!" Greene yelled. There was a lurch forward as the dampeners struggled to keep up with the ship, nearly sending Evie to the ground again. She glanced over at Cas who only stared at the screen, the two Sil ships disappeared behind them as they traversed the undercurrent. "How long until we're out of their space?"

"Forty-five seconds, sir," River replied.

"Blohm, push it. Give me everything they've got in Engineering."

She nodded, relaying the commands to the lower decks. Evie made it back to her chair to monitor the situation. "Ops did you get a good scan of those ships?" she asked.

Zaal shook his head. "Not much. Our scanners couldn't get past their armor. According to the information provided by Admiral Sanghvi, these ships were much more advanced than the one the *Achlys* captured."

"We're clear of their space," River said, producing a loud exhale.

"Give them a wide berth, and get us far outside their territory. I don't want to even *look* like we're close," Greene said.

"Aye, Captain."

"Commander Sesster is reporting the undercurrent generators are damaged. If we stay in here too long the current will collapse and crush us," Blohm said.

Greene stood, checking his own station for the damage reports. "How long can we sustain it?"

116

"Another ten minutes, tops," she replied. "Then we'll have to shut down for repairs."

"Can we use that gas giant system Robeaux mentioned?" Greene asked.

"It's too far away, but there's a binary star system close, heavy iron content with thousands of planetoids," Ensign River said before Cas could open his mouth. "It isn't perfect but it could provide some cover."

"Set course," Greene said. Ronde nodded, adjusting the direction of the ship. "Any sign of pursuit?"

"None," Page replied. "And I'd like to suggest locking up the traitor until we can properly dispose of him."

"What?" Cas said, "What are you talking about?"

"It's obvious you sent them a communication to tell them we were coming. How else could they have found our undercurrent so quickly? We weren't inside their space for more than a minute before they began attacking."

"I didn't send any *message*," Cas protested through his teeth.

"Just like you didn't send the message that got your last ship in trouble," Page said, pointing at him. "You better hope no one dies this time."

"That's enough, Lieutenant," Greene snapped. "We're not going to turn on each other, not when there are bigger stakes here." He turned to Evie. "Commander, get yourself down to sickbay and back as soon as you can."

Evie hated leaving her post in the middle of a crisis but fixing the arm wouldn't take long and she couldn't do her job properly with a useless appendage. She locked down her station and with a wince, headed for the hypervator.

"At least allow me to confine him to his quarters," Page said, indignant. Evie stopped on her way, spinning to face Page.

"He's the only one on this ship who might even give us a chance of success. Can't you see that or are you too stupid to get that through your head?" Evie said.

Page, momentarily stunned, only blinked at her.

"Lieutenant, return to your duties. Commander, sickbay. Now," Greene ordered.

With a huff she finally made it to the hypervator, the doors cutting her off from the tension in the room as they closed.

***

Evie passed two teams extinguishing fires on the corridors and one trying to contain a chemical leak close to Engineering. She thought about heading directly there to assess the situation but they probably didn't need her getting in the way. Sesster was no doubt in control of everything. Plus, she really needed to get her arm repaired. It was the same one she'd injured rescuing Cas the first time, maybe it hadn't healed correctly.

The doors to sickbay opened to reveal two people on the examination beds while Xax moved between the two of them, doling out diagnoses as she made her examination. She looked up to Evie, her aquamarine eyes probing.

"Arm," Evie said, holding it at a slight angle.

"Over here." Xax pointed with one of her smaller arms to the bed behind her. She crossed the room and sat on the bed, still holding the arm while she waited for treatment. The other two: Ensign Peters and Crewman Ulag'tcha seemed to be in worse shape than she was. They both worked in Engineering; they must be having a hell of a time over there. Once this was over she would pass by just to make sure there was nothing she could do. As she was staring into space the images in front of her eyes suddenly coalesced into a figure she recognized.

"Box?" she asked, staring over at the far wall where he stood, completely still. "What are you doing here?"

"You can't see me," Box replied. "I've adjusted my colors to completely blend in with the bulkheads."

"I can see you. The eyes give you away."

"Damn," he said, dropping his head. "It's always the eyes. I need eyelids."

She hopped down from the bed and approached him. "What's going on?"

"I...got lost," he said in the least convincing voice she'd ever heard.

"He's here to learn," Xax said from behind her. "Box, come over here."

Box stepped forward, past Evie over to Ensign Peters. "These are third-degree burns. See how the flesh has charred and necrotized?" Xax asked. "What sort of treatment would you give him?"

"Apply a level three dermal analgesic and monitor the response," Box replied.

Xax turned to Evie. "He's a quick study. Box, look at the commander's injury and report back to me."

Evie returned to the bed, taking a seat. "Does Cas know you're down here?" she asked.

His eyes blinked once. "No."

"I don't understand; is this some kind of experiment?"

He picked up her arm, probing it with his metal fingers. "Tell me if you feel pain," he replied, his voice low. "It's not an experiment. I've...found something here."

"Ow, right there," she said wincing.

Box turned to Xax. "Clean break of the radius. Check for splintering?" he asked.

Xax nodded without taking her eyes off Ensign Peters. Box turned back to Evie, taking a scanner from the tray of instruments beside him.

"So...is this what you're doing now?" she asked.

"Beats banging my head against the wall in our room. Without a ship to fly I feel…off." He ran the scanner over her arm.

"You haven't seemed like yourself since you came on board." Gone was the loud-mouthed, rambunctious robot she'd first met. He'd lost some of his oomph. "Is that what Cas thinks you're doing? Staying in the room all day?"

"I doubt he'd notice if I was gone when he got there. He's had too much on his mind lately. I'm assuming things didn't go well up there." He turned back to Xax. "No splintering."

"Next steps?" Xax asked.

"Reset the bone and inject two stitchers."

Xax turned to Evie. "He is excellent. I can't believe you had him holed up in a room somewhere. With the captain's permission I'd like to add him to my staff."

This seemed to surprise Box as much as it did Evie. The scanner hung limp at the robot's side as he stared at the Yax-Inax doctor. "I'll bring it up with him once we're out of crisis mode," Evie replied.

"Hold on to the bed, this will sting." Box set the scanner down. She grabbed the edge of the bed as he held her arm with both hands and made a swift twist. A jolt of pain shot through her, but she bore down and didn't scream.

One of the other nurses, Menkel if her memory served her correctly, brought Box a small syringe. "Thanks, Jimmy," Box said. He leaned into Evie. "They treat me so well here, it's *weird*."

She stifled a smile. He put the syringe against her skin and pushed. Evie felt the small prick and had the unnerving sensation of something scurrying through her arm even though technically you weren't supposed to feel them.

"Give them about ten minutes to repair the bone and try not to put pressure on it for a few hours as they reinforce it. We'll remove them tomorrow," Box said.

Xax walked over and inspected Evie's arm. "I assume you need to return to duty."

"As soon as possible," she said.

"Just take it easy. The stitchers have released a localized painkiller in the area, but you may still experience some numbness. Just don't go punching anyone for a while. And take it easy with that arm. I don't want to see you in here again."

Evie smiled, hopping down from the bed. "Thanks...to both of you." She headed for the door.

"Don't forget my request," Xax said.

She waved as the doors closed behind her.

17

Cas grabbed Ronde by the lapel, jerking him forward while he cocked his arm back, fully intending to smash the man's face in. But before he could execute someone else was on him, pulling him and his arm back. Ronde, for his part, looked half-terrified and half-emboldened, breathing a sigh of relief as Cas was forced to release his lapel.

"I knew you were trouble the minute you stepped on this ship," Page said from behind him, dragging Cas backward and away from the junior lieutenant.

It hadn't been the smartest move. But at the same time Cas was tired of all the needling, and after Evie had gone to sickbay and Greene retired to the command room to go over the damage reports, both Page and Ronde had started in on him and hadn't let up. Ronde placed the full blame for Blackburn's death squarely on Cas's shoulders. And it had been the last straw; the *ackmel* collapsing under the weight. But now he was most likely headed to the brig for threatening an officer. Unless he decided to go all in and shove the back of his elbow into Page's face.

As the man held him tighter, pulling him to the other side of the bridge, Cas was seriously considering it when the hypervator doors opened, revealing Evie. "What the hell?" she asked.

"He tried to assault Lieutenant Ronde," Page explained, still holding Cas in some kind of strange chokehold which didn't allow him much movement.

"Release him," Evie ordered. "Now."

"Commander," Page protested.

"Don't you have enough to worry about other than playing a bouncer?" Evie said. Page scowled at her, releasing Cas. He took a deep breath; he hadn't realized the man had had him in such a grip. It must have been the adrenaline. "And you." Evie shook her head at Cas. "Get down to Engineering. They need all the help they can get down there. Where's the captain?"

"Going over the damage reports," Zaal said, standing beside his station. When the scuffle began everyone had jumped to intervene, but Page had been the quickest.

"Everyone back to your stations, we don't have time for this," Evie ordered. Reluctantly Page returned to tactical. She scowled at Cas. "Don't make me tell you twice."

Cas shot a look at Page, who eyed him with an intense hatred like he'd never seen before. Why had he gone for the younger officer rather than the man who was determined to make his time on this ship a living hell? He didn't look at Evie again, instead made his way to the open hypervator and left the bridge.

Cas was lucky to have her on his side. Technically a move like that should have ended with him in the brig, officer or not. He never would have tolerated behavior like that aboard the *Achlys* or any ship he'd served on. Coalition officers were supposed to be civil and work together for a common good. But then again he wasn't an officer anymore, and the same rules didn't apply. Being back on board was harder than he thought, he'd become so used to living by the skin of his teeth, always on guard. If life in the Sargan Commonwealth did anything for him, it made him much more vigilant.

As soon as the hypervator doors opened he jogged down the hallway to Engineering. The massive room was in chaos as soon as he stepped inside.

Most of the Engineering teams were working on securing the large conduits that ran from the back wall through the space and out toward the generators that kept the undercurrents open and wide enough for the ship to pass through. Two of them had cracked from the strain. Cas had seen a similar problem when the *Achlys* had burned her engines for too long, but the *Achlys* hadn't had the advantage of Claxian-assisted speed.

In the middle of the room Commander Sesster, the only Claxian on board, moved three of his five identical-sized "arms" around, attempting to monitor and fix problems before they arose. Watching him work was mesmerizing. But it wasn't just his physical capabilities which made him unique among the Engineering crew. Sesster was the only being on board who had the capability to calculate the undercurrent parameters on the spot, which was what allowed the ship to move so fast. Even assisted by a computer any other ship would lose its vector once the speed reached a certain threshold. Cas thought he caught the commander make a slight pause before Ensign Tyler came running up. Tyler was Sesster's human counterpart, the one who performed the jobs Sesster couldn't due to his imposing size.

"He says you can help over here," Tyler said, out of breath. "We're having trouble containing the plasma. What the hell happened up there?"

Cas followed him over to the right side of the room where teams were working on building a sleeve to cover one of the cracked conduits. "We encountered the Sil. It didn't go to plan."

That's an understatement, Mr. Robeaux. Cas shuddered. Feeling Sesster's words flow through him was like water soaking into the ground. He wasn't used to the sensation.

"How long have we got?" Tyler asked. Cas wasn't sure if it was Tyler or Sesster asking the question. He glanced over to the Claxian still making the repairs. Without any eyes it was difficult to tell if a Claxian was ever paying attention to him or not.

I am always paying attention. Please answer the ensign's question.

"Not long. We're outside their territory right now, but if they come looking for us we won't be able to hide. Not long anyway. We need to do everything we can to get the engines back up to full capacity."

"Are we returning to Coalition space?" Tyler attached a piece of the sleeve to the conduit as another crewman held it in place.

Cas glanced to the units feeding the conduit and bent down, checking each connection one-by-one. The third one was bad and he yanked it out. "I don't know. It depends on what the captain decides. But I'd doubt we'd come all this way just to turn around and go back empty-handed." In fact, he knew they weren't leaving empty-handed.

Guard your thoughts, Mr. Robeaux. I don't want to inadvertently pick up classified orders.

Cas attempted to empty his mind. Maybe if Sesster didn't want to know he shouldn't go probing. But then again he might not have a choice; maybe it was like someone shouting in an empty room and unless your ears were covered, you were going to hear what they said whether you wanted to or not.

An apt analogy. And thank you for finding the defective connection.

"You're welcome," Cas said. Tyler glanced over, apparently having been alerted by Sesster.

"Bad connection? Any others?" he asked.

"Not that I see," Cas replied.

"Okay, let's finish getting this on to reinforce the conduit." He and the rest of the Engineering team finished attaching the sleeve, covering the cracks that had formed. "Captain pushed us too hard; when we got thrown from the undercurrent it strained the system. Then when we had to make a jump without a cooldown it pushed everything past their limits. When you get back up there do me a favor and remind him this is still an experimental system. We don't have all the safeguards and redundancies a normal Coalition ship would have."

"Is that coming from you or the commander?" Cas asked.

Tyler took once glance at Sesster then turned back to Cas, puffing out his chest. "Both," he said.

***

Keeping his mind clear was harder than he'd anticipated. Cas went from odd job to odd job in Engineering, struggling to keep his thoughts on his work. He kept wanting to drift back to the situation with Rutledge, but every time they moved in that direction he would pull them away, thinking instead about the ship, its design, or anything else. He even tried humming a few times but it did him no good. And the more he tried not to think about it the worse it got. By the time most of the repairs were done his hands shook.

"I think you have everything under control down here," Cas said, extricating himself from beneath a coolant unit. "You guys don't need me anymore."

"There's still a lot to be done," Tyler said from the control seat beside him. He was in the process of rebooting the coolant acceptance protocols which allowed the plasma conduits to run twice as hot with half the ambient heat.

"I'm sure you can take care of it." Cas threw a wave behind him as he headed for the doors, wanting nothing more than some mental relief.

Thank you for working so hard to safeguard your knowledge. Sesster said. *I know it isn't easy.*

"That's the truth," Cas uttered, leaving Engineering and getting halfway down the hall before he relaxed his mind. It was the most soothing relief and he felt better. As if bags of sand had been lifted from his shoulders.

In all the madness he hadn't had a good chance to process what had happened. The Sil obviously didn't want to talk, that much was clear. So how was he going to get them to listen? Was it even possible? This was what he'd predicted when he'd first started lessons with Laska. Fat lot of good those had done him. Maybe she should have been the one to initiate contact, though the Sil had barely allowed them to get a word in edgewise. If this was going to have any chance of working he had to find some way of reaching them. Something that they wanted.

Cas pulled his comm out, tapping it. "Box?"

"Here, boss," his voice was muffled.

"What's going on? Where are you?"

"In the room, why?"

"I was just checking to make sure everything was okay. We had some trouble with the Sil."

"You don't say," he replied, his voice emotionless.

Cas ground his teeth together. Why was this so hard? "But you're...okay? No damage?"

There was a pause on the other side. "No damage. I'm fine."

His voice was still muffled and Cas thought he heard another voice coming through the comm. "Are you sure?" Cas asked. "You sound...odd."

"Yep, everything's fine. Go save the ship."

Cas stopped in the hallway, furrowing his brow. Something was definitely off. "Okay, I'll see you—"

"I have to go," Box said, cutting the connection. Cas stood there staring at the device for a moment before taking a deep breath. Box was probably just pissed at being left in that room all day. Cas really needed to remember to request Box get his own quarters but he'd have to go through Evie since Page had apparently set up some kind of requisition net against him. And now wasn't the time.

He considered sending a comm to the bridge to ask if they needed his help anymore but decided against it, putting the comm away again. If they needed him they'd call. He needed to figure out how to get the Sil's attention without them destroying the ship. And as much as he hated to admit it, he needed to start taking Laska's words seriously. Which meant he'd have to go back to her. "Damn," he said under his breath. He didn't even want to know how much pleasure she'd gather from him crawling back.

Might as well get it over with.

18

Cas stood in front of the door to the classroom, gathering his courage to face her after his failure on the bridge. He tapped the button beside the door. No answer.

He pushed it again, holding longer this time. Still no answer. Running one hand through his hair he leaned down to the panel and tapped in a simple override code he'd had memorized from his days on the *Achlys*. Most low-security protocol doors worked on the same system and needed a little ingenuity to get past them. The high-security doors were another matter and Box was the one to take care of those for him.

The doors slid open to reveal an empty room. Of course. Why would she be in here if there was no one to teach? He tapped his comm unit. "Locate Negotiator Laska," he said.

"Primary lounge," the computer replied.

Cas raised an eyebrow. What was she doing in there? And during a ship-wide emergency? Weren't all the entertainment facilities automatically closed during ship-wide emergencies? He broke into a trot down a couple of hallways until he reached the hypervator, taking it to level twelve. He then broke into a full-blown sprint down to the lounge, thinking something must be wrong if she was in there while everything was shut down. As soon as he reached the large oak doors with glass circles embedded in them he stopped.

Inside the dark room the negotiator sat, sipping from a glass and staring out the large windows to the planetoids beyond. He stepped forward but the doors didn't budge. Instead, he used the same code he'd used on the classroom and they opened easily, swooshing closed behind him.

Laska didn't turn or acknowledge him, only took another sip from her glass.

"Negotiator?" he asked.

"I see I'm not the only accomplished lockpick on this ship," she said.

"Is everything…alright?" he asked.

She turned to him, her face dead serious. "You tell me."

Cas dropped his shoulders, standing beside the table she'd leaned up against. Her diminutive stature was subdued by the room, which was also on the small side. It was supposed to provide for a cozier atmosphere and Laska looked right at home. He shook his head.

"Take a seat, Former Commander," she said, indicating the table. He noticed she didn't have her stick he'd come to hate so much. Laska walked over to the bar at the far end of the lounge and pulled a second glass from the shelf and a bottle from underneath the counter. She returned, pouring him a small amount of the amber liquid into the glass. "They told me you can handle your liquor. Give this a shot."

"I thought my privileges were revoked," he said.

"Only until we reached Sil space. I always keep my word," she replied.

He picked up the glass, wondering if this was just another one of her tests. But what else did he have to lose? He tipped the glass, the alcohol coating his tongue then the back of his throat and all points south. It was so smooth and clean he couldn't believe he'd never had this particular brand before. His drinks tended to be harsh on his system, but this was like drinking pure bliss.

"Good?" she asked.

"Amazing," he replied, setting the glass down. "To be honest I thought you were going to give me something a lot harsher."

She smirked. "After all our time together, what was the one thing you took away about diplomacy?" she asked. He ran back through the rules of diplomacy in his head but those weren't what she was referring to. This was something simpler. Something he had missed. "*Everything* is a negotiation. You being on this ship. This ship even existing. The whole foundation of the Coalition. All of it is based on negotiation. On two or more parties coming together and making an agreement. Each time you have an argument you are negotiating your position." She took another sip from her glass. "It never ends."

"You were waiting for me," he said.

"I chose a location which I knew you would find amenable, somewhere you feel you have the home field advantage. How did I know that?"

"I'm assuming it wasn't a lucky guess," Cas said, eyeing the glass.

"It was because I did my homework. I know as much about you as there is to know, Former Commander. I probably know you better than you know yourself. And in that, I knew one way or another, you'd find yourself here."

"I didn't come here for a drink," he said. "I was looking for *you*."

She tipped her head back and barked a laugh. "Things didn't go well with the Sil I take it?"

There was no denying it. "I need help," he said.

"We don't have a lot of time left," Laska said. "One way or another we'll be drawn into another confrontation with them and we have to be prepared. If we even survive."

"You go up there," Cas said. "You can do a better job than I could."

Laska stared out the windows. One of the planetoids moved in between them and this system's star, temporarily sending the room into deep shadow before moving out of the way again. "It isn't my place. They're right. You're the best chance to make this work. But you have to work to your advantage. And you have to be willing to give the Sil something they want, to draw them in."

"How do I know what they want if they won't talk to us?" he asked.

Laska tapped the neck of the bottle sitting between them. "The same way I knew where you would show up."

Cas stared at the bottle, thinking. The hint of an idea passed through his head. He wasn't sure it would work, but it might give them what they needed. "I think...I might know what to do."

"Then I would get on it," she replied. "Because it may look like we're sitting out here peacefully drifting along, but time is growing short."

He nodded. "I know." Standing, he took one last look at her then made his way to the doors. It was a good thing he wasn't a Coalition officer anymore because he was about to break every rule in the book.

"Don't forget," she called to him as he reached the doors. "Every negotiation requires sacrifice. From *both* parties."

Cas nodded and gave her a quick wave, then took off running down the hall.

***

"You're back," Tyler said as Cas rushed into Engineering again.

"I am. I need to check on something for the bridge," he replied, jogging over to the right side of the room. Despite being a brand-new engine system, the room was laid out like every other Coalition ship. If there was one thing he could

132

count on it was the constant predictability of the Coalition. Things have to be in straight lines, and always in the same order. Cas already recognized the computer lockouts.

"I didn't see any requests come through," Tyler said. "Is it something urgent? I can get my team on it."

"Nothing like that," Cas replied. "I'll take care of it." He studied the computer a moment. Tyler lingered behind him before heading off to put out another fire somewhere else.

What are you doing, Mr. Robeaux?

You have to trust me, Sesster. Cas thought, hoping the Commander could understand him. *This is the only way to keep the ship in one piece.*

While I do not question your motives, I do question your methods. Should you not inform the captain of your plan?

We don't have time to debate this and I can't chance he'd rule against me. I have to do this on my own. He tapped a few of the controls, releasing the locks on the sensor logs from the bridge. *Can you help me route all the sensor information collected from our encounter with the Sil to this terminal?* He thought he caught a sigh, only to realize it was a mental one that had washed over him, not an actual verbal noise.

Humans. So complicated. Sometimes I question whether coming on this ship was the right decision.

"This helps," Cas whispered as the sensor log information came in. Normally civilians weren't allowed to see information like this but as Laska had reminded him more than once he was *former* Commander Robeaux. He had clearance, just…retroactively.

I hope you're right about that.

Pulling up the information Zaal gathered from the encounter, Cas looked for anything familiar. Not that there was much to go on. The energy signatures of the two ships were identical, making them indistinguishable from each other, though there was one small difference. On the outside of the first ship that had knocked them out of the undercurrent was a small, purple symbol painted (or maybe etched) on the side of the hull. The other Sil vessel had a different blue symbol in the same place. A ship name perhaps? Or some other kind of identifier.

Sesster, does the Tempest *have the logs of the* Achlys *Evie downloaded before the ship was destroyed?*

That sigh rumbled through him again. *There is a copy in the computer, but it is secured by the commander's personal ID code.*

That wouldn't do. He couldn't alert Evie to his plans. *If* he was right, that was. She would only try to stop him.

I don't suppose you'd—

No. I will not break into the commander's personal information.

Cas took a deep breath. *I know it's a lot. And I'm sorry I'm putting you in this position. Just give me access to that section of the computer. I can do the rest.*

If you do this, it is paramount to theft. I've seen your fears. They'll imprison you again.

If my plan works, they probably won't ever get the chance. But that doesn't matter. What matters is this mission succeeds.

Access to Evie's personal database came up on the screen. *This is a trick I learned from the Sargans,* Cas thought. *Once I've shown you this, you'll know how to combat it. You may need to rewrite the ship's security protocols when I'm done.* Sesster didn't respond. Cas went to work, putting the main system into a diagnostic loop which allowed him to create a quick and easy bot key in the computer which could produce a million password guesses per second. And because the system was in a diagnostic it didn't send a warning to the main computer someone was breaking in. Less than twelve seconds had passed before he was in.

I'll be taking that up with the captain as soon as we are clear of the Sil, Sesster said.

Sometimes the simplest things make for the biggest loopholes. Cas perused Evie's personal documents, resisting the urge to explore them in depth. No, he was looking for a particular file. "Here," he whispered, finding the copy of the database from the *Achlys*. Inside were all the sensor logs from when it had encountered the Sil. Both times. She'd backed up the entire drive on her personal database before handing it over to the Coalition. It seemed she didn't trust them as much as she professed after all.

Cas went back to the first encounter all those years ago, examining the visual logs of the Sil ship that responded to his original distress call. He found what he was looking for: the same purple symbol on the side of the ship.

It's the same ship. Sesster said. *You must inform the captain.*

It won't do the captain any good; he can't do anything about it. But I needed confirmation. Sesster, you have to give me twenty minutes. Can you do that? Just twenty minutes.

I'm not sure—

I know I'm asking a lot. But you know I only want the mission to be a success. You have to believe this is nothing insidious.

I can't see what you're planning but I don't feel any deception behind it. There was a pause. *Twenty minutes.*

"Thanks, that's all I need." Cas closed everything in the system and took it off diagnostic mode, returning it all back to the way he'd found it. He turned to find Ensign Tyler standing behind him with a scowl on his face.

"Did you get what the bridge required?" he asked, some sarcasm in his voice. How much had he heard?

"I did. Thank you. How long until the engines are back up and running?"

"Two more hours. We have to test to make sure we don't have any more leaks," Tyler said, eyeing him suspiciously.

Cas nodded, pushing past Tyler and exited through the large doors, doing his best to project confidence.

"I'll let the captain know," he called back as the doors closed again. People were much less likely to suspect someone who acted like nothing was wrong. Would Sesster stop Tyler from reporting him to the Captain? He didn't think so. He'd have to be quick; his twenty minutes might have just turned into five.

19

Cas jogged through the identical-looking corridors, thinking the Coalition could help everyone out if they color-coded the different sections of the ship. Every corridor looked like the last; an infinite series of dark gray panels and lit walls. He didn't have long, Tyler might have heard too much. He'd already turned off his comm in the event they tried to get in contact with him, but that cut off all his access. He had no clue how much they already knew.

He increased his pace.

Cas stopped as soon as he'd reached Bay Two, opposite where he'd originally parked the *Reasonable Excuse* back when she'd still been in one piece. It almost made him nostalgic thinking about sitting up with Box in the ship while they hunted the *Achlys*. What would they do to Box once he left? They'd be able to see he hadn't sent Box any coded messages, and hopefully they wouldn't suspect him of any treachery. Cas couldn't contact him now, not if he wanted to keep all suspicion off him. If his plan didn't work none of it would matter anyway and he'd be lucky to even get back alive.

Cas recognized one of the crewmen working on some minor repairs along the wall. It appeared as if some of the bulkheads had buckled in the short battle and he was in the process of replacing them. "Abernathy, isn't it?" he asked.

"Yeah?" Abernathy replied, looking away from his work.

"Can you help me a minute? We're headed back into Sil space soon and the captain wanted me to perform a readiness evaluation on the Spacewing fighters."

Abernathy's eyes narrowed. "We just sent up an evaluation before we entered Sil space."

"Were any of the units damaged? We took quite a few hits," Cas said.

"The fighters are fine," Abernathy said. "The pilots are all on standby."

"What about the shuttles?"

Abernathy sighed. "Look, if you're so concerned take a look for yourself. I have a job to finish here and if these bulkheads aren't repaired by the time we get underway—"

Cas put up his hands as if to say "say no more". He excused himself, catching glances from the pilots and technicians of the Spacewing fighters on the far side of the bay. Those would be his biggest concern. With the ship basically at a standstill he wasn't worried about it coming after him, but he'd need a few minutes with the long-range shuttle before he could open an undercurrent.

He did his best to ignore them and made his way to where the fourteen shuttles in this bay remained parked. They were in the back of the bay which meant he'd have to fly the shuttle *past* some of the Spacewings and Kor knew he wasn't the best pilot. In fact, if he got the ship out of the bay without hitting something it would be a miracle. He took note of the first shuttle's name: *Calypso*. Sounded like a winner to him.

Cas boarded the shuttle and shut the doors on the side, locking them in place. He made his way to the front and began the shuttle's startup sequence. It took a moment for everything to light up. "First things first," Cas said, reconfiguring the controls to Box's favorite settings. It would help him to know where everything was in a pinch. And there might be some pinches. As best he knew these shuttles had minimal weapons; they were most often used for dignitaries or moving cargo.

The Spacewings were the fighters. But somehow being back in the cramped space reminded Cas of his old ship. And this *was* technically a diplomatic mission so the shuttle was at least being put to good use.

Moving fast, he made a connection to the ship's computer and downloaded all of the information he'd found in Engineering to his personal server. He also pulled a copy of the telescope recordings and bundled them together. It was everything he'd need.

Double-checking the undercurrent drive Cas took a deep breath, staring out into the bay at all the people moving around, doing their jobs, not paying him much attention. If being on the ship for thirty days had been good for one thing, it was acclimating himself to the crew. They got used to seeing him around, which made them lower their guard.

He took one last look at the controls. If he did this there was no coming back. And if he didn't make it to the undercurrent before the Spacewings stopped him then he'd be in the brig for sure and the mission would be dead in the water. But traditional tactics weren't going to work with the Sil. He had to do something drastic.

Cas engaged the hover mode and the shuttle lifted off from the pad. He immediately threw the throttle forward, turning the small craft as he did and it jerked ahead, nearly slamming into the wall before rotating to the left to face the exit. People scrambled around the bay and two jumped in front of it waving their hands. Cas hit the accelerator and the shuttle shot forward faster than he'd intended. The two people jumped out of the way but he was sure he'd clipped one of them. He caught the surprised face of Abernathy as the shuttle rocketed past him through the force barrier and into open space. Other than possibly striking a crew member, it had been a collision-free exit. He could only hope they were okay.

Cas began the startup procedures for an undercurrent jump, heading for where the *Tempest* last came through. He could piggyback through the undercurrent the ship had made before it faded too much. As he was focused on flying the shuttle straight, the proximity alarm went off. He tapped a button showing him the rear view from the shuttle and three of the Spacewing fighters had been dispatched to follow him.

"Unavoidable," Cas muttered as a comm blast came through the shuttle's systems. He turned it off, not wanting to try and explain or listen to whatever Captain Greene had to say. Greene would never approve this mission and Cas didn't need to hear the threats; it wasn't like he hadn't heard it all before.

One of the fighters opened fire, the blast rocketing past him on the right. A warning shot. They would go for his engines first and they were already closing. His only chance was the undercurrent; the Spacewings didn't have generators on their own so they couldn't enter, not even an established current as the risk would be too great they could be crushed by the intense gravity inside. He pulled back on the accelerator and yanked up, sending the shuttle straight up with little time to adjust. His insides felt like jelly but he had to do something until he reached the current. He only needed a few more moments.

A blast struck the shuttle on the side and the computer blinked an indication of a breach. He could make it with a breach, he'd made much worse in the *Excuse*. "Not enough," he said, tapping the controls so the shuttle went into a barrel roll, though it wasn't really designed as a maneuverable craft. He could only imagine what the other pilots were seeing. Maybe if he made them think he was crazy they would back off.

That was it. Cas tapped the autopilot and jumped out of the seat, heading for the Engineering control panels in the back. He disabled the safety systems without pause and dropped two of the magnetic locks keeping the fuel stores away from each other. If the sensors on the Spacewings worked they'd see he was minutes away from a massive explosion.

The comm screamed at him again but he ignored it, returning to the front of the ship. The fighters were backing off, keeping a safe distance. All he had to do was keep them off him long enough to get to the current and disappear inside. He turned back to the panel. With the locks down he had maybe two minutes. Was the undercurrent close enough? He was already a good distance from *Tempest* but where had they come out when they'd entered this system? He put the scanners to work, searching for the remnants of the old current.

"There," he said, only it was too far away. He'd have to re-engage the fuel locks before he reached it, but if the fighters kept their distance...

Cas adjusted the course to match the old current so he'd enter right were *Tempest* had come out. Checking the rear monitor all three fighters were still there, hanging as close as they dared. It was a good bluff. People thought he was half-suicidal as it was, this would just confirm everyone's prejudices.

He ran back to the panel, counting down the seconds before he could re-engage the locks. He needed as much time as possible. "Eight, seven, six," he counted to himself, his hands over the controls. One false move or one incorrect entry would mean his death. But performing under pressure had never been a problem for Cas. And it wouldn't be one now. "Four, three, two," he said. At the same time he re-engaged the locks and shunted the additional material back to the holding units. The alarm on the system quieted. Jumping up Cas sprinted to the front and pushed the accelerator to its limit. The fighters were closing again.

"Here we go!" he yelled, initiating the undercurrent drive and the emitter at the exact spot *Tempest* had left. The undercurrent opened with ease, allowing the small ship into the tunnel and launching him millions of kilometers away from the fighters.

Cas slumped back in his chair. Now for the hard part.

20

He didn't. He couldn't have. It wasn't possible.

"Commander," Greene's voice snapped Evie out of her thoughts and she turned to him, his face burning. "Tell me you didn't know about this."

"He never would have left my sight if I had," she replied, just as angry. But she couldn't show her anger, not like the captain could. He had to be up to something. Caspian wouldn't betray them, not after everything he'd been through. She glanced over at Page who was doing a very bad job of keeping the smile off his face. He would never let this go now. Not after all of them watching that shuttle disappear into the undercurrent despite her and the captain's repeated attempts to contact him. She didn't have a choice, there was only one way to settle this.

"I tried to warn you," Page said. "When I had to pull him off Izak. I tried to tell everyone. Once a deserter always a deserter. He was a security risk from the moment he stepped on this ship. He's probably on his way back to them now with a shuttle full of tactical information to sell to them. We might have all just been pawns in his game to defect to the Sil. You should have let me blow him out of the sky."

Greene only shook his head.

"You're not that stupid, Jorro, so don't pretend like you are," Evie said. "The fact was Cas was ordered on this mission by Admiral Sanghvi. He was coming whether anyone else wanted him to or not."

Page's eyes flashed but he returned to his duties.

"I don't believe he would defect," Zaal said from ops. "He was too insulted by—" Evie cut him off with a hard stare. "He is no longer a deserter."

Evie locked down her station and made her way to the hypervator doors. "I'll get a shuttle prepped. And I want to bring some of the infantry soldiers with me. In case."

"Stay where you are, Commander," Greene ordered.

She screwed up her face, planting her feet. "You can't suggest we just let him go? I need to go after him. *Tempest's* engines won't be back online for another two hours and he could be anywhere by then. If his trail degrades for more than a few minutes…"

"I'm aware," Greene said. "May I see you in the command room for a moment?" His voice sounded calm and measured. Too calm considering what had just happened.

They made their way to the command room, Evie taking another look at Page and giving him the meanest scowl she could muster. Not only was it bad enough he'd been questioning her judgement ever since she'd been sent to retrieve Cas back in Sargan territory, but he'd made his concerns public to some of the other officers behind her back. And the last thing they needed was to lose confidence in their commanding officers. Had it not been against protocol she would have decked him already.

The doors closed behind them and she was so focused on her anger at Page she didn't realize the captain still hadn't said anything. He only stood, looking out his small window at the stars and planetoids of the system beyond.

"I need to go after him, sir. Unless you're willing to write him off as a deserter."

"He *is* a deserter," Greene replied, clasping his hands behind his back. "He abandoned the Coalition five years ago."

"Because of a crime he didn't even commit!"

"No, he committed it. He disobeyed a direct order, regardless if it was the right thing to do or not. He still committed a high crime. And he had to pay the price when he returned to the Coalition. But instead of serving out his sentence like he was supposed to, he ran, abandoning the institution he'd sworn to protect." Greene didn't move, only remained staring out the window.

"He was afraid Admiral Rutledge would do something else to him. Can you blame him for running?" she asked.

"Yes. I can," Greene replied. "Because serving the Coalition isn't just about living on starships and exploring the galaxy. It also means owning your mistakes—*all* of your mistakes—when you make them. Caspian made a mistake. Some could argue the bigger mistake was accepting a position from Admiral Rutledge in the first place. I looked it up. The terms of his parole were that he work on Axis Five, performing menial tasks six hours a day. For three years. That was all he had to do and he would have been free. Not exactly a hard job."

"But Cas was grounded. He couldn't leave. He'd just exchanged a small prison for a large one. If you knew—"

Greene turned and held up his hand. "We all live in prisons of our own making. Do you think it was any better he became indebted to a Sargan overlord? He was still in 'prison'." He paused. "No, if he'd finished out his time on the Axis Five facility and been cleared then I would be more inclined to send you after him. But I'm not about to lose my XO because a civilian decided to desert."

"Sir, you can't seriously believe he's leaving for good? He's crucial to this mission, maybe he's—"

"Spare me the excuses, Diazal. You aren't responsible for defending Mr. Robeaux from the rest of us. Do I think he's stolen a shuttle and gone off to live on his own? No. From what I've seen of Caspian Robeaux that seems very unlikely.

But I can't ignore the fact he modified certain systems and injured a crewmember in his attempt to…do whatever it is he's doing. And based on his past behavior, there is a real possibility he's gone rogue."

Evie clenched her hands. If she could just go *after* him, she was sure she could convince him to come back. "So, what do we do?"

"He made it very clear he wanted to do whatever he's doing alone. And I'm not willing to sacrifice any of my crew to retrieve him. But I do want to know what he knew before he left. Something made him jump and I need you to find out what it was."

She pulled her lips between her teeth, concentrating. "Sir, wouldn't Lieutenant Page—?"

"The lieutenant's objectivity has been compromised," Greene said. "I couldn't trust his report unless I read it with my eyes closed. I realize you're on the other side of the coin, but I hope *your* objectivity hasn't been compromised. I would hate to find out you covered up evidence that supports a case of desertion."

She stiffened. "I'd never do that, sir."

He nodded. "I know." The chime on the door rang, indicating someone was outside the door.

"Enter," Greene said.

The doors opened to reveal Chief Master Rafnkell, her helmet still in her hands. "He faked a generator breach, Captain," she said, storming in. "We had to back off. There was no telling if it was real or not."

Rafnkell commanded the Spacewing fighters and had helped provide invaluable assistance during the encounter with Veena, though Evie's only encounter with her had been when Evie had absconded with one of the Chief's ships to rescue Cas. From what she'd read of her record, Rafnkell was a brash woman, often charging head-first into a situation rather than waiting for the go-ahead. It made her an effective tactician if not something of a wildcard. But she was good at her job. The fighters tended to keep to themselves and weren't technically crewmembers as they each "captained" their own ships. But they did have duties on *Tempest*.

"It wasn't your fault, Chief, the fact you got out there as quickly as you did—"

Rafnkell winced. Her short, blonde hair was plastered with sweat to her skull. "I'm sorry I didn't wait for your orders sir, but we couldn't let him take the shuttle like that." She turned to face Evie. "*You* should have contained him."

"That's enough," Greene said. "Get your ships in order, Chief. If we're going back into Sil space we may need them, though…" he trailed off. Greene knew as well as anyone short-range fighters wouldn't do a damn thing against the Sil ships. If a Dragon Class starship couldn't even hold her own what were a series of smaller one-person fighters supposed to do?

"Don't worry, sir, we'll be ready with our teeth out. If you need us, we're prepared," she said.

"Thank you, though I hope none of this is necessary. Diplomacy is still my highest priority." Rafnkell nodded, out of things to say. "Dismissed," Greene added. She turned without another glance at Evie and left the two alone.

"How can we hope to go back in there without Cas?" Evie asked once she was gone.

Greene sighed, taking a seat at his desk. "I'll talk to Laska. I don't see we have much choice, do you?"

"I guess not," she replied.

21

"Give me a diagnosis," Xax said. "And be quick."

Box examined the young woman lying on the bed before them. They'd brought her in from Bay One, some sort of accident with a shuttle. Box hadn't heard the whole story as the room had been a flurry of activity when the emergency unit brought her in. All he knew was it involved blunt-force trauma.

"She's unconscious," Box said, leaning over her to examine her closer. "She may have a cranial fracture from this bruising pattern and her breathing is shallow which is indicative of a head injury. She may not be getting enough oxygen to the brain."

"I agree," Xax said. "Begin the full body scan, let's make sure we're not dealing with something else here." She waved Nurse Jimmy Menkel over to assist.

Box glanced up at the monitor over the bed, watching as the scanner covered Crewman Zorres from head to toe. "What happened? She was obviously struck but…"

"Unscheduled shuttle launch," Jimmy said. "They said it was your friend."

Box glanced over, taking his optics off the scanner. "What friend?"

"The traitor. Robeaux."

"He stole a shuttle?" Box asked. That didn't make sense. He'd been so invested in making sure these negotiations went well.

Jimmy shrugged. "That's what they said."

"None of that matters now," Xax interjected. "Crewman Zorres could become critical at any minute. We need to take care of her before worrying about what's happening on the rest of the ship. Box, take note. The patient comes first, no matter what."

This should have focused Box but he still couldn't comprehend Cas stealing a shuttle. He couldn't even pilot! Why hadn't he told Box about it? He could have helped. Though his time in sickbay had been pretty good so far. If Cas had asked, it would have meant giving up everything he'd built here.

"Scan complete," Jimmy said. "Looks like you were right, Box, she's not getting enough oxygen to her brain. We need to halt the processes otherwise she'll lose a good portion of her brain function."

"Prep for surgery," Xax announced moving over beside the crewman. Two more nurses joined them as Box set a tray of standard tools beside Xax. "I'm going to open her up here and remove the broken cranial bone," she said, indicating with one of her arms. "Go ahead and put her in temporary stasis."

Jimmy reached over to the bed and adjusted some controls. "Engaging stasis now." A blue glow emanated from under Zorres and the effect on the monitor was immediate. Her breathing all but stopped and her pulse slowed to two beats per minute. All of her natural functions had been slowed.

Xax picked up the incisor and made a cut around the bruised area of her skull, right above her left eye, peeling back the skin and discarding it. She then examined the fracture. "It's indented alright, like a bulkhead. Box, give me the solution."

"Remove the affected bone, examine the brain for injury and reconstruct the skull using calorcium growth to prevent rejection."

"Very good," Xax said, leaning down and not taking her eyes off Zorres. Humans were such fragile creatures, yet in other ways they were so resilient. Box found it fascinating. Xax took another tool, this one larger, and made an expert cut directly into the skull itself, taking great care to remove the broken bone. Beneath was Zorres' brain, but there was what looked like a blood clot in the center of the area they'd cut away.

"Regenerator." Xax held out her lower left hand. Box placed the regenerator in it, which was passed to the upper hand and held over the center of the clot. "Here's hoping we don't lose anything important," she said. As Xax waved the device over the clot it gradually disappeared until it was gone completely. "Give me another scan."

Jimmy tapped the button beside the bed and the monitor scanned Zorres again. "No indication of any more damage, doc."

"Then let's regrow this bone and get this woman back on her feet," Xax said. She placed the tip of a tube to the edge of the cranium and pushed, a small amount of gooey liquid coming out. Box watched as the liquid shuddered slightly until it was the same color as Zorres' skull then stretched to cover the affected area. It reminded him of a spider building a web. A strand would cross the center, then move around the circular opening and cross the center again, eventually making a tangled web covering the incision. Within a minute it had been completely covered.

Xax tapped it with an instrument. "It's cured." She held up one last device, running it over the edges of the skin she'd cut away. It stimulated the edges of the skin, making them grow at an accelerated rate until they had recovered the affected area. After a few minutes Box couldn't even tell there had ever been an injury. "Deactivate the field," Xax said. They turned to Box. "Here's the rough part, don't hold your breath."

Box stared at her, his eyes blinking.

"That was a joke. It helps to have humor in here." Jimmy deactivated the field and Zorres' breathing returned to normal. Xax watched the monitor closely. "Looks like everything is back within acceptable limits …let's wake her."

Box leaned over with a mental stimulator and pressed it to the base of Zorres' neck, activating the device. Her eyes fluttered open and she jerked.

"Easy," Xax said, her arms up. "It's okay, crewman."

"Where…?" She glanced around agitated at first, but began to calm down quickly. "Doctor?"

"How do you feel?" Xax asked.

Zorres touched her head with her hand, feeling the area. "Okay, I think. What happened?"

"You were in an accident. Nurse Menkel is going to take you to perform some mental tests to make sure everything is working correctly. Okay?" she asked.

Zorres nodded, feeling her head again. Jimmy helped her up and off the bed. She wobbled for a moment, but gained her balance and followed him to another section of the sickbay.

"Not bad," Xax said. "You obviously don't have a problem retaining information, and you also seem to be applying it correctly." She replaced all the tools back on the tray and moved it back into its sanitizing alcove.

"I find it fascinating. Organic life is—"

The doors to the sickbay opened revealing Ronde, a big grin on his face.

"Lieutenant," Xax said. "Is there something we can do for you?"

"I just need to take him," Ronde said.

Box glanced between them. "Why?" he asked, accusation creeping into his voice. There was no reason not to be suspicious after what Ronde had already tried to pull. And though he hadn't attempted anything since that day, Box had the distinct feeling Ronde was just waiting for another opportunity.

"Captain has ordered the machine confined to quarters," he replied, his grin even wider.

"Why?" Xax asked.

Ronde took a few steps forward. "His partner-in-crime stole a shuttle and took off to who-knows-where. The Captain feels this machine could be a liability or even some kind of infiltration unit and until more information is known, he's to be confined."

"This is ridiculous," Xax said. They continued arguing but Box had quit paying attention. All his focus was on picking up Ronde and tossing him across the room like a doll. They thought he was a traitor? The concept was ludicrous. As if they could stop him. And now that he'd found something he truly loved the Captain was going to take that away from him too?

"—esn't matter. For the security of the ship, he's coming with me." Ronde was saying.

"Where is Lieutenant Page? He's the head of security, why isn't he here?" Xax asked.

"He's occupied with other matters regarding the traitor's departure. He asked if I would be willing to help him with this."

Xax crossed two of her arms. "And he doesn't have any other security personnel who could do this for him?"

Ronde shrugged. "We're dead in the water at the moment, I had some time to spare."

Xax made a sound of disgust in her throat and raised one of her arms, activating her comm. "Captain, this is sickbay. I need to confirm you've ordered Box confined to quarters."

"Confirmed, sickbay. We can't take any chances at the moment. Not until we know what's going on," Greene's voice replied.

Ronde turned back to Box, his smile wider than ever. "Are you going to be a problem or can we be civil about this? I can have a contingent of guards here in twenty seconds."

"Afraid I'll break your spine?" Box asked, seething but unable to show it. "I know which vertebrae I'd need to shatter to rob you of your legs. Or your ability to pee." He leaned closer to Ronde whose smile faltered for the first time. "Wanna test my knowledge?"

"Box," Xax said from behind him. "I'm sorry but this is Captain's orders. I'm sure it's only temporary and you'll be back here shortly."

Ronde looked more triumphant than ever. He stuck his arm out toward the door. "After you," he said.

Box took one last look at the sickbay, all of the nurses and Xax staring at the scene before them. Even Zorres had turned from her chair. He wanted to smash something, or at least yell at the man wearing the shit-eating grin, but what choice did he have? Any outburst would be read as confirmation of their fears and without Cas he'd be taken down to one of the science labs and disassembled. It was a good thing they couldn't see his fear.

He walked ahead of Ronde out of sickbay without another word, accompanying him in the hallway where three other security guards waited for them. He didn't even look back at Ronde; the man was just waiting for any excuse to bait or taunt him and Box wouldn't give it to him. If Box couldn't do the work he enjoyed he needed to figure out what had happened to Cas and why.

And maybe that would keep him busy enough not to think about the humiliation he just suffered.

22

This was how he should have done it the first time. No *Tempest*, no Captain Greene, no other people to get in his way or trying to help him. The Coalition should have sent him in here alone.

Cas regretted leaving Box behind but bringing him along only would have made them both targets and he was doing much better on *Tempest* by himself. Cas chuckled. Box still thought he didn't know he was going down to sickbay every day. Frustrated with Laska last week Cas had come back early to find Box returning to the room ahead of him. The next morning, he tracked Box's movements using the computer, and every morning since. It was always the same thing. He'd leave fifteen minutes after Cas left for the day, spend it in sickbay, then return fifteen minutes before Cas was due to end his bridge shift, where he'd arrange himself in the exact same position as he was in when Cas had left to give the illusion he hadn't moved all day.

He considered calling Box out on it a few times, but decided his friend would tell him when he was ready. Cas was glad whatever he was doing down there seemed to be working out for him. Had there been a problem there was no question he would have heard about it by now. Pulling him out of that to get his help to steal a shuttle wasn't what was best for Box, and Cas could only hope he'd understand in the end. And Evie would take care of him; or at least she better. Cas put his chances at returning somewhere around twenty to twenty-five percent and if he didn't come back they better not take it out on his partner.

He took a breath and stood up, stretching. The shuttle wasn't spacious but it wasn't cramped either. Enough to walk around and stave off stiffness. A fair sight better than those Spacewing fighters, but then again people weren't expected to spend hours upon hours in those at a time. His journey back to Sil space would take at least as twice as long due to the limited nature of the shuttle's undercurrent drive. He couldn't help but crack a smile. A Claxian wouldn't even fit in here.

He accessed the rear sensor panel to check on the breach from the Spacewing, finding it not as serious as he'd first thought. *Calypso* should have no trouble getting him where he needed to go.

Cas returned to his seat, searching the shuttle's database for anything interesting. He'd been quite proud of himself for out-maneuvering those fighters back there. Having barely piloted anything it was comforting with how easy the controls responded. But a Coalition ship was designed to be easy and comfortable. Back on the *Reasonable Excuse* if he'd wanted to hit the throttle and break right at the same time he either needed very long arms or two people manning the controls. Perhaps he wasn't as bad of a pilot as he thought.

Cas leaned back in his seat, watching the stars pulse by as the walls of the undercurrent enveloped the ship like a protective cocoon. It was so deceiving that way. If even one of his stabilizing emitters failed the wall of the undercurrent could collapse, crushing him at any moment. It had been a minor miracle *Tempest* hadn't suffered more damage when the Sil ship knocked them out of the undercurrent. Somehow that ship had come up behind them with little warning. Like they'd known exactly where they would be. That was a trick Cas wouldn't mind learning.

"Maybe they'll honor a last request," he said to himself as he laid his head back and closed his eyes. Sleep came quick.

***

He was awoken by a warning claxon followed by the shuttle lurching to one side throwing him from the seat. "Damn seatbelt," he mumbled, pushing himself up and onto his knees. He was still in the undercurrent; somehow the blast hadn't knocked him out. The scanners showed a large Sil ship behind him, just like what had happened on *Tempest*.

Cas disengaged the drive, returning to normal space and upon checking the maps realized he was right at the edge of their territory. The large Sil ship exited after him, continuing to take shots at him but never hitting the shuttle. They seemed to be nothing more than warning shots. But he couldn't take that chance. He tried making some maneuvers Box had showed him but the shuttle was slow to respond and despite the controls being easy to use, the ship just wasn't doing what he wanted it to.

Cas hit the comm, trying to send a broadband message but he didn't get a confirmation of anyone receiving. "Pointless not to try anyway," he said to himself before clearing his throat. "My name is Caspian Robeaux and I'm here representing the Coalition but I am not *part* of the Coalition. I was the person who sent the distress call seven years ago which resulted in your ship being saved."

The blasts around him stopped at once. "Wow. That was easi—" The ship jerked forward and Cas realized something had penetrated the hull. He tapped a few of the sensor cameras trying to get a good look at it when the ship jerked again. They'd hooked on to him somehow and despite the thrust of his engines he couldn't pull away. He got a camera on the outside of the ship. Two long cables ran from the Sil ship to his hull where they had embedded themselves deep into the bulkheads with spikes.

Cas couldn't say he was surprised. He'd hoped to at least begin negotiations on the shuttle but there was no guarantee the Sil would work that way. And here was the proof. They would bring him in to interrogate him and that would be all she wrote. He hoped he'd be able to convince them of the impending threat before they sliced his head off. He just had to keep telling himself this was what he wanted. This was the only way.

Panic seized his chest. What the hell was he doing? Sacrificing himself for the Coalition? That hadn't been part of the plan. Somehow over the past couple of weeks Laska had wormed her way inside his head, made him think the Coalition was all that mattered. Had she brainwashed him? He couldn't be certain but something was definitely wrong. This *wasn't* how he was going to die.

Grabbing the controls of the shuttle Cas turned it to face the way he was being pulled and hit the accelerator. The shuttle shot forward and the cables pulling him went slack, until he jerked the ship up, attempting to wrap the cables around the "nose" of the Sil ship, hoping perhaps they'd snap. The shuttle jerked again and Cas realized they'd embedded a third cable and could now hold him in a steady position as they pulled him in.

Cas hit the controls with his hands as they flashed off and back on again, sending out an error message. He turned to the front window of the shuttle. He could at least get an idea of what he was going into here.

The Sil ship was sleek and black, like a series of knives held together by the handles. Exactly like he remembered from seven years ago. He wiped the sweat forming on his brow and took a breath. On the side of the ship he saw the same familiar purple symbol he'd seen in the video feeds. Just as expected. Whoever was on this ship they were obviously the designated "border patrol", tasked with taking care of any errant Coalition units coming across their borders. Cas had to admit, they had been fast to stop him. *Tempest* was lucky to get out of here. If he hadn't sent that comm would they still have spared him? They didn't seem interested in destroying him as he skirted their border, only scaring him off otherwise they could have plowed one of their missiles directly into the side of the shuttle. So, what did they want? To extract information?

The shuttle was pulled into a hangar not much larger than the shuttle itself. As soon as it was inside the hangar door closed sending the room into pitch black. The only lights were those inside the shuttle. Cas tried looking out through the windows but could see nothing. The only thing he could tell was the Sil did use artificial gravity because the shuttle was parked on something solid and wasn't drifting in any direction. Either that or those cables they'd used to pull him in were stronger than they looked.

The side doors to the shuttle opened without warning, causing Cas to jump back, pressing himself up against the main console. A figure stepped in, though it was unlike anything Cas had ever seen before. It was a bipedal creature, that much was clear, but as far as Cas could tell it had no face. It had a head, but where the face should be were only what looked like carvings or runes on a stone. As he looked further, the "carvings" were all over the creature, whose mono-color body didn't seem to have a seam or break anywhere. Could this be the natural form of the Sil? Above the creature's head was a small crystal or perhaps power source that glowed purple. It wasn't bright though it did seem to pulse every few seconds. And it seemed to be suspended directly in front of the creature's forehead, not actually touching anything.

The creature reached out and Cas noticed it had five fingers on the end of its long hand which he found oddly comforting. Behind the creature some kind of molded cape came down the back and wrapped back up in the front, becoming part of the full body. The cape reminded Cas of insect wings.

Unmoving, the creature held its hand out to Cas, as if to beckon him forward. He wasn't sure how to react. "My name is Caspian Robe—" he stopped talking when the purple glowy thing in the creature's head pulsed in rhythm with his words. Was that how they heard? But how could they see? Unlike the Claxians who were completely blind but had a large number of appendages and "feelers" this creature appeared to be not that different than any of the other bipedal races. The only difference was the distinct lack of a face. "I...uh...can you even understand me?"

The figure—roughly two meters tall—stepped forward and grabbed Cas by the shoulder. Pain surged through the connection point as well as the strange sensation of something absorbing into him.

"I understand you fine, you trash. Now come with me or suffer dismemberment," a voice said. Cas glanced around, not sure of the source of the voice. It was as if it had come to him in his mind, but he'd definitely *heard* it as well. It had to be the creature; there was no one else around.

"I'm here for formal negotiations," Cas said. "I need to inform your people of a threat—"

"Be quiet," the voice warned, louder now. Cas stared at the creature who hadn't moved other than putting its hand on him. He needed to do something.

"I'm not in the Coalition anymore. I only represent them," he said.

"Final warning," the creature said.

Cas dropped his head and put his hands up, relenting. He couldn't talk if he was dead. And the only way any of this would be worth it was if he made them understand before they killed him.

That familiar panic shot through him again. Had this been worth it? Why had he run off half-cocked on some suicide mission? Laska must have done something to him; inserted some kind of programming in him. If he made it back he'd see that she and everyone she worked for would face the same consequences as Rutledge. But now he needed to focus on staying alive.

Cas stepped out of the shuttle into the darkness. The only light in the room came from ahead of him where two more purple energies glowed. As he grew closer—his hands stretched out in front of him to keep him from smacking into the ground should he trip on anything—he realized the light sources belonged to two more Sil, flanking a doorway. Both these Sil looked different from the one who had come to retrieve him. They seemed to be made out of the same material, but it flowed and moved in different ways, neither of them with the insect wings on the back. And both of their head auras were slightly different as well; the energy patterns moving in different sequences and held by a different shape. They were mesmerizing in their own way.

One turned before he arrived and walked ahead of them through the corridor beyond; the second waited until Cas had passed and fell into line behind them. It was so dark Cas could barely make out any details at all, but they were in some kind of hallway. He could see the walls and the floor but not the ceiling. Either the Sil also breathed oxygen or they'd created this environment for him; he couldn't be sure. At some point the corridor curved to the right and Cas continued to follow the lead Sil. There was something very strange about this place, it felt different than where he'd parked the shuttle. It was as if when he passed through into the corridor everything changed, but he couldn't tell how. Their footsteps were so quiet it was almost silent. And the air was devoid of any smell. It was as if it had been purified so it contained as few particles as possible.

The corridor slanted up, causing him to work harder to get up the "hill", though it didn't slow down the Sil at all. Finally, they came to a door which they passed through into a long room. Despite its apparent size—as it was still dark as space—it felt claustrophobic. The Sil in front of him turned around, placing its hands with their long fingers on him. Cas glanced at both hands. "What...?"

"Quiet," a different voice said. The figure in front of him pushed him back to the wall, holding him there for a moment. As soon as the figure let go Cas attempted to relax, only to find his body immobilized.

"Hey, I can't, *ungh,* I can't move." It felt like his body was made of stone. His internal processes still working, but everything below his neck had frozen.

"Wait here," the voice said. The three Sil turned in unison and filed back through the doorway.

"Wait. I need to speak with a representative, I have urgent information I need to relay." But they were already gone.

"Perfect," Cas said, now enveloped in complete darkness. "Just perfect."

23

Cas couldn't tell how long the darkness enveloped him. He felt as if he was drifting into an infinite abyss. At one point he began to even question if he was on a ship at all. Perhaps he had died in the attack and this was whatever the afterlife was supposed to be. If he were alive shouldn't he at least be able to hear the hum of an engine or the movement of plasma through a conduit?

There was nothing. He'd close his eyes and open them again, hoping each time the nightmare would be over but to no avail. His appendages became sore, then tingled, then went numb. And at one point he needed to pee and had absolutely no way to mitigate the mounting pressure. All he could do was grit his teeth and bear down, praying to Kor he didn't piss his pants on the first diplomatic contact between the Coalition and the Sil.

When he wouldn't be able to hold it any longer a pinpoint of purple light appeared to his right. The longer he stared at it the more he thought he was hallucinating. But no, it was really there and growing closer. Finally he saw the form the light belonged to: another Sil, though this one was bigger than the other three, by an order of magnitude. It was at least twice as wide and almost another half meter tall. And its purple head aura was more intense than the others; it glowed with a subtle brightness that hadn't been present with the other Sil. Cas could only assume this was the…captain? Owner? Diplomat? It was impossible to tell.

The Sil touched him on his shoulder. "You're a human?" the voice asked. It was husky in a way, but with an undercurrent of empathy. Was it empathy? He couldn't be sure, but there was something under there. Something he didn't understand yet. But it sounded as if this person might be female, if the Sil even had genders.

Cas nodded.

"You have a buildup of waste," the Sil said.

Cas, embarrassed, tried to remember which of Laska's classes covered normal bodily functions and how to deal with them in diplomatic contact.

But only a moment after the voice had said it the pressure was gone. Cas tried to look down to see if he had let go all over the place only for the voice to return. "It's been taken care of. Why are you here?" it asked.

It's been taken care of? What did they do, suck it out of my body?

Now was his chance. "I'm here representing the Sovereign Coa—"

"You said you weren't part of the Coalition," the voice said. Cas felt as if the faceless creature was boring into his mind. All that were present were the runes on its face, but Cas could almost feel it *looking* at him. He really wished he could see something else in the "room". It would give him something else to focus on other than this strange…person.

"I'm their representative. I was arrested and imprisoned after I helped save your ship."

The figure swayed. "You saved nothing. That ship was captured."

Dammit. They *did* know about the *Achlys's* success in retrieving their ship. Rutledge's arrogance was going to cost him his life. No sense in pretending he wasn't aware of it. Cas narrowed his eyes. He couldn't worry about Rutledge's actions now; this might be his only chance. "I've come to warn you of a threat."

"There is no threat the Coalition could dream up that we wouldn't be prepared for."

"This isn't the Coalition. Our—I mean their telescopes have detected—"

"Your story is already false," the voice interrupted. "The evidence says you are an appointed agent of the Coalition. I don't even know if you are the person who made that distress call seven years ago. This is nothing more than a bluff. An elaborate attempt to infiltrate our borders."

"It's not a bluff," Cas protested. "I'm telling the truth. There really is a threat and it's unlike—"

"Present your evidence," the Sil said.

His heart sank. He'd been so stunned by the creature coming to collect him he'd forgotten the data on the shuttle. "I have sensor logs…on my ship. They can confirm—"

"Your information has been examined and no threat was present. Do you wish to advance any other evidence?"

The logs weren't there? How could that be? He'd made *certain* to bring the information with him knowing the Sil would want proof. He'd specifically downloaded everything before leaving. He remembered doing it.

"Lack of further evidence only confirms our position. You are charged with the death of ten Sil civilians and will face the appropriate trial and punishment." The Sil turned to leave.

"Wait." Cas tried moving to stop the Sil, only to find his head immobilized now as well. He only had his mouth to work with. The Sil turned slightly. "Wait, what is your name?"

"Zenfor. Consul of *Renglas*, this ship."

"Consul? Is that like a captain?" Cas asked. "Never mind. Consul Zenfor, please listen to me. I would not have violated your borders by myself without a good reason. What logical goal could I have by coming here alone?"

"Without evidence to the contrary your words mean little," Zenfor said.

"I'm telling you, the evidence you need is in the shuttle. The information has been downloaded on the ship's computer. I have astrometric data, images, video. Everything you would need to show that I am telling the truth." What could have happened to that data? Could they be bluffing?

The problem was he knew next to nothing about these people, though from his short experience with Zenfor they seemed to have a reliance on evidence. Or at least a strong inclination. Was that how their society was structured? Or was it this particular Sil? He needed more information and more exposure to them to understand.

"Your 'shuttle' has been searched. Must I tell you again? The data does not exist."

That isn't possible. She must be lying in order to give them a reason to fight him. The data was there, he was sure of it. But for some reason she wanted to pretend like it wasn't. "Then you tell me, why am I here?" Cas spat. "Why risk myself in a shuttle that is obviously inferior?"

"It does not matter. You have been restrained and will be dealt with in short order."

"Why go to all the trouble of capturing me if you were never going to listen in the first place?" he asked, struggling against the restraint.

"Your crimes require a trial. To which you will be subjected."

"Crimes?" Was crossing their border such an unreasonable offense they went to this much trouble for everyone?

"No wonder your species is so inferior. You do not listen. Your crimes are the deaths of the ten civilians. Prepare to be charged." Zenfor said.

"I had nothing to do with that," Cas protested. "I was the one who tried to save them. By the time the ship was captured

165

I was running for my life from the Coalition. They *betrayed* me."

The imposing figure stood before him for a moment. "This makes no sense. They betrayed you and yet you claim to represent them? Present your evidence."

"I don't have any evidence!" Cas yelled. "I did it for the benefit of all the innocent people who could be killed by this thing coming straight at us. And it's not going to stop with the Coalition."

Zenfor shifted in front of him, her long arm raising up and landing on his shoulder. "You will have another opportunity to present your evidence at trial," Zenfor said. "We won't meet again." She dropped her arm and left him in the darkness, with only his thoughts as company.

24

"Did you take care of it?" Page asked as Izak Ronde strolled up to him in the corridor. He kept his voice low, even though the corridor was empty.

"Yeah. I thought for a minute he might put up a fight, but unfortunately he went quietly," Izak said, rubbing his hands on his pants as he approached. "Got stupid lubricant all over my hands."

"You're not trying hard enough," Page replied.

"Hey, I got him to punch a wall before, *and* I reported it to the admiral and it didn't do jack shit. They're both still here."

Page smirked. "One of them is still here. My job is done. The other one; he's your department."

Izak sneered at him. "Just because you got lucky and yours decided to jump ship doesn't mean your job is done. I need help with mine; he's got some kind of weird Zen thing going on now. I can barely get a rise out of him."

Page sighed and pushed off the wall, taking a few steps down the hall. Izak caught up with him. "Maybe it won't matter anymore. With the traitor gone and the machine locked in his room this might be the best situation we could hope for. I already know the captain's faith in the traitor is shaky, no matter what our first officer says. He wouldn't have authorized my request to have the robot confined otherwise."

"What do you think Cas went off to do? Face them alone?" Izak asked.

Page shook his head. "No way. He ran. Just like he ran when they put him on parole. He's probably headed back to Sargan space though it will take him a season to get there. If he's even got that many supplies."

"I overheard one of the Spacewing guys talking about how he faked a shuttle breach to get them to back off."

"So what?" Page spat. "Are you impressed? Any rookie could have done that." Though, it would be a delicate bit of work to keep the ship from igniting and reallocating the matter back into their holding pods. Page hated to admit it, but maybe Cas wasn't all talk after all.

"Why do you have it in for him so badly anyway? I get he's a deserter, but as far as I can tell he's a competent officer. Well, not *officer* but former officer." Izak said.

Page could feel himself darkening. "The Sargan Commonwealth isn't just some jumble of Coalition-reject humans. They are a well-organized superpower controlled by a massive crime syndicate. Why anyone would ever want to live there is beyond me. But all that power comes with consequences. Especially when they run into people who don't agree with them.

"By the time I was your age I had spent fifteen years defending my home against border skirmishes from people who wanted to rob, rape and kill me and my family. My home, my friends, we were all part of the planetary resistance; fighting off the Sargans every time they landed looking for supplies, fuel or parts. You don't know what they're like. I watched a Sargan ship bombard an entire city from orbit because the city refused to allow the ship to land and take refuge from a skirmish with the Coalition. Sometimes they would try to sneak in during the night, take our fuel supplies. I learned to sleep with a weapon in my hands at all times. One night I woke to my mother's screams as a group tried to kidnap her along with all our food. My father killed three of them that night. I killed the fourth."

"*Fuck,*" Izak said.

Page turned to him. "When we encountered them back outside Car'pr was that the first time you'd ever faced Sargans?" Izak nodded. "Then yeah, you just don't get it. Out there, on the frontier where Coalition support is weak or non-existent, the Sargans will do anything they can to gain a foothold. I grew up knowing nothing else."

"You're from Meridian right?" he asked.

"Meridian Three," Page replied.

"That's technically not even in Coalition space, no wonder you were under attack constantly."

"I've been defending what's mine since I could pick up a knife," Page said, pushing the memories away. He couldn't relive those right now, though they were threatening to break through anyway. "And I'm not about to let some Sargan scum come on this ship and pretend like everything is okay. You heard him, he *worked* for them. A former Coalition officer!"

Izak shrugged. "I'm just saying, whatever he was doing with that shuttle he was determined to do it or die trying. I'm not sure that sounds like someone who is running away." Izak wiped his hands on his pants again. "I should get that machine disassembled for this," he mumbled.

Page needed to calm down or he was going to have another attack right here in the hallway. The drugs only did so much and the last thing he needed was another reprimand on his record. He needed to focus on something else; something other than bad memories. What had the kid said? Disassembled? "Maybe that can be arranged," Page replied, focusing his mind. "How did that happen?" He pointed to Izak's hands.

"Oh, I was escorting him back to his quarters with those security officers you sent and as soon as he got inside the door some port opened on his side and I got lubrication all over my hands. Then he made some kind of chuckling sound and a half-hearted apology."

Page furrowed his brow. "So, would you say he malfunctioned in front of you?"

"I wouldn't call it a malfunction," Izak said. "It was pretty obvious he was doing it intentionally."

"But *could* you call it a malfunction?"

"Yeah, I guess so," Izak replied. A young ensign jogged past them. Page avoided eye-contact even as the ensign acknowledged them.

"And my security guys, they saw it too?"

"It was hard...*fuck*...hard to miss," Izak said, still wiping his hands. "Whatever this stuff is it isn't coming off. I might have to go to sickbay to get them to remove it."

"Listen. As soon as you're done with that, file an official complaint to droid control. Tell them the new bot on board isn't working quite right. We might be able to get around the brass." He rubbed his chin.

"Do you think they'll pay attention? We are in the middle of an emergency at the moment."

"Yeah, I know. But maybe DC is having a slow day. Either way it can't hurt." He narrowed his eyes. "Oh, I hope he does come back. Can you imagine the look on his face when he realizes his 'friend' is in about a million pieces down in one of the repair bays? He'll never want to step on this ship again."

"Or he'll kill me for putting him down there," he said.

"Let me worry about that," Page replied, imagining Cas's shocked face when he came back aboard.

"Don't you think that's kind of extreme?" Izak asked. "Getting them kicked off the ship is one thing, but having the robot disassembled? Isn't that—?"

Page spun on him. "What? Harsh? Cruel? Did you already forget about Blackburn? The girl you told me you planned to date as soon as you got the courage to ask her out? If not for that scum and his robot you two might be strolling hand-in-

170

hand right now." Page was pushing too far but he'd run out of options. If the robot wasn't going to make a scene or cause any danger there had to be another way to get rid of him. And often the simplest answers were the best. Get the diagnostics teams on him. They'd have to take him halfway apart to figure out what's going on inside there and by then it will be too late. And even if they did get him back together he might not wake up the same machine he was when he went down. They might even be able to reprogram him to better serve the ship.

Izak's face had gone red but he wasn't saying anything. Only staring Page down. Perfect. "You're a bastard," he finally whispered.

"I know. It takes a bastard to do my job. My number one concern has always been this ship and I won't let these two disrupt what we have here. I will do anything to protect this ship." He resumed his path down the hallway.

"Anything."

25

Evie approached the doors to Engineering, still debating how to handle this. She didn't want to come off as an interrogator, but she didn't want to go soft on them either. The ship's internal sensors registered Engineering as the last place Cas had been before taking off for Bay One and the shuttle. If she was going to find anything it would be in here.

Her comm chirped. "Commander?"

"Box? What's wrong?" she asked.

"Did you know?" he asked.

"Know what?"

"About the captain's decision. To contain me to quarters."

She stopped in her tracks. "No. He never said anything to me about it. They confined you?"

"As of twenty minutes ago," he said. She caught the hint of not only anger but sadness in his voice. Did the captain really think he was a risk without Cas here?

"I'm sorry, Box, let me investigate this and I'll call you back. I'm sure there's a reasonable explanation. And if there's not I'll talk to the captain."

"But—"

"I'm sorry, I'll call you back soon. I'm on an assignment," she said. He didn't protest any further so she cut the comm. There would be no need for this assignment had Cas *talked* to her before going off half-cocked. Whatever he planned it had to be something bad; something he didn't want to risk anyone else stopping him over. Which made her job much harder because he probably didn't tell *anyone*. Between him and the robot Evie might soon find *herself* at the ship's bar if she wasn't careful. But to be honest she was glad she was the one investigating; she didn't trust anyone else to do it. Greene was right, everyone had their own prejudices and concerns and none of them could be trusted.

"Commander," Ensign Yamashita said, passing her in the hall. Evie caught a glint in her eye and a smile wider than most of the rest of the crew offered her as Yamashita passed. Evie turned, watching her as she made her way down the hall and couldn't help her eyes from drifting downward.

No. The last thing she needed to do was get involved with a junior officer. Not only would that make things complex aboard this ship it would give Page an unending stream of comments to hurl at her behind her back and she already knew she was on his shit list. It was obvious he was gunning for her job but as long as his temper kept getting the better of him it was unlikely he'd ever leave tactical. Unless he was reassigned altogether. Evie smiled at the prospect.

Ensign Yamashita turned to look back at her, her own smile growing larger in response. Evie whipped her head back around and cursed herself. She'd have to take the ensign aside later, explain nothing could ever happen between them. Though Yamashita had proved herself more than capable on the weapons of Cas's old ship. Maybe Yamashita could be the new tactical officer once Page had been kicked off. *That* thought made her smile even more.

She needed to focus. Depending on what Cas knew before he left could potentially influence how the captain was willing to react.

Stepping forward the doors opened for her, revealing Engineering. Most of the main conduits had been repaired and the crews seemed to be winding down, prepping to start everything back up again. Sesster stood in the middle of the room, his appendages on two consoles at once reprogramming the input parameters for the new engines.

"Commander Diazal," Ensign Tyler said, approaching. "I wasn't aware you would be supervising." He sounded strange. Worried even.

"I'm not," she replied. "I'm here to check on your status and I wanted to see it for myself. When can we be back up and running?"

Tyler turned so he was staring in the same direction she was. "Another hour, I think. Sesster says he can get it done quicker but I believe in being cautious." As if on cue one of Sesster's appendages turned to "look" at Evie. She hadn't been around many Claxians, but always found them an interesting species. No optical nerves at all and yet they "saw" better than most humans. Either with their appendages and how their tactile touch created an image in their minds or their otherworldly perception of things. She often wondered if Sesster could sense everyone on the ship at once.

Not everyone. Only those within a certain radius of myself. The words were like a bucket of cold water running down her back and she shivered.

"Did he talk to you?" Tyler smirked. "I used to have the same look on my face whenever he would speak to me. You get used to it."

She shook it off. "It's fine. An hour you say? I'll report it back to the captain." She surveyed the room as the crews continued to work.

"Is there something else, Commander?" Tyler asked.

"Yes. Did you or anyone else in here have contact with Robeaux before he left?"

The air in the room stilled. At first Evie thought it was just her, until she noticed the work crews glancing up and taking notice as well. As if they'd all felt the same thing at once.

"He was here," Tyler said, seemingly the only one unaffected by the strange sensation she felt. "But not for long. He worked on that terminal over there for a while. Ironically he said he was here to do an inspection for the bridge too." Tyler eyed her with a renewed curiosity.

"Relax, Ensign. I'm not going to run off with another shuttle. But I do need to know what he was looking for." The temperature in the room seemed to drop a couple of degrees and Evie rubbed her arms at the chill. "Is there a problem with the environmental units in here?"

"Not as far as I know." Tyler led her over to the terminal.

"Do you know what he was doing over here?"

"I couldn't tell exactly, but it seemed to me he was looking into something he shouldn't have been." Tyler opened the station. The screen glowed to life immediately.

"Why do you say that?" she asked.

"Just a feeling," Tyler replied. "I was watching him over my shoulder, and it seemed he was working hard on something but every time I asked him if I could help he said he'd take care of it. I'm not one of those people who necessarily blames Mr. Robeaux for what happened to him, especially not after all the help he gave us down here. But still, it seemed wrong to me. And then I find out he leaves from here and steals a shuttle. I have to think I made the right call."

"And what call is that?" Evie asked, scanning the screen. Nothing was showing up. "What did he access?

"I wiped the files he tried to transfer to the shuttle," Tyler said.

She turned to him. "You *what*?"

He took a step back, his face flushing. "I…uhh…erased the files. He left here in a hurry and I tracked him and once he was in the shuttle bay I knew what he was doing. So, I went back into the system and sure enough he'd sent a packet of files to the shuttle. I just deleted them. I figured if it was a sanctioned order then he had no business having those files, right?"

Her ears grew hot. "Did you see any of the data?"

He shook his head. "No, but I'm sure there's a backup copy in *Tempest's* computer."

If Cas had done what she suspected him of doing, then he would have taken the proof of the alien threat with him. But if Tyler deleted the files he wouldn't have anything for the Sil.

Dammit, Cas. This is why you don't go off to take care of shit on your own.

"I need to see what he was looking at," she replied.

"I don't have that clearance," Tyler replied. "You'll have to talk to the commander." He indicated Sesster. Evie wasn't sure but she thought she saw one of his appendages flinch as soon as Tyler mentioned him.

"Commander, could I have access to the files Cas was viewing please?" she asked.

He turned from the consoles, facing her in a way that only a Claxian could. *I tried to warn him not to access them. He wouldn't listen.*

"That's okay," she replied. "Just let me see what he was looking for."

Sesster made his way across the room, his massive frame moving with the grace of a bird. He ducked down to fit under the catwalk, stretching and contorting himself so he could "stand" beside them.

He needed information from your personal logs, Commander. I apologize. I didn't grant him access, but I didn't actively try to stop him either.

Her face softened. "Why not?"

Because his intentions were correct, even if his methods were not.

He knew. Sesster had seen something in Cas and knew of the threat. It was always hard to tell how much Claxians could read from certain people.

She glanced at Tyler. He wasn't being given the same courtesy of hearing Sesster as she was. He seemed bewildered by the conversation.

"Can you show me?" The terminal beside her automatically activated, showing her own personal files. Sesster highlighted the path Cas took and the files he copied. They were image and video files she had taken from the *Achlys*. Files she'd backed up before giving them over to the Coalition. "Was this all?"

Sesster led her down another path, this one showing the visual logs they'd recorded in their brief skirmish with the Sil. He'd copied files from both. He then showed her how Cas had copied the surveillance data from the unknown threat. Presumably to show the Sil.

He'd gone to try and convince them on his own. And he'd probably gotten himself killed in the process. Why did he have to be so hardheaded? Heat flushed up her neck and to her face and she had to work to keep her temper in check. "Ensign," she said. "You're temporarily relieved from duty."

"What?" Tyler said, stepping back.

"You should have reported this data to the bridge immediately. Instead, you saw fit to make the decision to delete it and tell no one."

"But...but he was...there was no time. If I'd waited he would have escaped—"

"—with the information, yes. Which he was cleared to do. Now we potentially have a man in the field with no backup and no bargaining chips. You should have informed your bridge officer immediately." She turned to Sesster. "The same goes for you."

I was unaware of the data transfer. After he had what he needed I stopped listening.

"Convenient," she said. "And it isn't as if I can relieve you since you are necessary for the engines to work. But be assured, the captain will hear of this." She turned back to Tyler. "Did I make myself clear?"

"Yes, Commander," he said, stiffening. He made an about-face and exited Engineering.

Sesster extricated himself from under the catwalk and stood his full four meters in height.

"I know you didn't mean any harm, but we should have known. We could have done something," she said.

You would have stopped him. Which was exactly what he didn't want. He didn't want any more crewmembers to die for him. He's lost enough because of his decisions.

Evie winced, thinking about the lost souls on the *Achlys*. First because of his actions of alerting the Sil to their presence, then after they tried to activate an untested weapon, resulting in the loss of all hands. There was no way Cas didn't feel that burden. No wonder he'd been so mopey on the way here. But that didn't mean he could make up the rules as he went along. There was a chain of command on this ship and everyone had to follow it. No exceptions.

"That wasn't his call to make, Commander," she said. "And it wasn't yours either."

With that she left Engineering, dreading her next meeting with the captain.

26

This darkness would drive him mad. How did an entire species operate without any sources of light? Perhaps since they didn't seem to have any kind of eyes they didn't need light. But they had to be able to see somehow, Zenfor had turned to him to interrogate him. That meant she looked at him. Maybe it was like the Claxians' ability. Perhaps they developed along a similar evolutionary curve, though the physical structure of a Sil was much closer to a human than he would have suspected.

Coming aboard he'd had no clue what to expect. They could have been beings made out of pure energy or amphibious creatures with their ship full of liquid. Or they could have been completely incomprehensible to him in every way and he would have stepped on the ship finding it empty. Creatures who lived on more than one plane of existence at once.

But no. They seemed to emulate the same body structure of many of the common species, two legs, two arms, head, hands. But there was also something very odd about them, and it had to do with that "aura" that surrounded their heads. Cas couldn't help but wonder if it was connected to the ship in any way. So far, every Sil had varying colors of purple auras, and that just happened to be the same color of the symbol he saw on the outside of the ship. Could they be connected? Were the auras not part of the Sil themselves but instead an enhancement of some kind? Or maybe even an insignia or rank for serving on this ship?

Even if he'd spent decades under the tutelage of Laska he couldn't have hoped to have been prepared for this. No one could. Diplomacy would only come with further contact and it would be impossible as long as he was stuck here against this wall.

Zenfor had said something about a trial. He hoped it would be like the trials he'd seen on other worlds, where the accused was allowed to speak. Cas needed to make his case before whoever was running the trial before he was executed. Which meant he needed proof. But without the data all they would have would be his word. He needed some other way in which to convince them he wasn't the enemy here. He shuddered to think what would happen if *Tempest* tried to enter Sil space again. Especially now that they had him as a captive. Though, to their credit, they didn't seem interested in using him as bait or as ransom. They simply wanted to kill him for something he didn't do.

Cas struggled; tried to move anything that would move but finding it impossible. Even his head had gone immobile after Zenfor left, which allowed him to breathe and little else. He had to admit, it was an effective way of keeping your prisoners from causing trouble. And since they were planning on killing him anyway what difference did it make that his arms and legs had long lost all their feeling? He could have a blood clot at any moment, leading to an aneurysm and Zenfor would come back to find him dead, hanging on the wall. Wouldn't that be a fitting end.

There had to be some way out of this. But without a way to actually see what was holding him up there was little chance he'd be able to find one. Perhaps the Coalition prison wasn't so bad after all. At least he'd been able to walk around. Go to the restroom. Eat on occasion. The simple things.

There was only one thing he could do, and he wasn't looking forward to it. Suffocation had always been a fear, whether it was the vacuum of space or the inhospitable atmosphere of a rogue planet. Cas'd spent his entire life always ensuring he'd be able to take his next breath. But it seemed like now was as good a time as any to stop. He sucked in as deep as he could since he couldn't expand his chest…and held, counting in his head. He had no idea if this would do anything or not, but it was better than nothing.

Ten seconds. No problem. Ten seconds was easy.

Twenty seconds. Little tougher. The desire to release the breath crept up the back of his throat.

Thirty. His pulse quickened, his body trying to figure out what had happened to the oxygen.

Forty. He could feel the blood rising to his cheeks and the pressure on his chest, willing him to exhale and suck in some sweet, sweet oxygen. But he couldn't. He had to remain strong.

Forty-five. The pull to release seemed to double every second. But he would not relent.

Fifty-five. Cas squeezed his eyes closed. *Forcing* himself to hold on.

Seventy. Thoughts were growing fuzzy. He was having difficulty focusing.

Seventy-five. He had to hold on.

Eighty.

Eighty-five.

Hold on.

Ninety.

Cas crumpled to the floor, sucking in gasps as hard as he could, risking hyperventilating. But slowly his breathing returned to normal. He snapped his head up, glancing around but still unable to see anything. It didn't matter; he could move again. He waited a moment for his breathing to return to normal before he decided to move. Slowly he scooted away from where he thought the wall was. There was no telling if he accidentally touched it when he tried to get up that it wouldn't pull him right back into immobilization again. As he moved all of his joints tingled and spasmed, having been immobile much too long. He had to also wait for all feeling to return before he could stand up again, though that might not be the best idea either.

Would he even be able to leave this place? He and the Sil had passed through a door when they'd entered, and Zenfor had left the same way, the door almost turning to mist for her. Would it do the same for him or remain solid? There was only one way to find out.

Wait, his mind said. *What's the play here? Get out of this room then…what? Go back to the shuttle?*

He couldn't go back. As much as he didn't like this place, returning to the shuttle and attempting to leave would be fruitless. They'd be on him immediately. They may even be on their way here now to restrain him again. But he couldn't let that happen. What he needed to do was find Zenfor, or someone else with as much power and influence on this ship and get them to listen for five minutes. Five minutes to avert disaster, that was all he needed. After ruminating everything over for hours he was convinced he could make it happen. He just needed the chance.

Cas crawled in the direction he thought the door should be, the metal beneath his hands cold. He was still unable to detect any vibration through the plates; just what kind of ship didn't produce reverberations when it was moving through space? There should be at least something. But this ship was like a tomb. No sounds, no smells, dark and lonely. It was the worst place he'd ever been and he wanted nothing more than to return home. Or at least let them shoot him out into space where he could see some stars before he died.

Maybe he should return to the shuttle. There would be a light inside he could use; it would at least give him some bearings on where he'd come from and where he was supposed to go. That was, assuming he could get out of here at all.

Still crawling he made his way forward until the plates sloped up slightly to what was definitely a wall. He felt around, wondering if this was the door or if he'd become turned around and was facing a different direction. He stood, making sure his hands led him up against the solid surface. This might not even be a door at all. In which case he'd have to make his way back around the room anyway. He tried to remember if he'd seen any other details in the dim light from Zenfor or any of the others' auras, but couldn't recall a thing.

He felt around for a seam, some way for him to tell this was in fact a door but only found smooth surface. He took a step back—making sure to keep his hand on the wall—hoping to trigger some mechanism that might let him leave. Unfortunately it made no difference. This ship was so odd; despite the metal plates he couldn't feel a seam anywhere, and hadn't felt one on the floor either. Was this ship just one continuous piece of molded machinery?

Cas took a deep breath and dropped his hand. The Sil wouldn't be stupid enough to allow him to leave this room, in the event he figured out how to remove the immobilization field. No, they would want to keep him in here until someone could come and restrain him again. He turned until he was facing one-hundred-eighty degrees from his previous spot and stepped forward. There should be another wall in front of him somewhere. He took another step. Nothing yet. He put his hands out in front of him hoping to feel something but they only swiped at air. Another few steps, still nothing. He had to be a good six meters from where he'd fallen from the wall. The room hadn't been that big, had it? Three more steps, each slightly more confident. He still hadn't run into anything yet. This was maddening. It was like being trapped in a midnight labyrinth. Someone would have to come for him eventually, right? He found himself wishing the person would come sooner rather than later, if for no other reason than to remind himself he hadn't gone absolutely mad in here.

Three more long steps. The room could *not* be this long. It wasn't possible; not from what he'd seen when they brought him in. Had he passed through another door and not even known it? He reached out with his arms, spinning one way then back the other hoping they would touch something but there was nothing. Somehow the lack of walls was even worse than being held up against one. Was this ship even real? By leaving his wall had he become lost in the folds between dimensions? And could he ever get out?

There was only one thing to do. He continued walking forward.

27

Box tossed the small device aside, the show playing within not drawing his interest at all. He'd tried to get into it, but something he'd once found enjoyable he now found dull and unexciting. It seemed like everything since he'd started spending time in sickbay had fallen to the side. Was it possible he'd finally found something fulfilling in his short life?

"Naahhh," he said aloud despite the room being empty. "Can you imagine? 'Hi Doctor Box, my balls hurt today.' 'Well, let's take a look and see if we can't find the problem'," he mocked in two different voices. First, he doubted anyone would let him see their balls and second, there was no way anyone in the Coalition would ever certify him for anything other than assistant work or maybe triage. Despite the fact he now had several centuries of medical knowledge stored in his systems. He'd even backed up the data to his secondary core in case he was in an accident and needed to be rebuilt. All he'd stored there before were his personality and memory routines, but now he had something much more important to store.

He was grateful for Xax for allowing him to work beside her, but if this situation showed anything it was how unevenly circumstances were stacked against him. If he could be pulled from anywhere and stored in a room with zero evidence and nothing more than a suspicion from the captain then how could he ever expect organics to see him as equal?

Before he'd come aboard the *Tempest* most people either ignored him or considered him Cas's helper/enforcer/love slave or whatever. The point was they never paid him any mind. Until they'd become involved with Commander Diazal. She'd been the first one to call for his assistance back on D'jattan, to help those people escape from the Sargans. Not many other organics would have done that. She'd even vouched for him once she'd finished his evaluation after the *incident* with Lieutenant Ronde. Maybe she thought she owed him for not giving her away that night she snuck on the *Reasonable Excuse*. Or maybe she really did see him as a fully autonomous person but either way she was the exception, not the rule. In his experience most people would toss him into a recycler before claiming he could think for himself.

He walked over to the comm panel on the wall, using it instead of his personal comm as it might be more likely to get a response since it would show as coming from the ship itself and not him.

"Commander Diazal? Hello?" he asked into the comm. No response. She must be otherwise occupied. She'd said she would get back in contact with him; perhaps she was making a case for him to the captain right now. It was ridiculous he was cooped up in this room when he could be down in sickbay putting his skills to good use. If they were going back into Sil space, whether they decided to go after Cas first or not he would be needed down there. They'd gotten away last time with barely a scrape. A second time they wouldn't be so lucky.

Cas, you stupid bastard. If they decided to leave him to his fate, wherever he'd shuttled off to, then Box might have a moral dilemma. He couldn't let him go off on his own forever. He'd have to find a way to get off the ship himself and go after him. Assuming he'd be able to track which way he went. He wouldn't have just left without a note or explanation if he wasn't planning on coming back. He had to have known how it would look, especially with a record like his. Box was lucky they hadn't taken more extreme actions.

As he was thinking the door to their quarters opened, revealing two people from the science wing—as designated by their uniforms—and three security officers.

"Doctor Amargosa, Doctor Stevens. Ensign Folier, Crewman Unak, Crewman Tes. What can I do for you?" he asked, trying not to panic. This could be nothing but bad news. And Box didn't have a lot of time to decide how he wanted to handle it. He began calculating his odds.

"Box, please come with us," Doctor Amargosa said. She was tall with clay-colored skin and dark brown eyes. He'd only ever seen her file but knew she was in charge of the team that worked on and repaired all the drones the Engineering team used for those tight spaces organics couldn't fit.

"Why? I've been compliant," he said. They had nothing on him. This wasn't like last time when he lashed out against Ronde, he'd been very careful to maintain his calm. No matter what he did these organics were going to do what they wanted with him. He took a step back.

"Now, Box," Amargosa said, putting her hands up. "I know we've never met before but we need to check some things out. We've been getting some reports you might have a malfunction."

"And how many other sentient machines have you 'checked things out on'?" he asked.

Amargosa fumbled over her words. "We're not...I mean there's no definitive proof... I tell you what, we can look at that as well while we're making sure everything is working okay," she said, her voice too cheerful. "Just come with us down to Science Two. We've got a really nice facility down there."

Box tapped his comm. "Commander? Commander, please respond. They're trying to abduct me."

Silence on the other end. What was going on? She wouldn't have turned it off. He took another step back. In response the three security officers stepped forward, one of them producing a sealing bolt from his pocket. Box knew his eyes must be blinking like crazy but they wouldn't know what that meant. All they knew was there was a machine on their ship they didn't have control over. And they meant to put him down. He could see it in the way Amargosa and Stevens' approached him with such caution. As if he were a wild animal. "Get Xax in here," Box said. "I'm not going anywhere without Xax."

"The doctor is preoccupied at the moment," Amargosa said. "You can speak with her later."

Box tapped his comm again. As he did, he felt the magnetic pull of the bolt land on his chest. As he glanced down he lost all control over his functions and crumpled into a pile on the floor, all his motor functions having been stalled.

"Wasn't that easier?" Amargosa asked. She turned to one of the security officers. "Let Page know we have him and we'll be transporting him down to Science Two."

Page. If Box ever managed to find his way out of this he was going to tear the man's head from his shoulders and bathe in his blood. The bastard deserved nothing else.

***

"You're telling me he went back to negotiate with the Sil. Alone?" Greene sat across from Evie in his command room.

"That's what I believe, sir," she said. "I also believe he was unwittingly aided by Commander Sesster and to a lesser extent, Negotiator Laska."

"Laska?" Greene said, his eyes going wide. "She's the last person I would have expected to help him escape."

Evie clenched her fists under the table and bore down, resetting herself. "Again, he didn't escape. He left to negotiate with the Sil. As he was ordered to do by the admiral."

Greene put up his hands. "Fair enough. Still. Laska's not one to skirt the rule of law. In fact, she often sees to it. What did she have to do with this?"

"I'm not sure," Evie said. "But computer logs track Cas going down to the bar before heading to Engineering. I checked the sensors and only one other person was in there at the same time: Laska."

"But all entertainment venues are closed during a ship-wide emergency," Greene replied. "How did they...?"

"They broke in. Or, as best I can tell, Laska broke in first and Cas just happened to meet her there. They spent a few minutes together then Cas made his way to Engineering where he stole the data and made his way to the shuttle."

"But the data was destroyed," Greene said.

She nodded. "Throwing any leverage he thought he had out the airlock. He went in there blind and defenseless. And he didn't even realize it until it was too late."

Greene leaned back, staring at the ceiling. "Which means he's probably dead."

As much as she didn't want to admit it, the captain was probably right. Still, she remained silent. There was no telling if he was alive or dead, since they knew so little about the Sil. Now the Sargans on the other hand...

Greene tapped his comm. "Send Negotiator Laska up to see me immediately," he said.

"Yes, Captain," Zaal replied from the bridge.

"What else? How bad is it?" he asked.

"Sesster, sir. I think he had an inkling of what Cas was doing but neglected to tell anyone. He told me he shut off his mind from Cas so he wouldn't see what was happening."

Greene slumped back. "Damn. But it isn't as if we can punish him. The brig won't even hold him, not comfortably anyway."

"I don't believe he did anything that would intentionally hurt the ship, he believed what Cas was doing was correct and you know how the Claxians are about their moral code."

Greene nodded. "I'm glad he has a hard time reading the two of us. If he knew what Rutledge had done—"

"—and it got back to the High Claxian Temple, I know," she said. The Claxians had always been big on full transparency; it had been one of the conditions for them sharing their technology with humans when they'd first encountered each other over two millennia ago. Rutledge's actions with the *Achlys* could threaten everything.

"Do you think he can read Cas?" Greene asked.

"I don't know. Maybe. Ensign Tyler said Cas barely talked the entire time. If he was communicating with Sesster—"

The chime on the door rang.

"Come in," Greene said.

The door opened to reveal Laska, a smug smile painted across her face. "You summoned?" she asked.

"Take a seat, Negotiator," Greene said.

"Thank you, Captain. Most kind." She strode around the chair and lifted herself up into it, her legs no longer touching the floor below.

"What do you know about Caspian Robeaux's disappearance?" Greene asked.

"What are you insinuating, Captain?" Laska asked, her steel gaze zeroing in on Greene.

Greene's eyes narrowed. "I'm not insinuating anything. I'm asking a question."

Laska turned to Evie, regarded her, then turned back to Greene. "I notice I am outnumbered in this situation. I would prefer to either have my own representative to assist me or you can ask the commander to step outside a moment," she said.

"I'm sorry if you feel as if I'm being unfair," Greene said. "But the commander stays. Now please, answer the question."

"As it is my right under section four of the Sovereign Judicial Code, I formally request this line of questioning be performed in the presence of a third-party arbiter."

Greene leaned forward. "Don't quote regulations to me. You know as well as I do the closest third-party arbiter is on Starbase Eight. Over thirty days away. And your reluctance to answer my question isn't doing you any favors, Negotiator."

He stared at her and she stared right back. Evie could feel the tension in the room increasing by the second. "You are quite right, Captain. But I must ask, are you denying me my rights as a Coalition citizen? One might say your determination to have your question answered in such a prompt manner is equally unfavorable."

"For Kor's sake," Greene said, standing and turning to his window. He clasped his hands behind his back. "I'm not trying to intimidate you here, Laska."

"Xerxes, please," the Negotiator said. "All of my friends call my Xerxes."

"All we're trying to do," Evie said, "is figure out where Cas went and what his plans were."

"Oh," Laska said, a smirk forming at the edges of her mouth. "Isn't it obvious? He went to perform his duty."

"Then he told you he was going after the Sil alone," Greene said.

"He didn't need to," Laska said. "I could see it in him. He wasn't about to let this mission fail. Somewhere under all that bravado and pain is still a Coalition officer. If spending the past few weeks with him has taught me anything, it's that."

"What did you talk about? We know you met in the bar shortly before he departed."

"We shared a drink," Laska said.

"Anything else?" Greene asked.

She only shrugged, extending her hands out in front of her.

"I should have you arrested," Greene said.

Laska hopped off the chair, standing before the desk and staring up at him. "It's never wise to imprison a diplomat, Captain. It always comes back around to bite you in the end." She didn't break eye-contact. "If there was nothing else?"

He gave a small shake of his head. Laska made a curt bow to both him and Evie and exited back through the doors.

"Damn, she's arrogant." Greene scoffed. "Negotiators."

"Regardless of what she told him, I'd say we can be certain of where Cas was headed when he left."

"Seems that way," Greene replied. "How long until the ship is up and running again?"

Evie checked her comm for the time. "Pearson down in Engineering says another forty-five minutes at best."

Green turned back to the window. "Then we can only hope it's not too late to save him. For all our sakes."

28

Evie walked back out of the Command Room and took her station. This whole thing had turned into a mess. Cas hadn't done himself or her any favors by leaving the way he did, even if he thought it was the right thing to do. And now because of an overzealous ensign there was a good chance the Sil had killed him on sight. They had no qualms about killing Coalition citizens, as evidenced by their actions with the *Achlys*. She double-checked the status of the ship's engines. Pearson had increased the timetable to another hour.

She tapped the comm. "Engineering, what is going on down there? We can't afford to wait."

"Sorry, Commander," Pearson said, having taken over to speak for Sesster from Tyler. "We found another leak right before we began the initiation sequence. We're plugging it now."

"Plug fast," Evie said. Every second they sat out here waiting was another second Cas lost out there. If he still even had any time left. It was an impossible task. At least they would be able to get back quickly; Cas's shuttle would have been twice as slow as *Tempest*. Which meant he wouldn't have been over there more than an hour at this point. She hoped they weren't too late. If anything happened to him Box would—

Shit. She'd forgotten to ask the captain about Box. It would have to wait until this mission was over. He'd be fine in his quarters until they were all out of danger. Still…she better check in on him, just to make sure he wasn't going to cause a problem.

She tapped her comm. "Box? Are you there?"

No response. That was odd. He always responded. She glanced over at Zaal. "Hey, Zaal, check the comms, are mine going through okay?"

"Fine, Commander," Zaal said. "But it seems something is blocking Box's comm from receiving you."

She arched an eyebrow. "What would be blocking it?"

"Looks like an override code," he replied, examining the data. "Someone has intentionally locked him out of the system."

"Who?" she asked.

He stared at the console a moment longer. "I am not sure if this is right but…Lieutenant Page?"

Evie swiveled in her chair to his station to find it manned by Lieutenant Uuma, who normally took second shift. "Where is he?" she yelled.

"Checking now, Commander," Zaal said.

The lieutenant looked stunned. "I only know he asked me to take over for him," Uuma said. "He said he wouldn't be long."

"He's in Science Two," Zaal said. "Along with Lieutenant Ronde. What would they be doing down there together?"

Evie tapped her comm again. "Diazal to Page. What the hell are you doing?"

"Commander?" he asked. "I'm…I had an—"

"Give me eyes on Science Two," Evie said. An image popped up on the viewscreen of Box laid out on a table, parts of him disassembled as his eyes blinked rapidly.

"Holy mother of Kor," Evie whispered. "Lieutenant, stop what you are doing right now!" she yelled into the comm.

"Science Two, this is Commander Diazal. Halt all procedures at this moment."

Greene stepped onto the bridge, taking a look at the screen ahead of him. "What's going on?" he asked. "Is that…the robot?"

The scientists on the screen disassembling Box stopped, staring up at the video feed. "Xax, get down to Science Two," Evie ordered. "And the rest of you stay where you are."

"Are they disassembling him?" Greene asked. "Why?"

"I don't know," Evie said, fuming as she shot out of her chair, headed for the hypervator doors. "But they sure as hell aren't getting away with it."

***

"Someone explain to me exactly what is going on and do it right now or all four of you are going in the brig and you're not coming back out," Evie said, fuming. Beside her Box lay on the table, his eyes still blinking while Xax, Nurse Menkel, and Crewman Zorres from Engineering worked to reassemble him.

Standing in a line were Ronde, Page, Dr. Amargosa, and Dr. Stevens. And the only one giving her any eye-contact was Page. "You can't do that," he said. "Izak and I are the best helm and tactical officers this ship has. And we're about to go back into hostile territory."

"Just try me, Jorro. Don't think I won't," she replied. He continued to stare her down but she caught the flicker of something in his eyes. Fear that she was serious, maybe.

"Commander, I never wanted it to go this far," Ronde said. "I only wanted him off the ship."

"Is that the reason for the admiral's request for an evaluation?" Evie asked. "Because of something you did to him?"

"It's not a *him*!" Page yelled. "It's a machine! Nothing but metal and wires. What is the big deal?"

"This *machine*," Evie said. "Saved our lives back on D'jattan. He's not like any other machine I've ever met, and he will not be treated as such. Do I make myself clear?"

"Commander, we thought we had authorization," Amargosa said. "Otherwise we never would have—"

"Authorization to what?" she snapped.

"Lieutenant Ronde reported it...he was having a malfunction and asked if we could repair it. Lieutenant Page backed up the order. I didn't know—"

"—you were being deceived." She turned to Box. "*Do* you have a malfunction?"

A sound like a laugh emanated from Box. "My only malfunction was thinking I could be part of this crew. This was never going to work," he said. And though he had laughed, there was a palpable sadness in his voice. It broke Evie's heart.

"Don't worry, Box," Xax said. "They didn't do anything permanent or hit anything vital, you'll be good as new in just a few minutes."

"We were being as careful as we could," Amargosa said. "*Despite* the insistence of the lieutenant that we just *rip everything out and start over.*"

Evie got right up in his face. And though he had a couple of inches on her she wasn't about to let him intimidate her. "I get you have a problem with Cas, but going after Box? Trying to *kill* him? That's too far, Lieutenant."

"They don't belong here," Page said. "They worked for the Sargans for five years. How can you trust them?"

"Because I've seen who they are, who they *really* are. And I don't let my prejudices guide my actions." She continued to stare at him, unblinking. "You're relieved of duty. And until I speak to the captain about this, consider yourself confined to your quarters."

His lip curled into a sneer. "You can't reprimand me, he doesn't have any rights. I didn't violate any rules."

"Conspiring with a fellow officer to do harm to another being? I think that qualifies," she said, dead serious.

"But he's *a machine!*" Page pointed at Box.

"Don't make me call your own security personnel on you," Evie hissed. "Return to your quarters. *Now.*"

He uttered a sound of disgust and stormed out of the room. She wasn't sorry to see him go. The only problem was he was right; he was the best tactical officer the ship had. And they would need him when they returned to Sil space. She turned to the rest of them. "All of you will be receiving formal reprimands on your service records. I don't care if you were following orders or not," she said before Amargosa or Stevens could protest. "This is a gross violation of Coalition standards. He isn't Coalition property and therefore does not fall under any Coalition guidelines. Do I make myself clear?"

"Yes, Commander," they both said at the same time.

"And you," she said, turning to Ronde. "Page I get. But what is so horrible about Cas you were a party to mutilating his friend?"

Ronde winced at her words. He wasn't as committed to this as Page had been. If she were a betting woman, Ronde never would have done this on his own.

"Something about it just didn't seem right, Commander," Ronde said. "He's a criminal. And we thought…I thought…" He turned to Box on the table where Zorres and Xax were re-attaching his arm. "If we hadn't had to go after him Blackburn would still be here."

Evie furrowed her brow. "Ensign, as a Coalition officer you know we all take risks for this job. Asha took the same oath you did. She knew the risks and she accepted them. Every morning when we put on the uniform, we know in the back of our minds it might be the last time."

Ronde turned away from them and Evie thought she saw his eyes shimmer. He'd done it all for nothing. Based on prodding and pressure from Page. "Am I..." he began, his voice shaking.

Evie took him by the shoulders, forcing him to face her. "I understand this is hard, and this is not entirely your fault. But you did have a role in it and you have to take responsibility for that."

He nodded, doing his best to maintain his composure.

"Take a few minutes for yourself then report to the bridge," she said. "We need you on the helm. We'll discuss your punishment later."

He nodded again and she dropped her arms, allowing him to leave the room.

Amargosa turned to Evie. "Commander please, you have to understand we didn't—"

"Save it," she said, putting her hand up. "I trust I've made myself clear on this matter."

They both murmured agreements.

"Then wait outside until the doctor is finished. I don't want you near Box again, is that understood?"

"Yes, ma'am," Amargosa said.

"Dismissed."

As soon as they were gone she turned back to Box. "How are you feeling?"

"Fine," he replied. But his voice was too even, too steady. She glanced up at Xax.

"Another ten minutes, then we'll be done and he'll be as good as new."

Evie reached over and took Box's working hand. "I'm so sorry they did that to you. And I wasn't there to stop them."

"It's okay," he replied, still emotionless.

"I don't think it is, but we're going to make it okay. Once the doc is done I want you to return to sickbay with them.

We're going back into Sil space within the hour and we need as many good medics as we can get."

"I think I'll just return to my room," Box said. "That way I won't be a distraction."

"You're not a distraction," Nurse Menkel said. "You're a great medic."

Box didn't reply. Instead, he turned away from all of them, staring at some unknown point in space.

Evie's heart fell, but she didn't let go. She was going to make this right. One way or another she would make it right for him.

29

It was hard to tell how long he'd been walking or that he'd been walking at all. If not for the solid floor underneath him Cas might have assumed he'd tumbled off somewhere, strolling along a corridor that no longer existed. Something was wrong; he should have run into a wall by now. Based on the size of the Sil ship when he approached there was no way it could be this long inside. In fact, the ship looked quite compact; smaller than the *Tempest* itself. If he'd been on board his own ship he would have covered about three decks by now.

Periodically he'd reach out with his hands, moving to the left and right to feel the walls but coming up empty. He had nothing to go by, and that made all of this stranger. When he'd entered with the Sil he had seen walls, hallways, but now without their auras there was nothing. What if instead of falling from the restraint he'd asphyxiated himself instead? Perhaps this was the purgatory of the afterlife, an endless, black path, leading nowhere. That theory made more sense than an infinite corridor on a decidedly non-infinite ship. Where was the crew? Where was anything at all?

So far, he'd been nothing but cautious. Perhaps he needed to take a few risks. Just as the thought crossed his mind he smacked face first into something hard and strong, knocking the air out of him and sending him tumbling backward. He cartwheeled his arms back and fell on the floor, wincing at the pain in his face.

He stood, rubbing the sore spots on his face and extended his hands, feeling for the structure he'd run into. As his hands felt the metal Cas felt a sinking feeling in his gut. This was his shuttle. Somehow he was back in the shuttlebay. Though he'd been walking for a good thirty minutes and the trip from here to where they'd restrained him took less than three. Had he really traveled in a large circle? He'd come upon the one thing on this ship he'd been looking for. His luck couldn't be *that* good.

Feeling his way around the outer hull, Cas slowly made his way to the door, which was still open. He climbed inside and felt for the controls, activating them as soon as he could reach them. The lights in the shuttle illuminated, prompting him to close his eyes. He turned the luminosity down to its lowest setting as he peered through the small slits of his eyes. When he finally opened them again he was glad to see everything in the shuttle as it had been; the Sil hadn't touched a thing. He went to the back and pulled out the emergency kit on board, complete with portable lights. He opened one and pocketed the second, affixing the first on the end of his forearm. There was also a blaster inside but he left it. Despite the Sil's threats to kill him nothing would be gained by trying to match their threats. With his luck the blaster wouldn't work on them anyway.

Cas turned on the light, shining it all over to the shuttle; it had a good beam and would at least allow him to navigate this ship. Maybe even build a mental map. Though he still couldn't figure out how he got back here.

The next order of business was to find Zenfor. Convince her of his claims. Cas returned to the control console and double-checked the databanks. Zenfor had been right, any trace of the information he'd downloaded was gone. Could the Sil have destroyed it themselves? There was no way to be sure.

But here he was without any sort of proof of his claims, except the information in his head. It would have to do.

He turned as the light caught the edge of something in the shuttle with him. Cas jumped back at the imposing black figure standing before him. "Fuck!" he yelled, his heart rate skyrocketing. It was like a physical shadow, completely devoid of any detail, standing at the door to the shuttle. Slowly its head aura began to glow purple, illuminating all the runes all over its body, though they didn't glow. But they definitely hadn't been there before.

The Sil stepped closer, its hand out. The long fingers curled around Cas's shoulder.

"They said you'd try to escape," the Sil said. This was a different one than the guards who'd brought him in. It sounded like a male.

"I wasn't trying to escape," Cas said.

"Your actions and movements have been logged since the moment Zenfor left you. We have seen everything."

The Sil let go of his shoulder. Cas ran his light over him, but the beam seemed to end as it passed over the Sil's form. As if his body absorbed the light instead of reflecting it. "All I want," Cas said, ignoring the strange phenomenon, "is to have an opportunity to speak. To prove what I have told you is true."

"Consul Zenfor provided you with the opportunity. You squandered it."

"She barely gave me the opportunity to say a word," Cas said. "This isn't something I can explain in one sentence. It requires someone to *listen* to me. I want to give you the information. To forge an alliance."

"Providing information and forming an alliance are two very different things," the Sil said.

"Who are you?" Cas asked.

"Pregūn Kayfor. I am ship's guard. I'm to escort you to your trial."

"You were there, with me while I walked along, weren't you?" Cas asked, cutting his eyes toward the Sil. He hadn't exactly felt a presence near him, but it explained why no one came to get him after he was free from the restraints.

Kayfor swayed, as though he was taking a deep breath. "We can't have you running around alone. It is my job to observe you. This may be the only opportunity we have to interact with the Coalition."

Cas dropped the light so it only shone on the floor. "Wouldn't it be better for both of us if that interaction was positive? On both ends? There's no need for a trial. I came here to warn you. Nothing else."

Cas caught what he thought might be a chuckle, though it was impossible to tell as Kayfor had no mouth. "Attempted escape overrides all previous interactions," he said. "And there must be a trial."

"I wasn't escaping," he protested again. "If I were why would I be holding a flashlight? I could've just tried to blast my way out of here." Cas furrowed his brow. "Are you telling me if I'd stayed where your people put me, I wouldn't have to defend myself?"

Kayfor's aura glowed brighter. "No. The previous charges against you for the death of the Sil crew would be applied instead."

Cas threw his hands up. "So, none of that matters now? Isn't escaping less serious than killing ten people?"

"Are you admitting you tried to esc—?"

"*No,*" Cas snapped. "No…I'm trying to understand your justice system."

Kayfor spread his hands wide. "It is very simple. A crime is committed and the person committing the crime pays for their error. The trial determines the punishment, independent of the crime. Now," he took one of Cas's arms with his outstretched hand, "accompany me."

"Wait!" Cas yelled. "Wait, look, if I was trying to escape, I would've either armed myself or tried to use my shuttle to leave. I'm still here and there's a blaster in that case back there. How do you explain that?"

Kayfor's "head" turned and seemed to stare at the case containing the blaster. They *had* to have a way to see, that much was certain.

"I came in here for a flashlight, and to find out what happened to my files." Cas shone the beam across Kayfor's "face", though it never quite reached him. "If I was going to find my way back to your captain I needed to be able to see. I need to explain." The Sil's "head" turned back around to face him.

"As I said, I am here to take you to punishment. There your life will end as it began: small and inconsequential. But you will have the sweet release of death to enjoy. We are doing you a favor."

"What?" Cas yelled. "My fate is already decided? But I haven't even had the trial yet!"

The Sil let out a noise Cas could only assume was exasperation. "It is our way for all inferior species. We are *helping* you. Your existence otherwise will only continue to be fruitless and inconsequential."

"It wasn't so inconsequential when I saved your ship!" Cas yelled as Kayfor pulled him out of the shuttle by the arm. The Sil was strong; his hand felt like it could be made of steel itself. If Cas pulled too hard, he could pop his shoulder from its socket, so he allowed himself to be led along. He wasn't going to get anywhere with this guy. Maybe there was someone else at the trial he could speak to. Laska's words flashed through his mind. *Understand the other side.* Cas stared at his feet, shining the light down. He'd never seen metal like this before.

"Pregūn Kayfor, could you tell me how the shuttle ended up here?" he asked, trying to keep the anger at his unfair treatment out of his voice. "When I left it was somewhere else, a much smaller room."

"This is a holding facility," Kayfor said. "A place where we store large items such as your shuttle. Our ship brought it here for us. To clear the way."

"Your *ship*?" Cas scanned the area with the beam of light from his arm. The room was huge, by an order of magnitude over the opening he'd arrived in. This was most obvious by the distance from the shuttle to the corridors, they had to be at least fifty meters away. His curious mind couldn't help it; how had this ship been constructed? And how could it seem to change on him? Ships were static, not dynamic. "I've never seen anything like this."

"Renglas isn't unique, but she is a wonder," Kayfor said, his voice reverential. Cas shone his light above him, finding the ceiling more than twenty meters above their heads, a purple sheen to its walls. There was something odd about the internal structure. The crossbeams running across the ceiling reminded him of fish bones. Evenly spaced "ribs" perpendicularly attached to a central spine piece. And they weren't all the same, some had variation to them. It was the strangest construction he'd ever seen.

Whatever it was made of, he'd love to see the schematics. But he couldn't focus on that at the moment; he had to try and figure out a way to prove his case. Kayfor wasn't going to let him go, not without something concrete. What had happened to those *logs*? They couldn't have just deleted themselves. Someone must have—

"Page. That son of a bitch," Cas uttered.

"What?" Kayfor asked, still leading him along.

"Nothing," Cas said. He didn't want to try and explain why some humans betrayed other humans and the screwed-up logic behind those decisions. But he bet anything it had been Page. He'd seen Cas flying away and unable to do anything to pursue had emptied Cas's databanks, without knowing the value of the information held within. He knew the man had it out for him, and it turned out Page might get his wish after all.

Not for the first time since he'd left Sargan space he questioned the wisdom of joining the Coalition. It seemed it had finally caught up to him, one way or another.

30

"Lieutenant, you have put me in a very precarious position," Greene said, facing Page in his quarters. Evie stood behind him along with Crewman Tes and Negotiator Laska.

"That wasn't my intention," Page replied, his attention focused on the wall behind Greene.

"Regardless of your intention, that is the situation. You have instigated a conspiracy with a bridge officer and two science officers to harm to another living being. If Box had been a human—or any other species for that matter—"

"Begging your pardon sir, but he's not human. He's a machine." Page kept his eyes forward and his body stiff. He'd stayed here ever since Evie had told him to report to his quarters while she spoke with the captain. Now here they were, less than ten minutes before the ship was up and running again, and their primary tactical officer was guilty of subterfuge and conspiracy.

Laska stepped forward, her tiny frame almost comical in contrast to Page's height. "Lieutenant, what is the difference between Box and all of the other non-human species we encounter? That we have alliances with?" she asked.

Page furrowed his brow, his eyes searching. "He's been manufactured. Built, by someone else."

"One could stay the same about you. Or me. We were 'built' by someone else and exist because of them."

"It's not the same," Page said, his gaze dropping.

"So, because he was built in a way different from you or me, you felt that gave you the right to do as you wished. To ignore any personal autonomy Box had and impose your will upon him without his consent."

Page shifted. "Well, I...I had concerns he was a security risk."

"Then why didn't you file that in your logs? There is no mention of removing Box from his quarters and taking him to Science Two. In fact, I believe it was only Commander Diazal's apropos timing that saved the machine's life."

"He doesn't have a life! He's not even a he," Page said. "It's a collection of parts cobbled together designed to pull cyclax from underground so no one else has to. We don't treat any other machine like this; why should it be any different?"

"The difference is Box has shown himself capable of individual thought and action, contrary to any initial programming. How many other Class 117 Autonomous Mining Robots do you see taking an interest in medical work?"

"They would if they were programmed to," Page replied, narrowing his eyes.

"Exactly my point. *If* they were programmed to. Box was programmed to dig in the mines under Kathora. Nothing else. How does working in sickbay correspond to that programming?"

Page was silent.

"Then we are in agreement. We agree Box does not follow his programming as most other machines do. Now let's move on to—"

"Negotiator," Greene interrupted. "I think you've made your point. We're short on time here."

She turned back to him. "I am sorry, Captain. If there is nothing else?"

"No, thank you," Greene replied. Laska made a swift bow to each person in the room, including Page, and left.

"So what? He gets the same rights as everyone else?" Page asked. "Is that how this is going to go?"

"I'm not here to make Coalition policy," Greene said, stepping forward. "But the very fact he is an unknown should have given you pause. I've never encountered another machine like Box and therefore I'm not so quick to dismiss him. And I certainly don't want to do anything that might endanger his existence. Suppose the Coalition does rule he has rights after the fact. Then you would have been responsible for a murder."

"That's not…it doesn't…" Page stumbled over his words. "I already told you, I wanted him pulled because I felt without his…friend…aboard I was concerned with the ship's security."

Greene dropped his gaze. "We both know that's not true. When you asked me to have him confined to quarters, I only agreed upon the assumption we didn't understand Mr. Robeaux's motives. Now we do, and Box should have been released on his own recognizance. The fact is you felt Box was a threat not to this ship, but to you, in some deep-rooted and perverse way. And you took specific steps to remove him."

Page only shook his head, glaring at Evie.

"I have to tell you I find this very concerning," Greene said. "Your behavior ever since Mr. Robeaux and the robot came aboard has been unbecoming to a Coalition officer. And as soon as we return to Starbase Eight, I will be requesting you to be transferred off my ship."

Page's eyes went wide. "Sir! Over a machine? You know I'm the best security chief and tactical officer you can find this side of Horus."

Evie couldn't help but smirk.

"I'm well aware of your qualifications. But you bring a lot of baggage with you, Lieutenant. And I'm not sure I can trust you to do your job without these issues clouding your judgement. Just look at what you've already reduced yourself to doing."

"This is ridiculous," Page said. "I've been serving this ship admirably for over a year. And this upstart comes in and throws everything into chaos? It's not right, Captain, and you know it."

"I'll make my own judgements on what is and isn't right," Greene snapped. "You're confined for the remainder of this mission. Lieutenant Uuma will be taking your place on the bridge. Can I trust I don't need to post a guard outside your door?"

Page gritted his teeth. "That won't be necessary, sir." He said it with such a seething hatred Evie thought he might go for the captain. But even Page wasn't that stupid. Not unless he wanted to throw his entire career away. At least this way he could still be assigned to another ship in the fleet.

Greene motioned for everyone to leave, Evie exiting the room first. Swift justice, just like the Coalition was supposed to deliver. Page had screwed up and this was his punishment. The only problem now was Uuma would have to step up, and though she was good, she wasn't the tactician Page was.

Greene joined her in the corridor as they made their way back to the bridge. "I can hear your enthusiasm in the silence, Commander," he said.

"He deserved it. After what he did to Box, who I think is emotionally scarred by the way. You should have stripped his rank."

"Don't think it didn't cross my mind. But we're still unclear about what to do with the robot. And until the Coalition makes some sort of ruling, I don't want to take an action that might be considered too drastic. Though this will be going on his service record."

"As it should," she replied, keeping in step with him. "With Uuma moving up to the primary shift we'll need someone to take over second shift."

"Anyone in mind?" he asked.

"Ensign Yamashita. Her skills back at D'jattan were impressive, to say the least." Hers had been the first name to pop to mind, despite there were probably more than a few qualified candidates on board. Why had she jumped to the ensign?

"Isn't she in exobiology?" he asked, raising an eyebrow at his first officer.

"She is, but wait until you see what she can do with a weapons array."

"Very well," Greene said. "Once this is over give her a few field runs. We'll try it out." As they stepped into the hypervator to go to the bridge he rubbed his forehead. "Do you think I just made a mistake back there? With what we're about to face?"

She pursed her lips, staring at the blinking lights indicating they were moving. "I think if you'd kept him on the bridge in an emergency you would have been questioning if you could have trusted his judgement instead of focusing on the task at hand. It's a lose-lose situation but I think you did the best you could, given the circumstances."

"You're probably right. I picked Page to serve on *Tempest* because he was the best at his job. But I neglected to see the darker side of him. The parts he hid so well."

"He's had a rough life," she added. "So, I understand where it comes from. It doesn't have a place on this ship."

He nodded, his eyes somber. "Let's just hope he finds what he needs elsewhere."

***

Box sat in his room, running it all over in his mind again. The sound of the drills and the saws, how they cut into him, extracting parts as if he were nothing more than a defective engine. He didn't want to think about what would have happened if Evie hadn't come when she did. They had come precariously close to his memory units, which could have completely wiped everything from the past five years, including everything he'd learned about medicine.

Damn Cas. If he hadn't gone off without Box none of this would have ever happened. No one would have ever suspected him, interrogated him, hurt him. But Ronde baited him while Cas was still onboard, so maybe there was no way to avoid it. Perhaps it had been the natural outcome of living on a ship full of organics.

Box was homesick. He missed the *Reasonable Excuse* and he missed flying around with just Cas. The man was an asshole but at least he showed Box a modicum of respect. There was no telling with these people. It was like the more organics he was around the worse things got. Why couldn't it be like it was back in the Sargan Commonwealth, where no one paid him any attention? Sure, maybe sometimes he had something thrown at him that he had to clean off later, but at least no one tried to kill him. At least, no one that he wasn't actively pursuing or trying to kill back.

The people here were too intrusive, too concerned with matters that didn't involve them. All they had to do was leave him alone and he would take care of the rest. But no, apparently some people found just the concept of him repulsive. And he'd definitely seen the hairy, pus-filled underbelly of the great and wonderful Coalition. After all this time he understood what Cas had been talking about all these years.

It didn't matter anymore. They didn't want him interacting with them and he couldn't stand to be around them. That was fine. He would stay in the room until Cas came back. And if he didn't, maybe Box would steal his own shuttle and head off somewhere. Somewhere no one cared if he was an artificial life form or not. That had always been the plan anyway.

He walked over and fished his entertainment center off the top of one of the unpacked crates, starting it up. He projected the image on the wall beside him and focused on one thing and one thing only: if Lady Penelope would find out about her husband's affair with the duchess. Nothing else mattered.

31

Cas was ushered into a large room, large enough so the beam of the flashlight didn't reach any of the walls. Behind him, Kayfor nudged him on. As best as he could tell it was circular in nature, with a four-meter-high wall on all sides, though beyond that there seemed to be alcoves or something similar that stair-stepped backward until he couldn't see them anymore. Directly across from him was a pillar about five meters high, upon which crouched another Sil, glaring down at him, its purple head aura swirling around. This aura was different; it seemed to leave the confines of the Sil's head, branching out in different directions like bolts of lightning. It was beautiful.

But when Cas glanced down his stomach dropped. In the floor was a dirty grate, caked with what looked like darkened bits of hair, blood and maybe even flesh. Was this an execution arena? After everything else he'd seen he wouldn't think the Sil to be capable of such gore. The entire ship seemed so pristine. What sort of other creatures had been in this exact same position, only to suffer a fate they didn't deserve? Did it even matter or was this all for show and nothing more?

Kayfor put his hand on Cas's shoulder again. "Take joy the life you lived brought you here, so it could be ended with swift dignity," he said.

The Sil above him on the pillar leaned over, "peering" down at Cas with a faceless head, which was unnerving. He wished they at least had eyes; it would give him something to focus on. He shifted from side to side, trying not to let his nerves get the better of him. He'd been in plenty of questionable situations before, places he thought he'd never get out of and yet somehow he had. But this was unlike any other place. And he barely held any of the cards, so negotiating would be difficult. "I would like—"

"Silence," the Sil atop the pillar announced. The voice was different enough from Kayfor, but at the same time it hung in the air. "Human, you have been found guilty for the crimes of attempted escape before, during or after an interrogation by the Consul. How do you plead?"

"I don't plead," Cas replied. "I don't agree with any of this." He shone the light up at the Sil but it did nothing but dissipate before it reached him. It was like this race was molded out of darkness. But he wasn't about to go quietly or easily. If they wanted to kill him, they'd have to get down here in the pit and get their hands dirty.

"Your plead is deemed irrelevant." The Sil's head lifted. "Ship guard, do your duty."

Cas turned to face Kayfor, shining his light on him, though the glow from his head aura had intensified. "Maybe Rutledge was right. Maybe when we were out there, waiting in that quaternary star system I should have let him take your ship. Because it's becoming obvious to me you're more worried about your borders than the sanctity of life."

Kayfor paused.

"If you really cared about justice, then you would be more interested in learning the truth, rather than just your version of it." He turned and flashed the light back up at the other Sil. "All of you. But I can see now that nothing I ever say will make a difference to you. You decide the fates of those less powerful than you before you even understand them. How can you profess to be an advanced race?"

"We don't need to understand them," the Sil above him said. "Which is what makes us advanced. We don't concern ourselves with the trivial matters of those beneath us."

"That's bullshit. If you didn't you would have blown my shuttle to pieces the minute you saw me. But you brought me aboard because you were curious about what I might have to say. It just so happened what I *did* say didn't match up with what you were expecting. And now, because it is an inconvenient truth rather than a comfortable lie, you will execute me and wash your hands of the entire situation."

Kayfor's head moved up to "look" at the other Sil, then back to Cas. He stepped back, his posture relaxing. "You say you were the human who sent the distress call three-point-one regulations ago?"

"I don't know what a regulation is, but if you mean seven of my years, yes." Cas replied.

"You have to prove it. In some way. We cannot allow this disruption to continue." Kayfor held out one of his hands, palm up.

Cas glanced down at his feet; they had smeared some of the errant fur and blood along the floor. "Do you know how my people measure time?"

"We downloaded your information. You base your cycles on the orbit of your planet around its sun. You then break those orbits into six seasons, which are further broken into seventy-three 'days'. Each day consists of twenty hours which can be divided into minutes and seconds."

Cas lost his attention span for a moment. "Yeah…yeah, that's it exactly."

"You also categorize a grouping of seven days into something called a week, though it seems superfluous," Kayfor added.

"According to our calendar, I sent the distress signal to your people on Dekaton 65th, 2593. Or in other terms, 2593.2.65. We were in the Quaval star system just inside your border, a quaternary star system consisting of a red supergiant, a white dwarf and two mid-level yellow stars. The massive gravity from the supergiant obscured our presence so we managed to find and surprise your ship. I sent the distress signal on frequency one-one-one-three-eight-two at fourteen hundred hours of that day."

Kayfor glanced up at the other Sil. "It is not enough. You could have obtained that information after the fact."

Cas shook his head. "I couldn't. The mission was classified by my people. Only those aboard on the ship would have had it. And I was the tactical officer that day. I had control over the weapons."

"Still, that does not prove you were there," Kayfor said.

"The proof is I am here now. Why else would my people send anyone else? No one has had contact with your race in over a hundred years. No one would be equipped to speak to you. Wouldn't they send the only person they thought you might be receptive to?"

Kayfor didn't respond, but he continued to hesitate.

"Listen to me," Cas said. "You have to be willing to trust me. I know you see me as inferior, but allow me to show you the evidence. If I'm lying *then* you can execute me. No one else other than me could tell you this."

"It isn't me you need to convince," Kayfor replied. "It's Zenfor. She has the ultimate say over your fate."

Cas cut his eyes at the form looking down on him from the pedestal. "She never gave me the chance. She had already made up her mind before she even came to talk to me."

Kayfor "stared" up at the other Sil. "Prejudice?"

"Agreed," the Sil replied. "Tainted questioning."

Kayfor returned his attention to Cas. "Zenfor had a relative on the ship your people took. We did not realize it would cloud her judgement. She should have given you the opportunity to explain."

"What are the risks?" the Sil above them asked. He shifted to the side of the pedestal, leaning over the edge.

"Risks, what risks?" Cas asked.

"The risk of not allowing you to make your case to her."

Cas craned his neck to the other Sil. "There is a threat that could potentially harm or destroy the Sil. And all the surrounding systems. I came to warn you and ask for your help." The other figure wasn't moving, but Cas caught the rise and fall of his chest. So they breathed after all, but how? He hadn't seen any way for them to take in oxygen. There was more to these Sil than what was on the surface.

"Allow him to make his case. It is a minor inconvenience," the Sil above him said.

Kayfor took him by the arm, leading him out of the center of the room back toward the door. "You don't know how lucky you are. A true rare gem in a field of common stones." The Sil Judge said nothing as they left, the door appearing behind them as if it had always been there.

"How often do you bring people aboard for execution?"

"Whenever one of the inferior races living in our space leaves their planets. Some evade us, others aren't as skilled."

"You mean there are other species living here?"

"Of course. My people come from a binary pair of planets orbiting what you know as Taurus Epsilon. But our home planet is called Thislea. Obviously there are others within our space." He led Cas down the dark hallway, though they hadn't gone through a different door there was something strange about this hallway. It wasn't the same one they'd taken to the judge.

"We have a binary set of planets in my system too," Cas said.

"We know. Amun and Mut, both Class J gas giants according to your own classification system."

218

"You know a lot about us," Cas replied, his arm aching from where Kayfor gripped it tight.

"We learned a lot more after you arrived. Your shuttle's database was very informative."

Cas shook his head, unable to believe all of that useless data was still in there while the thing he needed had been erased. "In order to get the evidence, I need to show your captain—I mean consul—about the attacks I'll have to go back to my ship. There's another copy of it there."

"Evidence gathering will be later," Kayfor said. "If you survive convincing the consul you are who you say you are then we'll discuss retrieving the information."

It was the best he could hope for in a tense situation. Maybe the Sil weren't as vicious as he thought. One thing was for certain. If Cas ever got back he was going to *kill* Page.

32

Page sat on the edge of his bed, fuming. How *dare* Greene take him off duty. The only thing he'd tried to do was keep the ship safe. It would have been different if had been a normal machine following its programming, but there was something strange about this one. It wasn't *alive*. But someone had done something to it to make it *seem* alive. Any machine who had threatened a Coalition officer would have been decommissioned, wiped, and reprogrammed. At least that's how they did it back on Meridian. Quite a few of the Sargans had machines helping them. They were easy cannon fodder and didn't complain when they got shot. Except the Sargans hadn't counted on the locals catching a few and turning them against their masters. Old Houck, he had been a technical genius at reprogramming. He told Page once he'd been the chief engineer on the Coalition flagship in his youth. But the thing with Old Houck was you could never tell when he was lying and when he wasn't. Half the shit he said had to have been made up.

Houck would even install remote cameras in the robots so he could make sure they would get back to where they belonged. Not to mention it allowed everyone to see the real prize: the face on a Sargan scum when his own robot came marching back to his camp and self-destructed. Those had been the days.

Not like now. When robots had *rights* and *feelings*. He'd never heard anything more ridiculous. That machine was an infiltrator for the Sargans and he was going to prove it if he had to rip its central cortex out himself and bleed the information from it. Box had already threatened Ronde with physical violence and with a passive-aggressive gesture. That would have been enough to get any Coalition officer put on suspension. By now he should be disassembled and in two hundred parts in the science lab. But no, it seemed that because this robot was good at emulating human emotions he was being given the benefit of the doubt. Was he alive? Was he just a copy of life? No one knew.

Except Page knew. That thing was nothing more than an automated utensil, programmed with a few quirks to make it seem more life-like. It was the perfect vehicle for stealing classified information. And it roamed the ship, *freely*. Any moment he expected to hear a BOOM, feel the ship shake from an internal pressure loss and a general alert come over the comms telling the crew the Sargans were closing in on them. Or the Sil. Or any of a hundred other organizations. The fact was the traitor and his machine were a liability, and it was Page's job to identify that threat and remove it.

But how was he supposed to remove anything with both the captain and the XO protecting it?

He slammed his fist down again, standing and pacing the room. There had to be something he could do. They hadn't left yet; he would have felt the ship jump into the undercurrent. Which meant he still had time. He couldn't be out of his room more than a few minutes before the automatic scanners all over the ship found and identified him. Unless...

There was only one recourse left to him.

He tapped his comm. "Izak. You there?"

"What do *you* want?" Izak whispered. "We're getting ready to depart, I can't talk now."

"I apologize you got in trouble because of me. But without you, this ship is in grave danger. We don't have any more time to spare."

"What am I supposed to do?" he asked.

Page wracked his brain. If left unchecked to his own devices, the machine could have the run of the ship as soon as everyone was preoccupied with returning to Sil space. There was only one thing he could think of.

"I need a favor. You're my last hope."

***

"Lieutenant Ronde, are we interrupting you?" Greene asked as he sat in the captain's chair. The voice startled Izak so bad he jerked his head back to the captain.

"No, sir." He'd listened to Page's request, thinking he was insane. Wasn't Izak in enough trouble as it was? And hadn't Page lied to him about the whole thing with Blackburn? Maybe not lied to him, but deceived him. If that was the case why would he ever consider helping him again?

"Prepare to depart," Greene said, looking straight ahead.

Izak tapped the controls, setting the course Ensign River had plotted. But his mind was on Page's call. Already his heart was hammering about the thought of returning to Sil space. The traitor—Cas—had gone in by himself and now they were going after him. And all this after they'd nearly lost the ship the first time. What could be so important the Coalition was willing to risk an entire ship and her crew? Page didn't know; he was convinced Cas was working against them. But Izak wasn't so sure anymore. Anyone with a head on their shoulders knew it was suicide to go into Sil space, much less go in alone. And if Cas had been working with them wouldn't they have destroyed the ship already? Or were they out there waiting, with Cas by their side, telling them all sorts of Coalition secrets?

None of this made sense. Maybe Page was right, maybe he was a threat. Izak wasn't stupid; he knew Page had used him. So where was the proof?

"Engineering reports ready, Captain," Blohm said from behind him.

Greene gripped the arms of his chair, leaning forward. "All hands, this is the captain. Alert level four. Everyone to designated battle stations. Spacewing fighters prepare to depart." He glanced around the bridge, Izak watching him. Both the Captain and Commander Diazal seemed calm, as if this was just another day. While he was a nervous wreck. The commander had essentially given him a pass. Maybe that was because they needed him for this mission or maybe it was because she really didn't believe he was at fault. But he was. "Deploy the emitter and let's make this happen," Greene said.

Ronde focused on the screen in front of him and moved the ship into position, scanning the space where they'd left the undercurrent the first time. His comm pinged again causing his heart rate to shoot up.

"Ready?" Ensign River asked, startling him. "You okay?"

Izak wiped the sweat from his brow, shooting her a quick glance. "Fine. Ready." His fingers moved over the controls as if on autopilot, sending them into the undercurrent. The ship lurched and space began speeding past them at an accelerated rate.

"Twelve minutes to Sil space," River said.

He couldn't do this. And it couldn't wait. There was no telling what Page might do now he wasn't answering his comms anymore. Izak turned around in his chair.

Greene's eyes flashed to him. "Yes, Lieutenant?"

"Sir, Lieutenant Page is attempting to contact me. He's asking me to wipe the internal logs of his movements."

Commander Diazal's eyes went wide and she jumped up, running over to Zaal's station.

"Have you?" Greene asked, his voice severe.

223

"No, sir, but I should have told you when I got the first request. Before we made the jump."

Greene turned to Evie. "Where is he?"

"I'm not sure," she said.

He turned back to Izak. "I thought you said you didn't help him."

"I didn't! I never accessed the internal sensors, you can check."

Zaal spoke. "He's correct. No one on the bridge has altered the internal sensors. However, sensor control on deck five has been altered. But I cannot tell by whom."

"Why didn't it show up?" Greene demanded.

"Because we were too focused on leaving," Evie replied. "And it's a good bet he's been to one of the weapon lockers."

"But those are coded only to open to active security personnel," Izak said.

Evie turned to him. "I doubt you're the only 'friend' Page has on this ship." She ran for the hypervator doors.

"Commander?" Greene said, turning in his seat.

"He's going to kill Box if we don't do something. I don't know who we can trust in security," she yelled back.

"Dammit," Greene said as the doors closed. "We should have just thrown him in the brig." He glanced at Izak. "Anything else you need to tell me, Lieutenant?"

He bit his lip. "I think the commander is right. I don't think Page will stop for anything now."

33

"I believe I have underestimated you," Kayfor said as they traversed the corridors. At some point he'd let go of Cas's arm and allowed him to walk on his own, though Cas was still so focused on seeing where he was going he hadn't paid much attention. The interior structure of this ship was something to behold. It was as if every time he entered the corridors they had changed on him. Despite the fact they had walked more than far enough to return back to where he'd been held. And they'd only seen one other Sil in the journey: standing outside an egg-shaped door. Cas hadn't bothered to ask.

"Why, because I didn't die in your dungeon back there?" he asked.

"Exactly. As I said, not many escape judgement. I haven't seen it in a few hundred regulations."

"What *is* a regulation?" Cas asked.

"Equivalent to two-point-three of your years," Kayfor said.

"How long do Sil live?"

Kayfor kept his "gaze" straight ahead. "It doesn't matter. What does matter is we reach the consul so we may resolve this discrepancy."

Cas turned to him. "What is going on with this ship? Why does it seem bigger on the inside? And why is it every time I leave a room I'm in a different place than where I started?"

If Sil sighed, Cas would have sworn that had been the noise Kayfor made. "It's hard to explain to non-Sil. Your perception of space and time is different. Think of this ship as a gateway into an interconnected series of pods. You are not actually on the ship, you are in these pods. And the corridors connecting the pods are…dynamic. As the ship moves in regular space it translates to a corresponding location change for the pods. The corridors have to change and adapt. It is an interconnected network of units."

"You mean to tell me we aren't actually in space right now?" he asked.

"No. We are in the *space beneath*. You have creatures on your world who stick their snouts out of the water while the rest of them remain below. Think of the ship like that. The part you encountered, the "ship" is a way we access your dimension. Everything you see around you is what lies below. Consul Zenfor *is* above, so we have to return the top where we can access it again. Sometimes the journey is long. Other times it is short."

Cas was flabbergasted. No wonder the Sil didn't want anything to do with other species; they had access to different dimensions. He now understood why they paid the Coalition little attention; especially if most of their society was here, in what Kayfor called the *space beneath*. "Is this where you're from?" he asked.

"It is where we developed," Kayfor said. "We found this dimension over ten of your millennia ago."

"Were *you* around? Back then?"

"No," he replied.

"Is this why everything is so dark? And why you don't have windows?"

"There's nothing to see in the void," Kayfor replied, sending a shudder up through Cas's spine. The more he learned about this place the less he wanted to do with it. He'd feel much better as soon as they were back in regular space. "This place troubles you."

Cas shone the light against the walls with their purple hue, trying to imagine what was beyond them. How had these corridors been constructed if there was nothing beyond? What had been here before? "It isn't what I expected," Cas replied. "But why do the corridors change?"

"The physics of the *space beneath* are too complex to go into at the moment. But remember my analogy. It is more appropriate than you may realize."

"Do you mean this ship...is alive?" Cas asked.

Kayfor's purple aura pulsed. "We're close. Prepare yourself to make your case."

Cas shone the light ahead of them but couldn't make out anything different. How could Kayfor tell where they were? It looked just like everywhere else they had been.

They passed through what felt like a fog and Cas found himself in a place he didn't recognize, but which felt familiar. The darkness was gone and he was on the bridge of a ship, or at least the Sil equivalent of the bridge of a ship.

A great big clear bubble showed a complete view of the surrounding stars and he felt himself relax for the first time since arriving. The bridge itself seemed to be on a wide catwalk suspended in the middle of the bubble without any supports except where it was connected to the back wall, though there was no door behind him. All of the purple interiors he'd become accustomed to were gone, replaced with more traditional ship bulkheads and stations.

Four Sil stood on the bridge. One on the very front, close to the bubble but still a few meters away from its surface; two more to the left and right respectively, and in the center stood Consul Zenfor, "staring" out into space.

"Pregūn Kayfor," she said. "What is this about?"

"The judge has deemed you were hasty in your evaluation, Consul. He asks you make another before he renders judgement."

"What?" Zenfor yelled, spinning around. Cas took a step back, despite the fact she still had no facial features. But it was as if he could feel her gaze boring into him once more. "My evaluation was resplendent."

"Your evaluation was tainted. You did not allow him to explain," Kayfor said.

"He does not need to explain. I understand the situation and I understand he is nothing more than an infiltrator. He needs to be dealt with. Especially after that escape attempt."

Cas stepped forward. "Consul, if I—"

White spots exploded in his vision as he was thrown backward. He felt himself skid along the floor until his back hit the wall. For a moment there was no pain until the rush of it bloomed all over his face. He blinked a few times, allowing his vision to re-adjust. Zenfor stood over him with Kayfor to the side.

"Consul, the judge will not approve your request if you continue to taint your argument," Kayfor said, boredom in his voice. Cas pushed up on his elbows, shaking his head and hoping she hadn't done any permanent damage.

"I will not listen to Coalition lies, and neither should you. You're too smart for that." Zenfor turned her back on him, "looking" back out into space. "I don't have time for this. Their ship is on the way back and we are preparing a surprise for them."

"Proof I'm telling the truth is on that ship," Cas said, though it hurt his jaw to speak. His entire body ached. *Had* she even hit him?

If *Tempest* was on her way back, then he didn't have much time. If he couldn't convince Zenfor of their intentions before they arrived he had no doubt she'd destroy the ship. If his assumptions about their justice system were correct, she had proper cause this time: sending an infiltrator into Sil space.

"We could download their database," Kayfor suggested, raising one of his long arms with his palm up. "Confirmation would—"

"I've heard enough," Zenfor said. "Get him back down to isolation. If the judge won't deal with him I will, after this is done."

"I know now why losing a ship is such a high crime," Cas said. "They're sacred, aren't they? They're living beings and my people killed one."

Zenfor turned on him. "Our 'ships' have the same rights as any Sil. When your people removed the crew and ejected them into space, the ship died, its body beneath disintegrating. What your people took back with you was nothing but a shell. We live in *concert* with our ships, one does not exist without the other. Your people killed one, and for that there must be a penance."

"Would it help if I told you everyone else that was on the ship that attacked yours along with dozens of others died because they tried to reverse engineer your weapons? Weapons they gleaned from that ship?" Cas asked.

Zenfor stood still. "It is not enough."

"How much revenge do you need, Consul?" Kayfor asked. "Allow the human to make his case then we can move on with this."

"Make what case? It does not matter if he was there that day or not. This *threat* he's come to warn us about, it isn't as if he even believes it himself, do you, human?" she asked.

Cas stood, his legs almost giving out underneath him. His thoughts betrayed him. Zenfor was right, he had wanted nothing to do with this threat. He wanted nothing to do with the Coalition or protecting it. But people who lived in the Coalition who still thought life under Coalition rule was a good thing. Who still relied on it for their livelihoods and who needed it to protect them. If he turned his back on the Coalition, he turned his back on them as well. And despite the attractiveness of such a prospect, he couldn't do it. Deep down he was still a Coalition officer, and he had still sworn an oath. It didn't matter if the organization he'd pledged himself to wasn't the same one he thought it was the day he began at the academy. He had made that promise to himself and it wasn't something he could just relinquish, no matter how hard he tried. Deep down, he *was* a Coalition officer, and it was his job to protect its citizens from all threats. Even those that seemed unbeatable.

"You're wrong Zenfor. Look at the evidence. If I'd wanted to run, I had plenty of opportunity. I came here in a shuttle with undercurrent capability. I could have gone off on my own and no one would have ever known, because you would have destroyed the *Tempest* anyway, wouldn't you? But I didn't. I came here, I put my life on the line to deliver *vital* information. Now it is up to you to accept that information."

Zenfor turned to her subordinate. "He escaped his imprisonment. There must be retribution."

"In fairness, Consul, he could not breathe."

Cas turned his attention to Kayfor. "You released my restraints? Why?"

"Because you are correct," Kayfor said. "You came here unarmed and at the risk of your own life, only to deliver information." He addressed Zenfor. "He knew he could not beat us, that he had no chance of stealing any secrets and giving them back to his people. When I found him he had picked up his flashlight, and left his weapon behind."

"I should have you sent to judgement for your insubordination," Zenfor said, her words seething with hate.

"But you won't. You know I am right."

"Consul," one of the other Sil said, its aura glowing bright. "The Coalition ship is coming through the undercurrent now."

Cas watched her featureless face. Her aura pulsed with an inconsistent rhythm. "What is your decision?" he asked.

34

The ship lurched into the undercurrent just as Lady Penelope revealed she'd been having an affair with both the butler *and* the coach driver. Box barely felt the rumble of the grav plating as the internal dampeners adjusted, but his internal systems logged the jump nonetheless. He couldn't help but be distracted by the fact they were returning to Sil space. Was Cas okay? Or had the Sil already killed him and disposed of his body? He had to be content with the fact he might never know. Without Cas to broker some kind of peace Box didn't believe any of them had much time anyway. He might as well spend his final few minutes enjoying himself.

He paused the program and put the device down. If he was honest with himself what would make him really happy would to be back in sickbay, helping Xax prepare the triage unit. Or practicing surgery on some cloned material. But he wasn't sure he could go back.

Box glanced up, not sure why, seconds before the door to his room opened to reveal Page, a wild look in his eye and a standard Coalition pistol in his hand. Box jumped to the side just as the pistol fired, diving behind the crates he and Cas still hadn't unpacked.

"You worthless piece of metal! You're not going to threaten this ship anymore. I'm going to expose you, then they'll all see I'm right."

"You don't want what's in my head," Box replied from behind the crate. "It's nothing but porn and drama."

Another shot hit the side of the crate, puncturing a hole straight through it which exited the other side close to Box's side. The crates were useless as cover. He jumped up, making a run for the other end of the room. Two more shots just missed him. "For the ship's tactical officer you sure are a bad shot. You'd think you'd be able to hit a two-meter tall machine." He ducked around the corner to the restroom.

"Shut. Up!" Page yelled, firing off three more shots. One came precariously close to the room's window. Box glanced over. If the pistol's power was turned up high enough it could destroy that window, then the entire ship's hull could be compromised now that they were in the undercurrent. He'd heard stories about what happened to material pulled into the current. And he wasn't keen to experience *that* as his last moment.

"You're ruining my show," Box yelled. "I thought we'd settled this when you tried to have me disassembled."

"Some people on this ship think you're more valuable than we are," Page said, his voice closer. Box estimated he was approaching at one meter per minute. Moving cautiously. He might be able to sustain a hit from the weapon, depending on its setting. Then again it could blow a hole straight through him. And knowing Page he no doubt had it turned up as high as it would go.

"I am," Box replied. "I can store a hundred times the information and lift twenty times as much. Couple that with my ability to think and feel for myself and you've got yourself one obsolete human and one superior robot."

"If you're so superior then why are you the one hiding?" Page asked.

Well, if he couldn't go out watching Lady Penelope at least he could go out with some dignity. He broke cover and stood in the middle of the arch separating the rooms. "If you're so superior why do you need a weapon?" he asked.

Page bared his teeth and tightened his hand on the pistol. For the first time in Box's life he felt himself involuntarily flinch. It was a strange sensation, but he was grateful at the last moments of his life he was able to experience something completely new.

"Page! Drop the weapon now." Box turned his optical circuits to see Commander Diazal standing behind Page with her own weapon trained on his back. Page didn't relax his grip or stop looking at Box. He only seemed to get angrier.

"Don't make me ask twice," the commander said, a steadiness in her voice Box rarely heard. It was the same as it had been back down in those caves on D'jattan. The commander was good under pressure, while Page was visibly shaken. Sweat poured down his face and the hand holding the pistol trembled.

"He's up to something, Evelyn, I know it. You know it too you're just not willing to admit it. If you stop me, whatever he does will be on your conscience," Page said.

"I'd rather his actions be on my conscience than yours. You're the one who is trying to influence junior officers to assist you in your conspiracy. I don't care about your problems with the Sargans. This machine is not your enemy."

Box kept his attention focused on Page. He still hadn't moved, and he had Box right in his crosshairs. Page had to know no matter what he decided to do his career in the Coalition was over. There was no recourse after this. Not because of his actions toward Box, but because he disobeyed a direct order to stay in his quarters. There was a very good chance he could see himself as a man with no other options.

"Commander, he's going to shoot me," Box said.

"We don't know that yet," she replied. Her arm was still steady.

"I'm pretty sure he is," Box replied. "He's got no other choice. His career is over, he'll be thrown—"

"Box, shut up!" she yelled.

Page's eyes flickered. He shifted them to the side then back to Box. His breathing had also increased as his chest heaved up and down with the fury of a man out of options. "Prove me wrong," Box said to Page. "Or prove me right. It's your choice."

Page creased his brow, as if studying Box. "What are you?" he asked, seemingly with genuine interest. His attention was so focused on Box he didn't realize Commander Diazal had come up right behind him. With one fluid motion she plucked the gun from his hand and drove the heel of her foot into the back of his knee, causing him to cry out as he crumpled to the ground.

"Grab him," she said and Box leaned down, pulling Page's hands behind him.

The commander studied Page's weapon. "Highest setting," she said. "He would have blown a hole straight through you."

"I was afraid of that," Box said.

"Then why did you goad him?"

Box shrugged, causing Page to wince as his own arms were lifted up. "I wanted to be as unpredictable as possible. Why didn't *you* bring your sword?"

"It's not exactly Coalition issue." She smirked.

The comm system came on over the room. "All hands, prepare for assault. Full alert!"

"*Shit*," Evie said, pocketing both weapons. "Get him down to the brig and make sure you set up the encryption yourself." She stared at Page who avoided her gaze. "Until we know who helped him, I don't know who on the security team we can trust. Get him stowed then get yourself to sickbay."

"Sickbay?" Box asked as she made her way to the door.

"If this goes badly, we're going to have a lot more wounded and we need all the medical professionals we can get. Now get moving." She left them there alone together. Wow. He could actually go back to sickbay. This was like a dream.

"I suppose now you have me in your clutches you're going to finally kill me," Page said, his voice distant. "Just tell me one thing before you do. What is your plan here?"

Box didn't even look at the man, instead he led him to the doors, a certain burst of pride filling him. "I'm not going to kill you. I'm going to be a *doctor*."

***

Evie stumbled down the hall as the ship lurched. In response to what she didn't know. She didn't think they'd been hit but she couldn't be sure. She tapped her comm back to the bridge. "Report," she said, making her way back to the hypervator.

"There is a Sil ship in sight, Commander. The captain believes it is the same one we encountered before. We are performing maneuvering abilities to keep them from locking on to us with their weapons," Zaal said.

"I'm on my way back. Zaal, make a note. Page is guilty of treason and is being held in the brig."

"Aye, Commander," he said, then cut the comm.

She made her way to the nearest hypervator, desperate to get back to the bridge. If they could see the Sil ship it meant they had come out of the undercurrent already. Which also meant the Sil hadn't attacked yet. That had to be a good sign. Maybe Cas made it after all.

The hypervator doors opened on the bridge and Evie made her way back to her station, unlocking it and checking all the incoming reports from all the ship's sections. Everyone was ready.

"Report," Greene said, keeping his attention on the screen in front of him. In the distance, barely visible against the field of stars, was a ship very similar to the one that had attacked them in the undercurrent.

"Lieutenant Page is guilty of treason, he's in the brig now." She caught Ronde glance back at her. "And Box is fine. I got there just in time."

"Fantastic," Greene said, his voice deadpan. "Perhaps now we can focus on our primary problem?"

"Yes, sir," she said. Ronde continued to perform complex maneuvers while the Sil ship sat in the distance unmoving.

"They've been doing this ever since we came out of the undercurrent. At first they were closer, but they've backed off, as if they're luring us deeper into their territory."

"You think it's a trap?" she asked.

He shook his head. "There's no telling what it is."

"What about the shuttle? Any sign?"

"Nothing on scanners," Zaal said.

"Should I try the greeting again, Captain?" Lieutenant Uuma asked. She stood in Page's place at tactical and Evie had to admit she felt a lot better with her there.

"Hold for now, Lieutenant. They haven't answered a damn thing," he told Evie.

"Do you want me to get Negotiator Laska up here? She might—"

He shook his head. "Not until they respond. I'm not confident about this. If they pull back again I'm going to order we break off pursuit and retreat back to the system."

"But what do we do once we're there?" she asked. "Are we supposed to keep trying until they stop humoring us and finally blow us out of the sky?"

"Captain, the helm is being sluggish," Ronde reported. "I can't get her to respond. It's like she's stuck in a swamp."

Evie narrowed her eyes, checking her inputs again. "Zaal?"

"I detect nothing," he said. "We should be moving at a normal velocity."

"Ensign River, anything on your end?"

"No, ma'am," she replied.

Evie glanced over the captain's shoulder to the Engineering station. "Anything?"

"Propulsion is working fine, we've got no idea," Blohm replied.

"We're losing velocity," Ronde said, his voice a pitch higher and tinged with a dash of panic. "We'll be at a full stop in a few minutes if this continues."

"Reverse, back us out of here, whatever this is," Greene ordered.

Ronde nodded and input the proper commands, though the ship only continued to slow. "Whatever we're in I think it's got us," he said as the ship drew closer to a halt.

Greene addressed River. "Did the Sil ship cross this boundary when they began baiting us?" he asked.

"I don't believe so, sir," she replied. "They must have been on the other side of it."

"Invisible net," Greene muttered. "Now what?"

Evie stared out at the dark ship slowly approaching them. "I have no idea." Then she felt a low rumble through the room.

35

"Consul, they are trapped. The gravity net has them immobilized."

Zenfor continued to "stare" at Cas, while behind her in the expanse of space the *Tempest* continued to slow down until it stopped completely. She hadn't said another word since the ship had come out of the undercurrent, only waiting and watching Cas. What was she waiting for? Even her own crew seemed confused. Kayfor stood off to the side, his attention focused on his consul.

"Consul?" one of the Sil on the bridge asked. "Shall we proceed?"

"Don't let your pride blind you, Consul," Cas said. "That was my captain's mistake. He thought he was the only one who could save my people by eliminating a non-existent threat. When he approved the mission to go after your ship we didn't know about the aliens. He was only doing it to strengthen Coalition armaments. And now, because of his hubris he'll rot in jail forever."

"Why didn't you kill him?" Zenfor said.

"Death was too easy. He deserves a long life thinking about how he could have done things differently. How if he hadn't been so foolish he wouldn't have ruined his life and how his actions wouldn't have led to the death of over seventy people, your people included. No, death is a gift for Rutledge. He's going to suffer."

"Will your people ever release him?" she asked.

"No. He has a life sentence for every soul that died. He would have to live over seven millennia before he was eligible."

"Consul, your orders?" the Sil asked again.

Zenfor cocked her head back behind her. "Hold."

"If there is one thing I can respect, it is a fair justice system," Zenfor said. "Present your evidence."

Cas straightened. "Using my calendar on Dekaton sixty-fifth, twenty-five-ninety-three, the *USCS Achlys*, registry FCE-1201 attacked your scout ship in the Quaval system. The attack occurred at thirteen-forty-five hours and I sent the distress signal at thirteen-forty-nine. The signal read as follows: 'To any Sil vessel in range, one of your ships is under attack by a Coalition ship. Respond immediately.' Less than four minutes later, you showed up. And when I say you I don't mean a general Sil ship. I mean you personally. You were there that day, Zenfor. As was I.

"I had hoped you being there would be enough to convince my captain to leave, but he decided to test his luck as he didn't want to let go of the ship. He opened fire on you, which I now understand was the volley that gave you permission to fire back, which you did, killing twenty-four members of my crew. My captain had no choice and ordered a retreat. That was the last time I was in your space."

"And what of the second encounter? Where you succeeded?" she asked.

"By then I was on the run and no longer part of the Coalition. But I spoke to my old captain. The new captain of the *Achlys* drew your scout ship into the Atrax system, where she had mined one of the planets. As soon as your ship was in range she detonated the explosives, destabilizing the precious balance in the system and allowing her to get a drop on your ship as they fought against the change in gravitational currents. She ejected them into space and towed the ship back into non-aligned space. It was a terrible tragedy that never should have happened."

"And the one in charge of the mission is being punished?"

Cas nodded. If he told her about the other admirals authorizing the mission he had the distinct feeling she'd kill him where he stood. But if he could limit it to Rutledge he might have a chance. And technically it wasn't a lie.

"Consul, the gravity net is beginning to crush the other ship. Do we allow it to continue?" one of the other Sil asked.

Cas glanced past Zenfor at the *Tempest*, locked out there in some invisible trap. He'd never heard of a gravity net before but it didn't sound good.

"Release the ship from the net," Zenfor said. As Cas took a breath, she stepped closer. It was as if he were being swallowed up by something terrible. Even Kayfor had never been this close to him. "Understand I am reserving a final decision until after I see this information you wish to present."

"I can accept that," Cas said, craning his neck to look at her "face". "Will you be able to...see a recording? I don't understand how your—"

"I see just fine. Better than you do." She grabbed him by the arm, pulling him to the center of the raised portion of the bridge where she'd been standing when they arrived. "Speak to your ship."

Cas scanned the area. He couldn't tell where to look. "Right here? Do I—"

"Straight ahead," Zenfor said, impatience in her voice.

"*Tempest*? Do you read me?" he called out.

A screen appeared as if it were plastered on the inside of the bubble, showing *Tempest's* bridge. "Robeaux?" Greene asked, his harried face staring at Cas from his seat on the bridge. Evie sat beside him though they both looked rough.

241

Debris littered the rest bridge behind them, had they been in another fight while he'd been gone?

"Is everyone alright? What happened over there?" Cas asked.

"As soon as we stopped our inertial dampeners went offline," Greene replied. "The ship nearly shook itself to pieces. What is your status? Have you been successful?"

"I need you to transmit the telescope logs back over. Someone deleted my copies as I was leaving."

Greene glanced over to Evie. "Transmitting now," she said, tapping some controls on her chair. "Are you okay?"

"We have the information, Consul," the Sil at the front of the bridge said.

"Display it," she replied.

In place of *Tempest's* bridge another image played. At first it showed nothing more than the long-range image of a starfield. The image clicked over to a zoomed-in image of a sector of space which seemed relatively empty. But when the image shifted to the left the entire field was taken up by a fleet of similarly-shaped ships. All dark gray in color they resembled a school of fish, with larger ones protected by the smaller versions. It was the exact same footage Cas had seen in the admiral's office.

The fleet of ships drifted as one, with none of them breaking off. The telescope flipped again to a wider view of the cloud of ships passing through a binary system. In the far corner two smaller ships red in color approached the cloud. Before they reached what Cas would consider weapons range the two smaller ships exploded. The entire cloud of ships made a turn, heading for one of the planets in the distant system. The telescope flipped again as the cloud of ships approached the planet's atmosphere. A moment later a blue beam erupted from the cloud but Cas couldn't tell where, and the planet began to collapse in on itself. Within a few minutes the planet was nothing but bits of rock floating in space. It looked like a disorganized asteroid field.

The cloud then moved again, turning its attention on one of the two stars in the system. The blue beam erupted again, this time at the star, causing it to collapse in on itself as well. But due to the massive gravity well left behind the entire system began to fall apart; the second star disappearing beyond the first star's event horizon. The cloud turned and resumed course. The telescope flipped again to a wide-angle image, extrapolating a course for the cloud based on current projections. It led to the center of Coalition space: Earth's star, Horus. The feed closed, and the image of Greene and Evie appeared once more.

Zenfor turned to her fellows on the bridge. "Can any of that information be confirmed?" she asked.

"I've sent a message to the Sanctuary, asking them to review and confirm the data," the Sil on the left said.

"The *star*," Kayfor said. Though he didn't have any features Cas detected some awe in his voice. Despite their power, apparently the Sil hadn't yet mastered the ability to destroy stars.

"If this is true, I don't know how to proceed," Zenfor said in a rare moment of vulnerability.

"We'll have no choice but to retreat to the space beneath," Kayfor said. "Assuming the aliens cannot penetrate the dimensional barrier."

"Our entire species? That's ludicrous. It is meant as an amendment, not a permanent home. If we were to leave this dimension for good…"

"What?" Cas asked. "What would that mean?"

Kayfor turned to him. "This dimension anchors the space beneath. It keeps us tethered. If our species were to let go and cut all connection with it, we could end up never finding another. Many dimensions are much more…chaotic…than this one. You should consider yourself lucky your species is native to it."

"That's enough, Kayfor, he doesn't need our society's history," the Consul said.

"The Sanctuary has confirmed the footage as genuine evidence, Consul," the Sil on the left said. Cas noticed his aura pulsed rapidly. "It hasn't been tampered with and is considered trustworthy."

"What system is that?" Zenfor asked.

"We don't have a name for it," Greene said over the screen. "It's so far away no Coalition ship has ever been there. We don't know anything about the species they just destroyed either, though it is out past Omicron Terminus. Ships have been on exploratory missions in that direction, but they never returned."

"How far are they from your borders?"

"At their current speed two hundred and nineteen of our days," Evie said.

"Assuming they move through the Coalition at their current speed, how long until they reach our own borders?" Zenfor asked.

"Sixteen thousand sqirms, Consul."

"What's a sqirm?" Cas whispered.

"Equivalent to three-fourths of one of your hours," Kayfor replied. "We don't measure days."

Right. No night cycle. He should have figured. "Which gives you a little over a year to prepare yourselves," Cas said. "We don't know they'll be hostile when they arrive, but we must be prepared for the eventuality. And we *can't* do it without you. It's like I told you before, I doubt they'll stop with us."

Zenfor placed her long hands on the console in front of her, leaning over it while her aura pulsed with an intense, regular beat. If she were human Cas would bet she'd be sweating. "Based on the evidence you've presented I'll have to confer with the Sanctuary on our next steps." She turned to Kayfor. "Send him back to his ship."

Kayfor led Cas back to the edge of the bridge. "Never did I think I'd see the day," the Sil said.

36

"Damage control teams to the bridge," Evie yelled. Whatever the Sil had trapped them in had nearly pulled the ship apart by its bulkheads, despite being short-lived. She stood and helped Ronde out of his station, tossing his arm around her shoulder and leading him to the back of the bridge where there was less damage. When the ship had begun shifting violently, he'd hit his head on his station hard enough to cause some bleeding, though he was awake.

"Find Ensign Cortez," Greene barked. "I need medical and fire teams right now, lock down all systems."

No sooner had the vibrations stopped than the image of the Sil had come up. Evie had almost let out an exclamation when she saw Cas standing on their bridge, though the appearance of them had her perplexed. From what she could tell they didn't have any faces, though it could have just been the darkness of the bridge. Greene had needed to postpone all other operations until the conversation with them was over— he couldn't afford to let anything get in the way of the mission. Which meant the lieutenant had ended up bleeding all over his console while Ensign River worked to keep the ship in one place.

"You're going to be fine, Izak, don't worry," Evie said. He moaned in response as she helped him down to the floor with his back propped up against the wall.

"All hands, we are still at full alert, I repeat full alert," Greene ordered. Evie turned back to look at the view screen. The Sil ship was still out there, holding position. It seemed they had made some progress, but it was too early to tell. All she knew was their ship hadn't been destroyed yet. Now if only they could continue to defy the odds.

The hypervator doors at the back and side of the bridge opened at almost the same time. The fire crew exited the side, running to some of the bridge conduits that ruptured when the ship nearly tore itself apart. To her surprise, Box exited the back doors, headed straight for her and Ronde. "Box? Are you—?"

"You told me to get to sickbay, Commander," he said, leaning down and focusing his attention on Ronde. "And you were right. We do need as many medics as we can find. Sickbay is already filling up." He placed his metallic fingers on Ronde's head, inspecting the wound. "Good thing I have experience with head injuries."

Evie nodded, her heart bursting with pride. If nothing else Box being here was a reward within itself for a job well done. "Looks like you finally made it to the bridge. Officially." She smirked.

He turned his head, as if only now realizing where he was. "Oh. I guess I did. Okay, Lieutenant, hold still. This will hurt for only a second." He placed a small black device on the wound. Ronde winced as his eyes fluttered open.

"You," he said, his eyes flicking back and forth between Box and Evie. "I…"

"Yes, me. Unless you'd rather me leave you here. There are plenty of injured people on this ship."

"N—no, I…I didn't expect…"

"Many times life isn't what we expect." Box removed the device which had stopped the bleeding. He inspected the wound again. "It looks superficial, I don't think you'll need surgery. But you do have a concussion. If you'll come with

247

me, please." He turned to Evie. "He can't return to duty right now."

"Understood. Thanks, *doc*." She pushed up on her knees to stand as Box helped Ronde up.

"I'll get him down to sickbay. Has there been any word on—?"

"He's alive," she replied. "And he may have just succeeded."

Box's yellow eyes blinked three times. "I'm very glad to hear that." He turned and led Ronde back into the hypervator.

"Captain, we have a ship approaching," Ensign River announced.

"The Sil?" he asked.

"No, sir. It's our missing shuttle." Evie glanced up to see the shuttle appear as a small silver dot in the view screen, headed straight for them.

Greene turned to her. "Grab a security contingent and get down to the bays. I don't want any surprises." Lieutenant Uuma glanced up as he gave the order, which didn't escape Greene's notice. "I need you to stay on the weapons, Lieutenant. In case we're not in the clear yet. Diazal can handle this."

She nodded. "Yes, sir." But there was trepidation in her voice.

"Do I arrest him when he comes aboard?" Evie asked.

"*If* it is him, bring him back here," Greene replied. "I don't want him anywhere near the brig."

*　*　*

Evie watched as the shuttle made its way back into the bay, clipping the ceiling as it maneuvered into the space. Three security officers stood behind her, weapons drawn, and she still had the two pistols tucked into her belt. But she wasn't about to brandish them unless it was necessary. She took a few deep breaths in through her nose and out through a small part in her lips. There was no telling what was in that shuttle. It could be Cas. Or it could be a Sil raiding party and Evie was willing to bet no matter how many weapons her officers had they wouldn't be effective against them.

The shuttle finally landed hard, causing the room to shake. Evie glanced past the shuttle at Chief Master Rafnkell who had boarded her Spacewing fighter with the cockpit still open. Rafnkell nodded in solidarity. Though she hadn't been ordered to, Evie bet the woman had her weapons lit and ready.

The side door of the shuttle opened to reveal a very dirty and smelly Cas. His face was a shade of pale she hadn't seen on him before and dark circles colored under his eyes. On his arm he wore a portable flashlight from the shuttle's survival kit that was still on. "Hey," he said. "Miss me?"

"Are you alone?" she asked.

"Kor, I hope so." He hopped down from the shuttle. "I don't know how much more of the Sil I can take."

Evie turned to the security team. "Stand down." She also put her hand up to Rafnkell, who returned the wave but didn't get out of her ship.

"What happened over there?" Evie asked. "And what is going on?"

"I need to talk to the captain," he replied.

***

"I should have you arrested," Greene said, taking his seat behind his desk.

"If you think that's best," Cas replied, taking his seat on the other side with Evie. On the way they'd stopped by one of the food dispensers for a protein bar. Apparently the Sil didn't eat. Or if they did he didn't know how. And they weren't planning on keeping him long enough to feed him in any capacity. From everything he'd described on their trip to the bridge it sounded like a hellish labyrinth over there and that was something Evie never wanted to experience.

"What is the situation?" Greene asked.

Cas took a bite of the protein bar, chewed, then made a face. "We're on hold," he said, his mouth half-full. He leaned over to Evie, "I thought you said these things were good."

"Good *for* you," she said.

"And what does that mean? Have they agreed to help us?" Greene asked.

Cas shrugged. "They weren't clear. But I think I got through to the Sil captain. She's…well, she's formidable, let's put it that way. But considering I went from almost being executed to being allowed to return to you unharmed, I would take that as very good news."

"What is their goal? What do they want?" Evie asked. She couldn't believe he'd made it back in one piece. There might be hope for this after all.

"They're highly xenophobic, they won't even allow other species that reside in their own space to leave their planets. But they seem to want to preserve life, so we have that much in common. Though, they have some strange relationship with their ships. I didn't quite understand all of it, but the ships are alive. And the crew forms some sort of bond with them."

"So, when Rutledge captured the Sil scout ship and ejected its crew—"

"—he killed the creature. The ship, whatever it is," Cas finished for her.

"How does this help us?" Greene asked. "What are we supposed to do?"

"They didn't formally request anything of us," Cas replied. "But I wouldn't try to leave the area. You'll have to ask Laska, but I don't think the negotiation is over yet. I know the captain is speaking with her superiors about the situation. And they believe the footage. They know it's real."

"That's a relief," Evie said.

Cas took another bite of the bar, chewing as he spoke. "The guard, Kayfor, he seemed to be more on our side than the captain. I think he'll put in a good word for us. But the fact is the Sil know if whatever is headed our way plows right through the Coalition its next target will be them. And I got the distinct impression that is a problem, as much as they don't want to admit it."

"Whatever they do I hope they do it soon. It isn't like we have the luxury of time," Greene replied. "How long did it take Rutledge to develop that weapon?"

"Four years? Five? Something like that," Cas said.

"And we have less than one."

"Presumably with their help it will go faster," Cas said.

"Unless they decide to take care of this problem themselves," Evie said. "What's stopping them from sending their own armada across our borders to meet them head-on? If they left now, they might make it to Valdera before running into them. But by then they'd already be deep in Coalition territory."

"I think our only hope is if they give us the schematics we need to defend ourselves and we transmit that information out to the border. Hopefully by the time the threat arrives, Starbase Five and its defenses will be ready." Greene turned in his chair to watch the stars out his window.

"Against something that can implode a star?" Cas asked.

"I don't know," the captain replied. "I just don't know."

"Captain to the bridge," Lieutenant Uuma's voice said across the comm. Evie sensed the tension in the room increase tenfold as they stood and headed for the bridge.

37

Following the captain and Evie, Cas took the empty specialist's position behind tactical. Page wasn't at his post. Probably a good thing as someone would have needed to restrain Cas from strangling the man. Ronde wasn't at his post either, which was strange.

The captain and XO took their seats and Greene nodded to the lieutenant at tactical. The screen filled up with the image of Zenfor on her own bridge. Kayfor stood behind her, his long arms crossed as he leaned against the far wall.

"Coalition representative," Zenfor said.

Evie turned to look at Cas who only just realized she was talking about him. He stepped forward, positioning himself between the helm and navigation stations so he was in the middle of the room. "Zenfor."

"I take it your trip back was uneventful."

"Fine, thank you. Have you had a chance to confer with your superiors?" This felt so strange. When he'd been young, he'd always dreamed of being the contact person for a new race; of being the first face an alien species saw when they first encountered the Coalition. But all that had been destroyed when he'd lost his commission. And yet, he found himself standing here anyway.

"I have. The Sanctuary cannot make a decision, they are at a deadlock."

"What does that mean?" he asked.

"It means nothing changes."

Cas tried to hide his disappointment. But he couldn't let this opportunity pass them by. Not while they had the opportunity for dialogue. "Zenfor, I want to thank you for hearing me out. I know that took a leap of faith on your part and it wasn't a leap we necessarily deserved."

"It turned out to be the right decision," she said.

"What will you do if the Sanctuary can't make up its mind?" He stared straight at her glowing aura. It pulsed, slow and steady, reminding him of a heartbeat.

"If no decision is made by the time the threat reaches us, it will be up to the individual consuls to decide how to proceed."

"Does that power extend to you right now?" he asked.

She took a moment. "In moments of indecision, if an agreement cannot be reached, then yes, a consul may make a decision as long as it is in the best interest of the species."

"Then may I suggest you make the decision for them? Your ship has met ours, we have spoken, had dialogue. And you know the stakes; you know what we're up against."

Zenfor's gaze broke and she turned her head a moment before returning her attention to him. "Before today we have never been interested in your kind. Your alliance is not something we wish to be a part of. For the most part you have left us alone, which is what we want. Were it not for your Rutledge invading our property and killing our people, we might even be more inclined to help. But your actions have consequences. We must sit back and wait."

"Zenfor, please, you can't wait for us to solve this problem for you. For all you know they could pass us by entirely and just want to get to you. Allow us to help each other, to get involved. It doesn't mean this would be anything permanent, but I can think of no better reason for an alliance than that of a common foe." Maybe he was going about this the wrong way. Maybe he needed to make things more personal.

"You and I are very much alike. I was preparing to board a ship headed for deep space when I first found out about the threat. I was called back in to watch the footage, and afterward they told me the plan: go speak with you, see if you'd be willing to help. And I didn't want any part of it. I just wanted to get on that ship, fly to Procyon, and get away from everyone. Because I don't believe in the Coalition, not like I used to when I was an officer." He turned back to glance at Evie. She was on the edge of her chair with her eyebrows drawn together in worry. He winked at her.

"But then I realized if I turned my back on the Coalition, I could be potentially sentencing trillions of people to death. Which would be a far worse penalty to pay than to spend time helping them. I didn't have to agree with the organization to want to help. And I also realized there was nowhere I could go where the effects of what was coming wouldn't reach me. If these aliens are as dangerous as they seem, it's going to take the combined efforts of every species in this quadrant to even slow them down. That means we can't do it without you. No one else is going to take care of this problem for you. But if you'll let us, we *will* help."

Zenfor took a step back. Kayfor uncrossed his arms and moved closer to the screen, standing beside her. "Your words ring true," the consul said.

"They are true. Thirty days ago getting me to stand here in front of you seemed like an impossibility. For many reasons. But here we are."

"Here we are," she said. "Very well. In the interest of preserving life, I am willing to help. Conditionally."

"What is the condition?" he asked.

"I will not interface with anyone except you. I will not be passed around like a tool to be used. Do you understand?"

Cas's ears had grown hot and he could feel the perspiration dripping down his back. "I do."

"Return with your shuttle. It will take me some time to disengage from my ship."

He didn't quite understand what that meant but he wasn't about to question it. "I will be there in less than a sqirm."

She nodded and the screen clicked off.

Cas took a breath, trying not to hyperventilate in front of the rest of the crew. He turned his attention back to the captain and Evie.

"What did you just agree to?" Greene asked.

Cas furrowed his brow. "I'm not entirely sure. But wasn't the mission to get their help?"

"Not by them coming on board. We know little to nothing about these people, how can we expect to host them? Do they even breathe oxygen?" he asked.

"I didn't have any trouble breathing over there," he replied.

"Captain, isn't this a good thing?" Evie asked.

"I need to confer with Coalition Central. These people are potentially a mortal enemy. By allowing them access they could—"

"Captain," Cas said. "They can destroy us whenever they want. They don't need to steal our secrets. There is no security issue; they already downloaded everything from the first shuttle, which was a good part of our history and database. How do you think they figured out how to speak our language?"

Greene shook his head, pinching the bridge of his nose. "It's been a long few days and I'm...you and the commander prep the shuttle. Let's take a few minutes to figure out how best to welcome them on a Coalition ship."

***

"Did you ever think we'd be doing this?" Evie asked as she maneuvered the shuttle close to the Sil ship.

"I thought we were all dead the minute we crossed into their space." Cas had taken five minutes to shower and put on clean clothes before jumping back aboard the *Calypso* again. Evie took the helm and, with a precision he could never hope to match, had piloted them out of the bay and toward the Sil.

"So, each of their ships is alive? But we can only see part of them?"

"As far as I understand it. The rest of it is in a place they call the *space beneath*."

Her eyes went wide. "I'm not sure I like how that sounds."

"It's eerie," Cas said. "Like the absence of life. I'd rather not go back if I can help it."

"What are they like?" she asked.

"Not as strange as I thought they would be, once they started talking. I think we have a lot in common, though it concerns me they subjugate all the other intelligent species in their space. Especially since they have the ability to cross dimensions."

"Leave things like that up to the diplomats," she said. "Let's see if we can work out an agreement. Maybe they can help us meet this thing head-on."

"Do you think a hundred years ago, when the first war broke out, that either side ever thought there would be peace?" Cas asked, remembering what he'd learned in school about the Coalition's disastrous attempts to come to an agreement.

"I doubt it. But it's because none of them had sacrificed for the Sil. They went in wanting something for nothing. But you put yourself on the line for them. It's hard to ignore." She peered out the window. "Is this it?"

He nodded. It was the same small door on the side of the ship where they'd pulled him in the first time. Evie guided the shuttle inside, setting it down in the inky blackness. "They like it dark, huh?" she asked.

He shuddered, thinking about walking through all those corridors with nothing to guide him, when he felt like he'd lost all tether on reality. "Too dark for my tastes."

The doors on the side of the shuttle opened, revealing the dark shapes of Zenfor and one other Sil Cas hadn't seen before. He stood to greet them. "Are you sure you wouldn't be more comfortable coming on your own ship?" he asked.

"Considering what happened last time, no," Zenfor said. "I'm not willing to risk another of our ships to you."

The comment stung, but Cas understood. He turned to Evie who had also stood. "This is Commander Diazal, second in command of the *Tempest*."

"Welcome," Evie said.

Zenfor ignored her, and her own companion. "Let's get this over with," she said.

Evie paused, then returned to the controls. The ship lifted as the doors closed, returning to space. Cas noticed both Zenfor and her companion hunched slightly as they exited the Sil shuttlebay, as if they were in pain.

"Are you alright?" he asked.

"It takes considerable effort to voluntarily disconnect ourselves from the ship," Zenfor said. "It's a painful process."

"And you're sure—?"

"*No,*" Zenfor said. "Just proceed. It'll subside soon." Both she and her companion reached up to the gem suspended in their auras and plucked them away, their auras going dark. Concerned, Cas moved closer but Zenfor held out her hand for him to stay.

There was a hiss and four clicks as both Sil reached up with their slender fingers and pulled *their helmets* from their heads. The helmets unlocked in the back with tiny hinges on the sides and completely unclasped from around their faces. They had *faces*.

Their skin had a purplish-blue hue and they had two eyes, small noses and even mouths. Zenfor's face was slimmer, with a chin that ended in a point while the other Sil, also a female, had rounder features. Both their eyes were a sharp gray, with pupils that sparkled. And from the sides of their eyes, running back along their head where they disappeared into their dark purple hairlines, were two identical ridges, almost like scales on top of one another, leading from the front to back. Of all the species he'd encountered, they were remarkably human-like.

"This is what you really look like?" he asked. Evie turned in her seat and did a double-take at the Sil.

"When we are in our ship, it regulates all our functions," Zenfor said, setting her helmet beside her. Her voice had a less ethereal quality about it. "Now because we are no longer connected, we will need to resort to our natural biological processes."

Cas' eyes narrowed. "Do you mean to tell me you evolved in another dimension, and yet you look more like my people than ninety percent of the species out there?"

"I never said we evolved there. I said we were *from* there. Note the difference," Zenfor said, taking her eyes off him and staring straight ahead. He couldn't articulate what a relief it was they actually had faces. A face he could read. A blank mask he could not.

"How long do you think this will take? Will we need to call other ships to come assist?" Cas asked.

Zenfor turned her attention to him again. "Why would you need other ships? We're returning to your territory with you."

38

"Congratulations, Mr. Robeaux," Admiral Sanghvi said.

Cas stared at the admiral's image on the screen in the conference room. No one else had arrived yet. "Thank you, but I can't take all the credit," he said.

"Captain Greene tells me you took the initiative and went off on your own to try and convince them," Sanghvi said, a smile plastered on his face. "It's reminiscent of what you did back on Nullox when your fellow crewmates were in danger of burning up in the atmosphere. And it's the kind of behavior I would expect from a dedicated officer. Whether you want to admit it or not, you are a valuable member of the Coalition."

Cas sighed. "Admiral, half the reason Zenfor even agreed to speak with me was because I'm *not* a member of the Coalition. And I would appreciate it if you quit trying to shoehorn me into someone I no longer am."

The admiral put up his hands, but the smile stayed. "Loud and clear. Though I just want you to know you deserve your commission back. Especially now. The offer still stands."

"Thank you. I appreciate it."

"Before everyone else arrives, give me a status update on the Sil. Greene tells me they won't talk without you around."

"They're prepared to return with us and Zenfor seems willing to at least help for the time being. What that entails I don't know. But Greene is right. They won't interact with the others, at least not without me being close. It's like I'm—for lack of a better word—a security blanket."

"It's because you are the only one who has proved themselves to them. And until the other members of the crew can find a way to do that, I think you are our best hope for garnering their help. Looks like you'll be staying on board for a while longer."

"I expected as much," Cas said.

The doors to the conference room opened to reveal Evie, Greene, and Zenfor. Her Sil companion hadn't accompanied them. "Everything okay?" Cas asked, standing.

"Their quarters are all set up," Greene replied. "We had to make some adjustments."

Cas glanced at Evie, then Zenfor, who was still in her suit, just without the helmet. "They are satisfactory," she said.

"Consul Zenfor, this is Admiral Sanghvi," Cas said, indicating the admiral on the screen.

"Pleasure to meet a Sil. I look forward to meeting you in person," Sanghvi said, his smile growing even larger.

"You don't interest me. Will the one who invaded our space be at your Starbase?" Zenfor asked Cas.

Cas flicked his eyes to Evie who subtly shook her head no. "Yes, he's there. Under heavy guard."

"As another condition of my help I want to see him. In person," she said.

"I'm sure that can be arranged," Sanghvi replied. "But you have a long journey ahead of you. Let's start with what we would like to accomplish."

"We will work to improve your defensive and offensive weapon capabilities," Zenfor said. "Using *only* your own technology. You won't have any of ours. We won't let this become a prelude to the destruction of the Sil. When this threat is over, we expect things to go back to the way they were, and for the Coalition to leave us alone."

"Consul, do you think there is a possibility—?" Greene began.

"No. On this there can't be a compromise. Those are our terms. If you find them unacceptable take us back to our ship."

"We appreciate all the help you can provide," Sanghvi said. "*Tempest* will be our first line of defense against whatever is out there."

Greene's head snapped up. "Admiral? I wasn't aware—"

"This came down the pipeline, Cordell. As soon as you get back to Eight and reset, we're sending you out there. *Tempest* is the only ship we have that could possibly reach them before they hit our borders."

"But we're still thirty days away from Eight, which means we're at least another what, three and a half seasons from their projected position?" Greene said. "There must be someone closer."

"Let me rephrase that," Sanghvi said. "*Tempest* is the only ship that could get out there and back before they arrive. You're going to be our scout. According to our calculations on how fast they're moving, you should meet up somewhere around Omicron Terminus."

"I hope you are aware weapons development takes time. It will take more than thirty of your own days to design and build anything substantial," Zenfor said.

"Would you consider making the trip with them? Continuing the work as you travel?" Sanghvi asked.

Zenfor's eyes scanned the room and she leaned back in the chair. "I will accept, but only if I can send information about them back to my own people. We also need to prepare."

"Captain?" Sanghvi asked.

"I'm sure we can accommodate that. You can use our communications network and send back updates as we get closer."

"Acceptable," Zenfor said.

"Very good. Then I won't keep you. Get back to Eight as soon as you can and we'll be ready and waiting for you," Sanghvi said. "I'm looking forward to seeing what you come up with. Sanghvi out." The screen went blank.

Greene turned to Zenfor. "Thank you for agreeing. I realize this might be longer than you were originally expecting."

"It doesn't matter. My people have three times the lifespan of yours. I have the time to spare."

Greene stood. "Commander, tell the helm to set a course. Let's get back as quick as we can."

"Aye, sir." Evie nodded, though Cas noted a hint of worry behind her eyes. For some reason she seemed more anxious. Was it because the Sil would be coming with them?

Cas turned to Zenfor. "If you don't mind, I need a good night's rest before we get started. And there's something else I need to do first."

**

"Are you okay?" Cas asked as they made their way down the corridor.

"I'm not thrilled about going out there to meet those…things, but yeah, other than that, why?" Evie asked.

"You seem worried."

"I'm not."

"Is it the Sil? About them coming along with us?"

"Nope. All good."

Cas knew she wasn't telling him something. What was going on with her? He'd have to investigate later. Right now, he needed to do something he'd been putting off for much too long.

The doors to sickbay slid open, revealing Xax standing at one of the terminals while a few nurses milled about. Most of the injuries from the dampener failure had already been discharged though Lieutenant Ronde lay on a bed in the corner. Standing over him was Box, performing an examination.

He turned when Cas and Evie entered the room, his eyes blinking rapidly. "Holy shit, you're not dead."

"Box," Xax said, warning in her voice.

"Sorry, I'm supposed to work on my manners," Box said, coming over to them. He smacked Cas on the shoulder.

"Ow! What was that for?"

"For not telling me your plan. *Or* including me. There is no way you could have left without needing a pilot."

"Oh, he needed one alright." Evie grinned. "Tore the paint right off the bulkheads."

"*And* almost put Crewman Zorres in a coma," Box added. "Which I had to fix for you."

"Is she okay?" Cas asked. "I thought I barely clipped her."

"Yeah. With a *shuttle*. Thanks to me she's just fine."

Cas sighed. "I didn't want you to get into trouble because of me. And I wasn't sure how the Sil would respond to an artificial life form. Though I really could have used your navigation skills while I was over there."

"What, you call almost getting ripped into a thousand parts not getting into trouble?" Box asked, placing his metal hands on his hips.

"What?" Cas asked, turning to Evie. "What is this about?"

"I was going to wait to tell you, but Lieutenant Page tried to kill him. A few different times while you were away. He's safely in the brig now."

Cas clenched his fists. "That motherfucker. *And* he nearly got me killed when he deleted all that info I took with me."

"No," Evie said. "That was Ensign Tyler. He thought he was stopping a criminal."

Cas hung his head. "Of course. Is Page—?"

"Locked away until we get to Eight. Then Coalition Central will decide what to do with him. It's nebulous since the Accords don't specifically include artificial lifeforms. But Greene ordered him off the ship. Lieutenant Uuma took his post."

"And the captain offered me a *personal* apology," Box said, his eyes blinking twice. His pride was showing. "So as long as I don't break into the brig and strangle that asshole—"

"Box!"

"—that *inconsiderate person* I'm in good shape."

Cas glanced around the room. "So, this is where you are now. And this is what you want to do?"

"It's better than ferrying your butt around," Box said. "And they treat me well here."

"Not to mention he's a fair medic," Xax said, approaching them. "The fastest study I've ever known. Other than myself, of course. He's even managed to convince our helmsman he's not so bad." Xax glanced over at Ronde, sitting up on the table. "How is he?"

"Mild concussion. No internal bleeding. He'll be fine in a few hours," Box replied.

"See?" Xax said. "He'll make a great doctor one day." She returned to her station.

Cas couldn't help but grin. "Not bad. Beats sitting in the room all day watching net dramas, huh?" Box shrugged. "You could have told me. It's nothing to be embarrassed about."

"It wasn't that," he replied. "I wanted to be sure this was what I wanted before I made it official. I guess now that the mission is over you'll have to find a new pilot. Maybe Commander Diazal would prefer to go off with you into deep space." One of his yellow eyes blinked in a wink.

Cas narrowed his eyes. "What is he talking about?" Evie asked.

"Nothing. He's being annoying." He returned his attention to Box. "No, it looks like we're both sticking around. They need me to stay to assist the Sil."

Box leaned forward. "And you're *okay* with that?"

Cas let a smile slip across his face. "Yeah. I am."

Thank you for reading **TEMPEST RISING!** If you enjoyed the book, please consider leaving a review on AMAZON. And look for future installments in the series! The easiest way to keep up is to sign up on my website, and you get access to all the INFINITY'S END short stories, absolutely free!

The adventure continues in **DARKEST REACH**. Turn the page for a sneak preview!

DARKEST REACH: INFINITY'S END BOOK 3

PREVIEW

It was like staring into his past.

Caspian Robeaux stood, facing the only occupied cell in the brig of the *USCS Tempest*, watching the tall man inside pace back and forth. His dark hair was unkempt, and his hard visage reflected a hatred Cas had come to expect over the past few weeks. Though he hadn't been down here to visit Lieutenant Page since his arrest. Now that they were only a few hours from reaching Starbase Eight again, he'd figured he better take the opportunity while he still had it.

Once he'd entered the room Page had stood, and with a palpable sneer on his unshaven face, had locked his eyes on Cas and hadn't removed them. Page didn't say anything, only watched Cas from the other side of the force barrier keeping them apart. He was still in his uniform, though it looked wrinkled and showed sweat stains on the chest and armpits. Cas was glad smells couldn't penetrate the force barrier.

He'd managed to avoid this confrontation for almost thirty days—their entire trip from Sil space back to Coalition territory. But as the moment of their arrival grew closer, he found himself drawn to the man who'd tried to betray him and his closest companion: Box, an Autonomous Mining Robot who had been with Cas ever since his exile from the Sovereign Coalition of Aligned Systems. Cas had been off the ship when Page had enlisted the help of some of the other crew that hadn't been happy about Cas's arrival and used them to get rid of him and Box, in the most inhumane way possible. It was a crime Cas wouldn't be able to forgive.

"I suppose you've come here to gloat," Page finally said. His voice sounded raspy, as if he'd been shouting a lot.

"I just wanted to—" What? What had he wanted?

"You're the one who should be in here, not me." Page stopped pacing but kept his stare on Cas.

"I'm not the one who tried to illegally disassemble a life form because of his own prejudices."

Page scoffed. "That thing's not alive, I don't care what anyone says. It's a collection of parts built to imitate life. Disabling it would have done nothing but saved some energy."

Cas had known Box for over five years and to him the robot was as alive as any organic being. He had independence of thought, full autonomy and a sense of humor. "How many times do I have to tell you we're not a threat? I didn't want to be here anymore than you wanted me here, but like you I had a job to do. If you want to hate me for trying to help then go right ahead. It doesn't matter to me what you think."

"I don't hate you," Page said with the same intensity. "You *are* a threat and you don't even know it. A threat to this ship and you don't deserve to be here. Anyone who violates their commanding officer's orders and then runs away has no place on a Coalition ship. Especially not when it's mine."

"It's not yours anymore," Cas replied, unable to keep the man from goading him.

"We'll see about that. Out of the two of us, I'm the one who still has his rank and his commission. Just check my record. It's virtually spotless. What do you think will happen when I go in front of the review board? That they'll just dismiss me?"

"When you picked up that weapon and tried to kill Box you gave up all your credibility. You disobeyed an order from *your* commanding officer. I guess we're not that different after all." Box had told Cas about how Evie had come to his rescue, stopping Page at the last minute from shooting Box by getting the drop on him.

Page balled his hands into fists. "The commander didn't understand the situation. She's been compromised because of her relationship with you."

"The commander and I don't have a relationship," Cas said, on the defense. He hated Page for goading him, but he couldn't stand the thought that Evie was giving him preferential treatment because of their brief history together.

"Oh please. I'm not blind. She never should have been the one to retrieve you from the Sargan Commonwealth. That job should have been mine. I wouldn't have been as *understanding.*"

Cas hadn't come down here to talk about Evie. He'd only wanted...what? Closure? The odds were Page was going to prison after a court-martial, just like Admiral Rutledge. Somehow, Cas was making an impact. Ridding the Coalition of its less-than-ideal elements. Was it pride he felt at coming here? At having accomplished something?

"Wipe that smirk off your face," Page spat. "We'll see who's laughing as soon as Coalition Central hears my side of the story."

Cas shook his head. "You idiot. You don't even know what you're arguing against. Do you understand the kind of people you're working for? They won't hesitate to toss you in jail and throw away the key. Believe me, I know."

"You committed a capital offense." Page turned his back on Cas. "I'd never put my own interests above those of my crew."

"What about the interests of innocent people then?" Cas said, heat rising in his cheeks. "What if you were ordered to open fire on an innocent civilian ship? To capture it and eject its crew? Would you still be so high-and-mighty?"

Page glanced over his shoulder; a frown spread across his face. "Is *that* what Rutledge ordered you to do?"

"On a Sil vessel," Cas replied. It had been a classified mission, and very few people in the Coalition had known about it, including Cas himself up until the moment when then Captain Rutledge had ordered him to fire on and disable the smaller Sil ship so they could capture it. The mission had been to obtain the Sil technology to bring it back to Coalition space in order to reverse-engineer it. To learn the secrets of their destructive weapons so the Coalition could build its own. The entire mission went against everything the Coalition stood for. Cas had refused his captain's orders. And because of Rutledge's stubbornness, it had cost the lives of twenty-four of their crew before they narrowly escaped.

"There must have been a reason," Page said. "He wouldn't have given the order without a purpose."

Cas knew he shouldn't be telling Page this, but he'd had enough of the man blaming him. "Rutledge was the face of those in the Coalition who wanted to get a look at the weapon systems. Build some of their own."

"So it was to protect the Coalition," Page said.

"By violating everything it stood for." Cas ground his teeth together.

"That's easy for you to say. You grew up on Earth, didn't you? Never having to worry about anyone invading your perfect home? You never woke up in the middle of the night to marauders tearing through your home, looking for fuel or food or worse. On my homeworld I had to fight every day to stay alive. I didn't have the luxury of taking the easy way out."

"And yet you joined the Coalition," Cas said. "An institution based on principles. We don't attack civilian vessels and we don't build weapons of mass destruction."

Page laughed. "Listen to you. *We.* Like you belong to it anymore. No, *we* do what we need to survive. And if that means adapting to new threats then so be it. Admiral Rutledge did what was necessary to survive. And as one of his officers you should have seen that. Instead, you saw yourself fit to make a moral judgment over something you had no knowledge about. You were a bad officer."

270

Cas screwed up his face. "I didn't—"

"Did you know all the facts? Or were you just going off intuition?"

Cas hadn't known what was going on at the time. He hadn't known Rutledge and others in Coalition Central were trying to prepare the Coalition for future unknown threats, and they were trying to do it in the most clandestine way possible. All he'd known was his captain wanted him to fire on and disable an innocent vessel and Cas couldn't get on board. No matter the reason. Unfortunately Rutledge's fears came to pass when Coalition telescopes picked up an unknown alien threat headed their way a few seasons ago. Somehow Rutledge had known, or at least known they would need to be prepared. The entire reason Cas had been on the last mission had been to convince the Sil to help the Coalition. Despite the fact the Coalition had eventually succeeded in capturing one of their ships and attempting to reverse-engineer its weapons.

It hadn't gone well.

"I didn't think so," Page said. "You disobeyed an order without knowing all the facts. And it resulted in the deaths of your crewmates. If that doesn't define a bad officer then I don't know what else would."

Cas wondered if Page was right. What if he *had* followed Rutledge's order? They would have captured the ship and begun the experiments earlier. Rutledge had revealed the entire reason Cas had been chosen to be on the crew was his extraordinary engineering experience. Rutledge had wanted Cas to head up the team that reverse-engineered and constructed the Coalition version of the Sil's weapons. As it turned out Cas hadn't been there, so when the weapon had been tested, it had resulted in the loss of all hands on his old ship. If Cas had been there maybe he could have figured out how to make it work. Or at least prevented a catastrophe.

It wasn't *right*. The Coalition wasn't like that, at least he had believed that back then. He'd since discovered the

Coalition was just as corrupt as any other massive space-faring organization, they just hid it better behind messages of peace and goodwill. It was the whole reason he'd fled to the Sargan Commonwealth as soon as he'd been released on parole. At least the Sargans didn't pretend they were something they weren't. The Commonwealth was a massive crime syndicate and everyone knew it. You *expected* them to try and kill you. Up until his parole Cas never would have thought the Coalition capable of such a thing.

But was working to make a corrupt organization better than leaving it in the hands of those who would only make it worse? After all, not all the trillions of citizens of the Coalition were bad people; most didn't even know what was happening within the inner politics of the system. Cas had been a Lieutenant Commander on a starship and even *he* hadn't known. But instead of staying to help combat the corruption, he'd fled. And the all the innocent souls who were part of the Coalition didn't deserve that. They deserved to have someone fight for them; to stay inside the system and work from within to make it better. Wasn't that what he'd tried to do from the beginning?

"Not so sure of yourself anymore, huh?" Page smirked. "Like I said, let's just see what happens when the review board hears my side of it."

Cas knew it wouldn't matter. Evie would back him up and all the evidence pointed to Page disobeying orders. The Coalition couldn't sweep that under the rug. The *Tempest* had become too important in regards to the encroaching threat. Even now they were due for a stop-off on Eight before moving on to the next leg of their assignment.

"I hope it was worth it," Page called as Cas moved to leave, pressing his finger against the pad beside the door. "I hope setting the program back a couple years and getting all those people killed was worth an eased conscience."

Cas ignored him, allowed the door behind him to slide shut, cutting the man off. Once in the corridor Cas closed his eyes and took a deep breath.

"Well?" The voice made Cas jump as his eyes shot open to see the robotic body of Box standing beside him. He could be scary quiet when he wanted to be.

"Well what?" Cas asked, trying to keep his heart from thrumming out of his chest.

"What did he say?" Box asked, his yellow eyes blinking in anticipation.

Cas narrowed his eyes. "Aren't you supposed to be on duty?" Over the past few weeks Box had ingratiated himself to the ship's doctor and had provisionally become part of the medical crew. Just until they left again. Though he seemed to enjoy the work more than anything else Cas had seen him do.

"I took a lunch break."

"You don't eat."

"Are you saying I shouldn't get a break?"

Cas couldn't help but smirk. "He's as dickish as ever. He agrees with Rutledge; can you believe that?"

Box turned toward the door, though he didn't go through. "Considering he tried to have me disassembled...yeah, I can. Even though I'm practically a doctor now, I have a strong urge to reach through that force barrier and choke the life out of him."

"Don't let Xax hear you talk that way; she'll take you off-duty for sure." Cas moved away from the door and down the hallway. Page's words rang through his head. What if he *hadn't* disobeyed orders? How might things be different? "How long until we reach Eight?"

"Two hours, fifteen minutes." Box fell into step beside Cas.

"Sounds like the perfect amount of time to visit the bar."

To be continued in DARKEST REACH, available soon!

Glossary

Planets

Quaval – One of the few charted systems in Sil territory, discovered by the USCS Achlys

Cassiopeia Optima – Sargan homeworld (settled by humans millennia ago)

Claxia Prime – Claxian homeworld

Earth – Human homeworld

Atrax – system where Captain Soon overwhelmed a Sil civilian ship

Starbase Eight – Coalition stronghold and first line of defense against Sargan incursions

Meridian – non-aligned colony world subject to raids by the Sargans

Thislea – Sil homeworld, inside the Taurus Epsilon star system

Kathora – Coalition planet used for cyclax mining

Species

Human – one of the founding members of the Coalition and central to its operation. Humans can be found on any of a hundred different worlds in the Coalition and often hold high positions of power within the organization. Worked with the Claxians to be the founding members.

Claxian – Founding members of the Coalition and pacifists with advanced technology. Lived as isolationists until first contact by the humans two thousand years ago. Helped form the Coalition to spread peace through the galaxy.

Untuburu – Early members of the Coalition. Highly religious to their god Kor. Untuburu are the only Coalition members not required to wear uniforms as their religion requires the sacred blue robes be the only garments worn off world.

Yax-Inax – Early member of the Coalition. Studious, have perfect memory and can retain huge amounts of information. Often integrate themselves into other cultures to learn as much as possible.

Sargans – Generally human but can also pertain to other species who have joined the Sargan Commonwealth. Sargans are humans who want to be lawless, or at least out from under the thumb of the Coalition.

Sil – Unknown species of great power. The Coalition has reached a tentative treaty with the Sil not to violate their borders under any circumstances. Their empire is large.

Miscellaneous

Scorb – a heavy-type drink
Firebrand – liquor close to whiskey
Rank – a drink brewed from the hops of Caldonia
Galvanium – a type of metal used in ship construction
Cyclax – a type of metal used in ship reinforcement
Yaarn - protein synthesized to approximate the texture of an animal on Earth
Ackmel – a lumbering mammal used to traverse desert worlds

Author's Note

Thanks for reading TEMPEST RISING! Crafting a universe as large and complex as this is no small feat, but the challenge has been one of the greatest of my life. Back when I first began writing I wasn't even sure if I could write a trilogy and now I've not only written a five-book series but I am hard at work on making the universe of the Sovereign Coalition expansive to hold many, many more stories. But I couldn't do this alone. Despite the fact most of my time is spent at my desk, there are always other people who have helped me along the way.

To my beta readers and ARC team: Meenaz, Kay, Katie, Brian, and Lori in particular, you keep me on my toes and do the hard job of searching for all my mistakes. Thank you for all the time you dedicate to making my work better.

To the Charlotte Writers Group: when I joined back in 2014 I had no idea what kind of path this career would take me on. Thank you for all the insight and advice you gave me over the years. It made my writing excel far beyond what it was when I began.

To the Sterling and Stone Team: your enthusiasm for story and willingness to help others no matter their skill level was a game-changer for me. Before I found you, I found it daunting to write more than two books a year. You made the process so much better for me and without it I never would have gotten this far. Thank you.

To my family: you have always supported me, and never believed I would achieve anything other than what I set out to achieve and beyond. Thank you for always being there and never giving up.

To Tiffany Shand and Dan Van Oss: you guys turn coal into diamonds. Without you, this would be a rough smattering of words and Tiffany made them better while Dan brought beauty and images to my ideas.

And finally, thank you to my very patient wife, you're the reason I do what I do and I love you more than anything.

Until next time!

-Eric Warren

About the Author

I've always been an author, but I haven't always known I've been an author. It took a few tragic events in my life and a lot of time for me to figure it out.

But I've never had a problem creating stories. Or creating in general. I wasn't *the* creative person in any of my classes in school, I was always the kid who never spoke but always listened. I was the one who would take an assignment and pour my heart into it, as long as it meant I could do something original.

I didn't start writing professionally until 2014 when I tackled the idea of finishing a novel-length book. Before then I had always written in some capacity, even as far back as elementary school where I wrote pages of stories about creatures under the earth.

It took a few tries and a few novels under my belt before I figured out what I was doing, and I've now finished my first series and am hard at work on my second (which you hold in your hands now!). I am thrilled to be doing this and couldn't imagine doing anything else with my life.

I hope you enjoy the fruits of my labor. May they bring you as much joy as they bring me.

Having lived in both Virginia and California in the past, I currently reside in Charlotte, NC with my very supportive wife and two small pugs.

Visit me at my website

Made in the USA
Middletown, DE
14 August 2021